Humans have become an endangered species

Fortunately, someone built

THE

The End series

Freda Lewis-Lombardo

HABITAT

THE END SERIES

For Sandra
Best of luck with
your book!

Frieda
Lewis Lombardi

2020

Printed in the United States of America
First Printing, 2019
ISBN 978-1-7332479-0-0

Lancaster House ink ☀

Editing by Sam Wright
Cover Design by Ranka Stevic
Interior Book Design by Roseanna White Designs

For my brilliant daughter, Liz.

You are such a marvelous example of perseverance and achievement.

I am so proud of you.

Without your love, support, and absence

(source of my empty-nest syndrome),

this book could not have been

finished.

You are my heart.

HABITAT

Oh, sweet ignorance,

My one true guardian,

Do not abandon me

In this world of deceit.

THE END

I was named *Savannah, Georgia/March 2, 2032/ Female/4-21 days old/Survivor 3* by the military team who rescued me twenty years ago. I'll never learn my birth name because my biological parents didn't survive the nuclear war that destroyed our world. I was one of the lucky ones, having no memories of family or life as it once was. Neither do I remember the horror of war nor the joy of rescue. I can only imagine the relief of being brought to the town of Horizon with the other 4,999 survivors.

Many adults married days after meeting—a prerequisite for adopting an orphaned child. The town's leaders thought our best chance of success lay in creating new family bonds. We were a group of devastated strangers thrown together in the darkest time of man's existence and given the monumental task of rebuilding civilization.

Years before The End, the government designed and built a network of secret refuges across America to shelter politicians if Armageddon occurred. Doomsday came, but they weren't rescued, nor were our families. Everything and everyone we loved was gone. No other government bunkers have contacted us and now, two decades later, finding survivors is unlikely. I hope that someone saved other groups, just like the Horizon 5000 and they, like us, were now somewhere safe and happy.

Because the bunkers beneath our town were fully stockpiled with necessities for any emergency, we didn't struggle initially. However, those supplies couldn't last forever. We learned to make some essentials, but conservation was crucial. Who could have imagined creating ways to make clothes last for twenty years? In Horizon, we needed each other's skill and knowledge to survive.

Two decades after The End, our new goal is about more than mere survival. Now, we look for ways to thrive in what remains of our restructured society. We acknowledge sadness comes from missing life from before the war. Those crippling memories held on to from the last world stand between success and us. The constant reminders of all we lost drain our spirits; therefore, we practice releasing old memories to avoid emotional instability. Naturally, the older you are, the more memories you have. The more memories you have, the more you have to release. Our regulated therapy program helps manage everything considered harmful. I'm thankful I don't have memories of the other world. How can we move forward if we are chained to the past?

Although we are protected inside Horizon, I am still frightened when I hear the machines clean radiation from the air—just one additional reminder of lingering danger beyond our walls. My father says that war will never happen again—those inclinations vanished with The End. We hope he is right.

I believe we live in a better world, and it's called The Beginning.

—Ellis Bauer, graduation essay excerpt
Horizon: A Look Back, A Look Forward
July 2052

CHAPTER 1

It was July 4, 1986, at one of those low-country mansions in Charleston, South Carolina. That place was square in the middle of nowhere I cared about, and yet it was the only place I wanted to be. She was, without a nickel's worth of doubt, the most beautiful woman I'd ever laid my eyes on, and she was way outta my league. My daddy worked his whole life on a horse farm, and I'd probably end up doing the same. Her daddy was a millionaire banker.

It was Friday night, and she wore this flowery, mini skirt with a pale pink sweater slung over her shoulders. Lillian Rose Stallworth—Lilly Rose, for short. Giant chandeliers hung from the ceiling of an old, southern ballroom that had no purpose any more than just to show off. Charleston's cream of the crop mingled about pretending to have more money than everybody else.

Lilly Rose gave me my invitation while I shoveled manure out of her Arabian's stall. Mutan was a big, fierce, black stallion who didn't think I was good enough for her either, and he let me know it by giving me a kick to the thigh when she walked away. That horse bout near broke my leg, but I would have shown up to that party in a body cast if I had to.

I wasn't ever shy before. Heck, that wasn't my first rodeo, but my knees wobbled as I shuffled over to where she stood talking with her girlfriends. After a tap on her shoulder and a bunch of stammering, I somehow found the courage to ask for a dance. Without saying a word, she smiled and gave me her hand. Out of all those Citadel College boys with their turned-up-collar polo shirts and silver-spoon trust funds, she chose me.

It felt like heaven to hold her in my arms. She smelled like wild honeysuckle on a breezy, summer night. That was it. She was mine for the next forty-five years.

When you're still a pup, you think you'll live forever. The End War took my Lilly Rose. Now, the only thing left is the memory of her I keep secret. Memories are dangerous things. They're forbidden here in Horizon, and they're trying to take 'em from us.

—Henry A. Parsons
Release Sleep Therapy Recording
July 4, 2052

RELEASE

THE SIRENS BLASTED DURING THE NIGHT FOR THE second time this month. As usual, I got out of bed to shelter with Mom and Dad in the safe room. Who knew we would still have these threats twenty years after the war? I wouldn't have minded so much, but this time I couldn't get back to sleep. The window-less room had soft, thick sleeping bags, always comfortable, but the stupid, red nightlight had me in a trance. I tried to will it to change color with an attempt at mind control. Finally, at 5:00 am, we got the green—no more red. Either the radiation dispersed, or my superhero powers finally kicked in. I suspect it was not the latter.

I stumbled back to my bedroom in the dark, tripped over my dataport, and banged into the nightstand. From then on, I laid in bed, trying to will my toe to stop throbbing. Yeah, it's official; I have no mind-control over anything. Since the radiation alarm activated during the night, school would be canceled. I was grateful because getting back to sleep was difficult.

"Wake up, Ellis." I tried to block out the voice.

For a millisecond, I was walking through a dazzling city of high-rises and streets bustling with cars. I was so happy, and then it vanished into some vague memory, melting like ice cream on a hot, summer day. Sadness washed over me. Now, a persistent knock at my door stole the final shreds of the magnificent dream. I sighed. Time to get up and leave behind places I'd never seen and never would. After all, that world died long ago.

"Ellis, you will be late again. Hurry, so the doctor won't need to rearrange her schedule. Tardiness is inconsiderate." My mother opened the bedroom door. "I agreed to let you nap because of sirens in the night, but I won't allow you to miss your appointment—no matter how tired you claim to be."

Had other people heard her, they might have assumed I was a child instead of a twenty-year-old future graduate.

"I'm awake," I said. I sat up in bed, and she turned to leave.

My dataport alarm chimed, "The time is 3:30 pm, July 15, 2052."

"Dataport, alarm off," I said. A small beep acknowledged my voice command.

I sat on the edge of the bed shaking off sleepiness and dreams of cities that no longer existed, except in pictures. I looked for my clothes. At the foot of the bed, a suspicious mound lay under the covers. "Gotcha," I said aloud. Sure enough, the missing shirt. Now if I could find my shorts, I could be on my way. I still had thirty minutes.

"Ellis," my mother yelled from the kitchen.

Where are my sneakers? I didn't hate my weekly release sessions; I'd spent hundreds of hours with Dr. Adler. Our visits were helpful. She supported my goal to become a release therapist. Helping people find relief from negative emotions appealed to me. If I scored high enough on my placement test, I would begin training in the fall.

With graduation and career placement consuming my thoughts, I'd been somewhat irritable. On the most hectic days, I never completed school, homework, my daily activities list, and release therapy without exhausting myself mentally and physically.

Now dressed, I stuck my tongue out while standing in front of the full-length mirror. I tried to make peace with the image staring back, but she wasn't cooperative. Five feet-four inches was the most I could hope for, and if I didn't stop sneaking to the Fountain for real food, I'd never lose the extra ten pounds. *I* didn't have a problem with my weight. I had a problem with the problem my *mom* had with my weight. She lived life as an organic, naturalist, vegetarian, neat freak, exercising, yoga-doing type of person.

I stepped back and made my final analysis. My clothes weren't backward or inside out (wished I could say the same for other days). I had no blemishes this week, and my auburn ponytail was straight with curls surprisingly well behaved. *Congratulations, you're not a total mess today.*

Aromas drifted from the kitchen reminding me today was baking day. *Please let it be edible.* I rushed in at the exact moment Mom removed cookies from the oven—rutabaga-wheat germ. *Crap.* When she turned her back, I grabbed two and juggled them from hand to hand. Heat was nearly a successful deterrent for food theft. The front door was on the verge of closing when I remembered to say goodbye. I jammed one cookie into my mouth and held it between my teeth as I jumped on my bike. *Steam burn*. Mom's rant about stealing the cookies without asking reached my ears as I hurried to get away. I gobbled the first cookie while steering and came close to choking because it was the worst *goodie* I'd ever eaten. To be honest, the name *baddie* would have been a compliment considering the flavor. An accurate taste description was a cross between tree bark, dried leaves, and dirt. This might set the diet revolution on fire. If I kept eating this garbage, I'd lose those ten pounds in no time.

Then again, I could end up hospitalized.

From our enormous mountains, exhilarating air swooped in gentle gusts. Fresh and scented with the last gardenias of the season, I gulped in great lungfuls. Sweet freedom. Why hadn't I spent more of my day outside enjoying this beauty?

Mother Nature was remarkable and just as resolute as the Horizon 5000 to survive. Years ago, the town celebrated the return of the first white-tailed deer. Professor Zhào explained, after the war, nature needed rest to plan its comeback. Now, every time an animal reappeared, it renewed hope for the future.

The End War claimed responsibility for many living organisms becoming extinct but not humans. Five thousand wasn't an enormous number, but we survived and continued to grow since the war. Many people thought radiation might cause infertility. However, our determination and the luck of having survivors with medical knowledge saved us. We hoped other groups of people might be outside Horizon fighting to make their comeback as well.

Arriving on time for my therapy appointments had never been an issue, despite Mom's incessant warnings. I quickened my pace and rocketed through our quiet street when I noticed my neighbor, Henry Parsons. Dad and Mom expected me to address older adults by mister or missus, but Mr. Parsons and I worked out a deal a long time ago to call him Mr. Hap.

"This way it makes us seem more friendly-like," he told me once, "and makes me not feel like such an old fart blossom."

Today, my friend focused on picking up an oak leaf with the audacity to fall onto his well-controlled lawn. Mr. Hap must have spent hours taking care of his home, although he was in his eighties. All houses in our neighborhood were one story with two bedrooms, their exteriors varied. Mr. Hap's white New England cottage with blue shutters and blue roof represented one of fifty designs. My home was a craftsman design with a natural stone exterior. The government thought of everything when planning this community.

Despite living in a post-apocalyptic world, the town administration expected our homes to be kept in rule-abiding, pristine condition. Nothing ever looked neglected. I complimented Mr. Hap on his colorful garden one day, and he told me his wife always loved a well-kept yard.

"It was her favorite hobby," he explained. "That little gal of mine loved flowers better than a poor hog loves slop. Back before everything went to hell in a handbasket, she'd sit on the porch and watch me cut grass. She'd meet me on every third turn around the yard and bring me a sip of homemade lemonade with fresh mint and crushed ice served in a mason jar. My little gal declared there wasn't nothing more soul-satisfying than a freshly mowed yard and a good-looking devil with an honest sweat. So now, I keep on doing this for her, cause she's looking down on me every moment."

I wondered if someone would love me enough to keep my memory alive twenty years after I'd gone. I doubted if I'd have a marriage last fifty years. My parents' union wasn't the best example of supreme felicity.

As a child, I once asked Mr. Hap if he might marry again. I remembered he said, "Once you've found your soul mate, no one else can come close. You smile just thinking about them, and your heart lights up when you see them. Remember that, and you'll find a love that lasts forever."

I couldn't go past him today without stopping—even if time was running close. He was one of my favorite people to talk with because he told me stories of life before The End.

"Hi, Mr. Hap," I called out. I slowed and glided onto the sidewalk. "How are you today?"

He walked toward me with a small garden tool I didn't know the name for. "Well, I'm a tad-bit down in my back, to tell the truth." He rubbed the area and smiled through weary eyes. "The curse of being a darn fossil," he said with a hint of a sly grin, "but hard work ain't never killed nobody."

"Cookie?" I held up the remaining one.

He shook his head. "Thanks, but I'll pass. No offense, Ellis, but your Ma ain't no cook."

"You've got a point, Mr. Hap." He belted out a hearty laugh as sweat dripped from his face. "Maybe you should rest today. I bet your wife wouldn't mind you taking a day off from her garden," I said. I finished the remaining cookie, including the crumbs on my faded, tie-dyed T-shirt.

"My wife? Shoot, she woulda wanted me to dig up this whole place. Lilly Rose told everyone I spent too much time in the yard. To be honest with ya, little Miss, I stayed outside to get a break from her," he explained.

I grinned and waited for one of his famous punch lines. He didn't even cut a smile.

"But Lilly Rose loved tending the yard with you," I said, "and your story of the roses and how she always wore floral printed clothes…"

Mr. Hap chuckled. I relaxed and smiled; I hadn't misunderstood the wonderful love story he told me so many times in my life.

He raised the tool in his hand and aimed it toward the ground. He flung it straight into its intended mark. His laugh faded, "Make no mistake, Ellis, if my wife had a tender side, she musta kept it locked in a box somewhere." He took a stained handkerchief from his back pocket and wiped the sweat from his brow. "Gardening was the only time she wasn't in my ear with hellacious—pardon my French—naggin' about something or other. No, ma'am, there wasn't ever a moment's worth of peace with that woman. I suppose some folks just aren't meant for each other, and I wish it hadn't taken me so long to find out." He replaced the handkerchief in his pocket, "We divorced twenty years too late if you ask me."

I leaned half on and half off my bike, fixated on an altered version of this man's marriage. Mr. Hap and Lilly Rose never divorced.

"You okay there, Ellis? You look like you done seen a ghost. Why don't you park yourself in the shade for a spell? Come on and sit here by this butterfly bush and I'll bring you something cool to drink." He pointed back toward the house to a chair sitting by an enormous plant.

"No, I'm fine," I lied. "I…have my release session," I added. Why did he contradict every sweet story he'd ever told me?

"Well okay, if you're gonna be all right. Stop by and see me again." He looked around before leaning closer and whispered, "I'll make us lemonade with mint and crushed ice. We can sneak and talk about stories from the old days." He took one more look around with his eyes narrowed and his brow creased. His voice lowered just enough for me to hear. "I'll tell them stories to you before they take 'em," he said before standing upright again. His expression changed, and he smiled the same sweet Mr. Hap smile as always. He took a step backward and raised a hand to wave goodbye.

Confused by his complete change in demeanor, I wasn't altogether sure I even said goodbye. I may have ridden away with no acknowledgment whatsoever. My mind raced through possible explanations. Weird chills traveled down my spine, and I was, for the first time, glad to be leaving my old friend.

In health class, we studied several memory ailments that affected the older generation. I didn't recall these illnesses took effect within such a short time span. Last week, he shared the memory of celebrating his fortieth wedding anniversary. Mr. Hap said he took their entire family on a cruise ship (a giant recreational boat that sailed on the ocean and took people to different places around the world).

Dad would solve the mystery of Mr. Hap's odd behavior when I told him later today. Farther away from my neighbor now, I comforted myself by concluding *Mr. Hap* had been in the sun too long and needed shade. I re-focused and biked toward downtown.

I came to Park Center—the heart of Horizon. In the middle of the park was a fountain where kids loved to play on hot days. Today was quiet except for the two children who squealed splashing each other.

The unknown Horizon architect loved symmetry. Every aspect was laid out in perfect balance. The black iron park clock showed me I was still five minutes from being late to my session. The street surrounding the circle-shaped park was Main. Off Main, branched six streets, also symmetrical, leading to the other parts of town. From high above, I imagined Horizon's park must have resembled the shape of a sun with the streets being rays stretching in every direction.

Today, two workers made repairs on the solar-paneled lampposts, and a few people strolled along the shop walk. This part of Horizon, a replica of downtowns existing in the 1940s, contained many shops. The Barbershop shared space with Cuts & Curls and operated by appointment only. Décor & More employed six of the best artisans in Horizon who designed and built decorative pieces for homes such as art and furniture. Recycled items donated to Second Time Around next door provided work materials for the decorators. Mr. Fix-it took your broken items and repaired them. Many other tiny shops filled the town, but Horizon didn't use money. I had never seen dollars except in pictures. Citizens used cards that tracked Gives and Takes. Instead of measuring value in dollars, we measured value in time. We gave our talents and time equal to what we took. A person who stayed at home without contributing didn't deserve to take all of his living necessities. By performing required volunteer work every week, even the youth earned Give credits. Seniors, who were physically capable, volunteered or worked. Twenty years after The End, our system operated smoothly. Mr. Hap said it wouldn't have lasted five minutes in the old world because of greed. He volunteered at the Hobby Center teaching classes on gardening and landscaping. When Horizon was new, and he was twenty years younger, he worked at Horizon Farms raising newly-cloned farm animals.

Dad and Mom tried to abide by the "let memories stay in the past" rule, but I yearned for stories describing how the world before looked and worked. Mom said we should be grateful we weren't living the way cavemen did thousands of years ago. She said the government was more generous than we deserved, and I shouldn't question our condition, but be thankful someone had the forethought to provide us with so many luxuries. Dad called our life utopic because we were safe, healthy, and had people to love.

Outside the Orchard building, my bike took the last available slot in the rack. Horizon had racks everywhere. Solar-powered carts replaced bikes when graduates got job assignments. When I get my placement, I'll be eligible for a cart. Riding my bike was still an option; many people did. But why bike when I could drive?

I scurried up the steps of the grand, stone edifice. The Orchard appeared to be a century old but was just slightly older than I was. The massive three-story construction was even larger than the Horizon House of Prayer. As a child, Dad said I rubbed the rough exterior of the Orchard and described how each stone was special.

Inside the vaulted, sunlit lobby, I saw Sarah, who greeted me with a smile and a wink. She answered calls and messages from the dataport at her reception desk. Without a word, I pointed upstairs, and she nodded. She was accustomed to my being consistently *on the verge* of late.

The aroma of polished wood filled my nostrils as I climbed cherry-stained stairs leading to the second floor. I liked the sound of steps creaking beneath my feet, and every time I came to a particular spot on the grand staircase, I expected a tiny squeak. I often wondered if the builder designed the stairs to make those noises. Shouldn't a building that looked a hundred years old, sound a hundred years old? Every bit of the Horizon design seemed perfectly orchestrated.

Forty release physicians shared the Orchard for their office space. When I practice therapy, it will be here. *If I practice therapy.* Dr. Adler assured me although I remembered nothing of life during The End; I might still aid those who did. My goal was to help people become happier and emotionally healthier. Before The End, psychology helped people with those issues. I worried release therapy might become obsolete. Life was perfect now. What could the next generation have to release?

We learned in health class life will get easier for society when our older generation moved forward—once called death. That phrase always sounded silly to me. There was no *moving* when someone was dead. If therapists frowned on using the term death, I think a better rephrasing would have been *stopped. Mrs. Smith stopped moving today.*

I laughed way too loudly and caught myself. Acting loopy in the therapy building was probably not a good idea.

For now, doctors used talk therapy to help us maintain emotional stability. Our goal was to release negativity from our lives. A sign at the stair landing read, Release the memory—Release the pain. I had read it every week for as long as I could remember.

As I came closer to the doctor's office, I passed familiar faces. Horizon now had over seven thousand people, thanks to the brave, military soldiers who rescued so many. Chances of surviving were one in two million. The last time scouts found anyone was ten years ago. One survivor, from a group of three, came to my school, after a period of confinement. She was a teacher's assistant before The End. She did intervention, helping students who struggled. To me, she acted friendly and not traumatized. Many classmates asked her for details of life beyond the wall, but she'd suffered amnesia and couldn't give us any information.

I arrived at the doctor's door, located at the end of a long hall.

"Ellis, you are prompt." Dr. Adler smiled and welcomed me. Her office always gave me a mental picture of eating summer peaches by our lake. Bizarre.

She looked the same. Today, she wore her sleeveless black dress, medium black heels, and a strand of white pearls around her neck. She was the prettiest woman I'd ever seen. Her short, dark hair contrasted against her pale skin. She was tall and thin with a flawless appearance. If she ever had a frizzy-hair, puffy-eye allergy, wrinkled clothes from the bottom-of-the-hamper day, I'd never seen it. She might have been forty-five, but in the fifteen years of memories with her, she never changed. I imagined, before The End War, she could have been one of those people called models. She trained as a psychiatrist, a profession similar to release therapy, which used medicinal intervention. She motioned for me to take a seat, and I chose my usual spot on the brown leather sofa. Sometimes, I laid down or sat in an oversized chair. Today was a kick-your-shoes-off-and-plop-down-for-a-chat kind of therapy. She had an over-stuffed leather chair opposite me. This had been our routine year after year.

"So tell me, how was your biology final assessment?" she asked.

I looked at my faded blue jean shorts and noticed a loose string. "Ninety-one," I said, wishing I'd scored higher.

"What happy news, congratulations. I'm proud of you, Ellis. What other news do you have?"

"Nothing, much. I slept over at Ana's house for her birthday. It was good."

"Just good? It makes me wonder whether the visit was enjoyable. Did you sleep well? Any dreams?"

"No." *What? Why did I lie? I never lie to her.* I looked up at the doctor. She sensed what I had done. I opened my mouth to correct my answer, but she spoke.

"I'm glad you slept in a different place and didn't have your rest interrupted. When you sleep away again, remember to journal any troubling dreams. We can discuss and clarify them. This will help you. Agreed?" Her face changed its expression, and now she looked as if she believed me. "What are your thoughts on the final placement tests you took last week?" she asked.

I asked her to repeat the question. Thoughts were flying through my head like daggers. The immediate guilt was crushing me. She was one of three people I trusted, but now, I had ruined that bond. I scrambled to find the words to answer her question. "I'm…nervous, I mean…I've studied and paid attention, but I'm terrified one test will determine my career. What if the results place me in a job I hate?"

"Ellis, I'm familiar with this examination. The questions measure your aptitude for different careers but considers your preferences. If you don't receive a release therapist apprenticeship, you will be assigned employment to a field in which you've shown interest and skill. Our small town needs many talents to keep it running. I'm confident your assignment will suit you, and you will be successful. Remember Ellis, every job is important, and every job depends on every other to hold Horizon together."

I looked down again at the small, loose thread I'd been playing with on my shorts and wondered if that insignificant string was important enough to hold the other fabric together. I grasped it and yanked. It came loose from its place with no resistance at all.

I looked up and waited for the next question.

CHAPTER 2

This community will be innovative. When the time comes for emergency evacuations to begin, this complex will be operational. The area will serve as a safe zone and ensure the survival of mankind. Every security measure imaginable will protect the inhabitants. Monitored entrances and exits will have double-layered barriers providing extra security. Hidden layers of defense will guarantee a normal, tranquil appearance so leaders can focus on restructuring a world thrown into apocalyptic chaos and ruin. In no way should this haven resemble a military installation. Instead, the architecture will create a small town, USA—a model community evoking feelings of comfort and hospitality. Homes in sectioned neighborhoods will have front porches and sidewalks. The traditional American backyard will no longer exist. Outside gatherings will be in full view of other homes. Interaction and so-

cialization will be the catalyst for success. Eventually, shops, markets, and diners will service the town.
Here, society will rebuild itself. Mirrored glasses will...

—Reece Briggs, Architect
Classified Doomsday Project Horizon
2016

HORIZON

MY MIND RACED—I LIED TO MY DOCTOR FOR NO
apparent reason. At Ana's house, I dreamed something strange
but had forgotten it until the doctor asked. So why did I lie? For the
rest of my session, I was a mess. I stuttered, jumbled my words, and
spoke in babbling sentences. She could not have been more aware
of my dishonesty unless I had taken a marker and written the words
big, fat liar across my face.

Dr. Adler asked questions about my relationship with Mom and
Dad and any changes I noticed in their behavior. The subject of
reading came up, so I asked her to suggest psychology books relat-
ing to release therapy. The visit was positive except for walking away
burdened with guilt.

I descended the massive staircase, passing the next group of patients for the day. Once outside, I tried to take cleansing breaths to
lighten the weight of my guilt. It wasn't working. After leaving the
Orchard building front steps, I hurried across the square toward a
place I loved. After every session, Ana and I met at the Fountain for
a snack. She met with Dr. Webster during my same time slot. While
crossing the street, I strained to see through the large restaurant
windows if Ana sat at the corner booth—our booth. The Fountain

looked empty, so I assumed she hadn't finished her session. While waiting, I soaked up vitamin D. Dad always told me I should get sunshine every day because it made the body stronger, and I believed him. I always felt better when I'd been outside, and in the winter, being indoors more than normal made me sluggish and grumpy.

A black, iron bench outside the restaurant seemed the perfect place to watch life. That's what I called it, but Mr. Hap said the term was stopping to smell the roses. Whatever the correct phrase, I thought life slipped by us sometimes, and we should attempt to appreciate every moment. I imagined people my age took these little pleasures for granted.

Horizon was astonishing, although the history of its construction wasn't fully known. The rescue team, stationed here for two years before the war began, shared a few details. State-of-the-art materials used in construction resisted horrific conditions—weather and war. Our power, generated from solar, wind, and water technologies, provided clean energy. When I heard that term, I wondered why anyone used dirty energy.

Had our location taken a direct hit during the war, nothing would have survived, but here we were. The façade of our town had a purpose. The simple, pleasant look promoted tranquility and continuity. A familiar environment lessened our anxiety. Now, Earth was deserted rubble—the leftovers of war. Thankfully, we didn't have to live on a military base. An army compound would have reminded us normal life wasn't so normal anymore.

The design for our new (but old-looking) community was an excellent plan. A member of the town council called it a "brilliance of forethought" our government designed such a perfect place for civilization to rebuild. The citizens of Horizon wished our government had the brilliance of forethought not to blow up our world in the first place. However, it reminded me of the Norman Rockwell drawings at the Archives. Ana, who volunteered there, showed me copies after finding them in a dust-covered box. Someone saved these relics and put them in storage. Perhaps with these artifacts, the government assumed we could rebuild a better society. I was happy the town wanted a tranquil existence. Mr. Rockwell thought life should be peaceful and simplistic. In a magazine he illustrated was one of his quotes, "All of us who turn our eyes away from what we have are missing life." That was my philosophy, or so I intended. This notion aligned with Mr. Hap's idea of smelling the roses. Even as I worked to attain this harmonious outlook for life, I still had two questions without answers. Both were about The End. Why didn't Mr. Rockwell's world stay like that forever? Why would people choose war over peace? How and who didn't concern me, the *whys* perplexed me more than anything did.

Now, we lived in peace. War was such an absurd notion I had trouble imagining such an act. Perhaps we learned our lesson. Horizon, for us, was paradise. Sadness rushed over me, reflecting on the billions of people who never lived a life free from war.

The government constructed towns like Horizon in secret areas of the United States. These refuge designs allowed communication with one another, but war likely destroyed most of these sanctuaries. Billions of dollars in taxpayer money gone. Horizon was built in the Chattahoochee National Forest, in the northern part of Georgia—one of the southern states in America. Soldiers said the enemy targeted a city called Atlanta during the war because it was home to a government facility that studied diseases. As far as we knew, the war left little behind except for Horizon and five thousand strangers.

In the distance, Ana walked out of the Orchard. I could tell she had been crying. Her eyes were red, and her pale skin was blotchy. Lately, she left every release that way. She needed a diversion. I stood and walked to meet her halfway.

"I lied," I said.

"What?"

"I lied to Dr. Adler about not having any dreams the night I slept over at your house."

"Why?" She wrinkled her nose, which was her mannerism during deep thinking. My plan worked. Mission accomplished.

"I hoped you might have the answer," I said, with an honest exhale of exasperation. "It fell out of my mouth before I realized what I was saying."

We walked into the diner, and the familiar tinkling of the silver bell over the doorway caused Mrs. McCoy to come from the kitchen.

"Lookie there. Hello, cutie-pies," she said. "I was wondering where you two were today. I told Phil you'd be here and here you are. I'm telling you my psychic ability is fine-tuned today."

I could hear Phil, the cook, howl with laughter in the back. "Then tell me what I'm thinking now, Josie," he yelled.

We took our regular booth at the window, giggling. Mrs. McCoy, the mother of a friend from school, was the jolliest woman I'd ever met. At Christmas, she always played Mrs. Claus. It was a good fit for her.

Mrs. McCoy never brought us menus because she said we knew what was written on them better than Phil. "So, what'll it be today? Wait, don't tell me," she said, with her hand to her temple, "a nice chocolate milkshake. Is that right, Ellis? Phil isn't burning those today, are you Phil?" she yelled over her shoulder toward the kitchen.

"Ha, ha, Josie, hilarious," said Phil, with his thick Spanish accent, sounding much like Ana's mom.

"You did read my mind, Mrs. McCoy. That is exactly what I want today. I've been eating raw vegetables and fruits this week to drop a little weight."

"Well, there's your problem right there, honey. God don't make no mistakes. He meant for you to look just the way you do. Can you imagine how boring life would be if everyone looked alike? Besides, when I was your age and worrying about my weight, my mama told me nothing but a dog wants a bone. You remember that. Now, I'm gonna bring y'all toasted pimento cheese sandwiches. Bobby, from over at the dairy, brought me a block of cheddar. I made up a batch fresh this morning. It's so doggone good it'll make you slap your granny. But if it'll make you feel better, I'll put pickles on top, and they can be your vegetables." She walked away before I could say no. "Phil! Order up if you ain't too busy looking at yourself in the mirror, Casanova. Honey, let me tell you, Sylvia ain't interested in dating you, why she'd just as soon…"

Her voice faded out as she hurried back to the kitchen, talking non-stop. I loved Mrs. McCoy. You couldn't help but smile and laugh when you were around her.

The Fountain was a soda shop right out of the 1940s where kids sat at a bar and ordered drinks called floats and egg creams. Those items weren't on the menu but sounded delicious. I longed to know how soft drinks tasted and why they were called soft. I saw pictures of diners that existed over a hundred years earlier. For a school project, I did a compare and contrast report on the 2040s and the 1940s.

I looked at Ana. In the few moments it had taken me to talk with Mrs. McCoy, tears pooled in her eyes. I've never been one to stick my head in the sand, so I said, "Why are you upset, Ana?" She took her napkin and covered her face.

"My session was intense," she said, with the napkin still in place to hide her emotion. "The headaches are worse, and I…I can't get a grip. Dr. Webster tried sleep therapy."

I had sleep therapy one time, and it didn't help me to remember or forget anything, so my doctor never tried it again. Doctors, before The End, used hypnotherapy, a style of treatment. Our doctors told us it helped with the release of memories from that time. Oddly, Ana carried more memories with her, even though we were the same age. She convinced herself she remembered birth parents and a brother that was most likely wishful thinking than an actual possibility. Therapists told us not to discuss our memories, but Ana and I did. Dr. Adler called it dangerous but said I should listen to her if she talked. "The best way to help your friend," she told me once, "is to relay any memory she might tell you." Each doctor at the Orchard worked together and compared notes. Although not each therapist had been a doctor before, survivors with medical, psychological, or social work experience were trained.

"First," I said to Ana, in my best Mr. Hap accent, "I'm gonna need you to take that napkin off your face, okay? This ain't no round of peek-a-boo." She tried to stifle a laugh. "Second, I'm gonna need you to perk up cause if you don't, I'm gonna be forced to eat your sandwich. You've seen my butt. It's that giant thing that follows me around all day." She couldn't hold back the laughter and let the napkin fall back into her lap. "Thank ya, sister." This was a temporary fix, but at least her mood lightened.

"I'm sorry, Ellis. At one time, after therapy, I always felt clearer, but now I'm worse than before going," she said. "The doctor tells me I might progress quicker if I attend more sessions per week."

"Ana, everyone goes through down periods. You're normal."

"That's what you think?" she asked. Her nose wrinkled again. "You believe I'm depressed?"

"I…I didn't mean it in an ugly way," I stammered. "It's common to get—"

"Ellis, I'm not sad," she said, "I'm angry. But who should I be angry with?"

Her hands balled into fists. I reached out to touch her. At once, she relaxed. "Look, I'm your friend and want to help. I'll always be here for you."

"I wish I were sad, and I could mourn whatever family or life I've lost. But who were they? They are faceless and nameless. I'm not sad. I'm angry, and I don't know who to be angry with, so I'm angry at everyone and everything." She took a deep breath and a sip of water. "Who started the war, Ellis? Who pressed the button? Should I be mad at the person who rescued me? If I'd died, I wouldn't be suffering now."

I froze. I didn't want to make it worse, so I said nothing. With perfect timing, our food was delivered. We ate, without talking, except for Mrs. McCoy chiming in a few times. Ana looked out at the park. There was nothing to see, so I figured she was deep in thought. We finished the last of the milkshakes in calm silence except for the enormous burp I forced out to get a laugh from her. It worked. We said goodbye to Mrs. McCoy and Phil and walked to our bikes.

We rode part of the way home together. I lived in the Lakeside neighborhood, and Ana lived in the Parkview neighborhood closer to downtown. The Town Place neighborhood was behind the Orchard. These were apartments for singles and families without children. My dad compared them to something called brownstones, famous in New York City neighborhoods. Mountain Springs neighborhood was at the base of our largest mountain. Brook Haven was an assisted living home for our seniors. It was near the hospital and overlooked a little meadow with a stream. The Meadows was the neighborhood farthest from town. It shared the same area with Horizon Farm, where we raised animals and grew foods. The government thought of everything. They left behind instruction manuals for every aspect of survival.

"Are you mad at me, Ellis?" Ana asked.

"You're extra nuts today, aren't you?" I said. "Tomorrow, it's my turn. Just so you know…" We laughed.

I had become lost in my thoughts when I should've been thinking of ways to console my pal. We'd been best friends forever. I remembered the second day of kindergarten. I tried going the first day, but I cried so much my dad brought me back home. (But not before taking me for ice cream.) The next day, I cried again, but this time, Dad left me after being coaxed by the mean assistant teacher. I still hated her. *Horrible, old witch.* I was still crying when the sweet teacher took me by the hand and walked with me to where Ana was playing. She was smaller than I was and had golden blonde pigtails that hung in corkscrew curls. The teacher bent down to me and said, "Ellis, I want you to meet Ana. Ana likes to search for treasure in this sandbox. Can you help her discover what goodies might still be hidden?" Ana reached out to me, her hands covered in sand. I reached out expecting her to give me a treasure, but instead, she took my hand and pulled me closer to the sandbox. We dug holes, searching as a team. Although I was too young to realize, I had already found something more valuable than treasure.

Even now, we experienced times where one of us was reaching out to the other. Life would have been so much easier if a dig in the sandbox solved our problems. Ana suffered so much, and I wanted to help. I should've had the answers as a future therapist.

At the cut-off for her street, we said goodbye, and I continued home. Why did she have more intense memories to release? Just like me, she was a baby when The End occurred. I'd always felt sorry for her. Her adoptive dad died when she was four years old, and her mom raised her without talking about him. A long time ago, I asked her what happened, but she only would say that he was sick. Although Ana's mother was widowed at a young age, she never remarried. If I'd lost my dad, I don't think I'd have survived. If permitted,

I would've wanted Ana for my sister. One adoption per family was the limit. Singles weren't eligible to receive a child—a choice Mom and Dad considered unwise. People rushed to get married so they'd qualify to adopt an orphan of the war.

I looked ahead and saw my house. I breathed a sigh, thinking how lucky I was to have a stable, normal family.

CHAPTER 3

It must not have been easy for everyone to lose their families. During The Beginning, the orphaned children were given away to any survivors who agreed to marry first. Officials were eager to have everyone settled into normal lifestyles and placed children with those couples as soon as possible. Many adults rushed into loveless marriages to escape grief. Fear of lonesomeness fueled a need for the family unit. Men replaced dead wives. Women replaced dead husbands. Couples replaced dead children. Not every circumstance was satisfactory. The cases that failed needed correction. Secretly, many of us wished for something far different.

—Greta Bauer, Horizon adoptive mother
Personal Statement Transcript
February 2038

HOME

I ZOOMED INTO THE GARAGE AND PARKED MY BIKE alongside the solar-powered cart. Only a few officials drove cars. Each home received one cart, but if you saved your Credits, you could buy another. Our garage was immaculate. Dad arranged his tools and supplies in rows because he liked working on renovation projects to help neighbors when he had time off from work.

"Hi, Ell," called my dad from under the cart. He finished tightening a bolt on the door. "Good day?"

"Okay, I guess." I knew he'd question me further. For obvious reasons, I wanted to unburden myself. Dad would worry why I lied to Dr. Adler, but I needed to talk, and I wanted to be coerced into doing it.

"Well, I'm all ears, and both belong to you." Dad understood the entire psychology behind my response. Laying aside the tools, he sat on the brick steps leading from the garage to the inside of our house, smiling and waiting. This was Dad. His stare told me nothing else took precedence over whatever I wanted to say.

I closed my eyes and took a deep breath. "I lied to Dr. Adler."

My dad didn't change his expression. "Let's discuss why."

"I'm not sure. I've never lied during release. Dr. Adler has always been a friend, but I didn't want to tell her the bad dream I had when I slept over at Ana's house."

"Well, I'm no doctor," he said, "but I might have an idea."

"Dad, be serious." He was a doctor who had worked at the largest hospital in New York before The End, and he was a doctor now. His old joke made little sense to me but was funny because he was king of the nerds.

"Come, sit," he said, still chuckling. He moved over, allowing me space on the step. "Something in your dream made you uncomfortable. By choosing to keep silent, you are not experiencing the details again. Therefore, *deliberate* avoidance of the discussion indicates concerns that should be explored."

"Non-doctor-talk, please."

"Sorry. You should talk about the dream because you *didn't* want to talk about it. Remember, a dream is only a dream. It is not flesh and blood—it can't hurt or kill you. Don't let it take control of you. You must control it." He put his arm around me and squeezed. "I love you, Junior." *I love my pet name.* "It is admirable you take your therapy seriously; I hope you'll discuss the dream, with me or the doctor. Only then, can you move forward."

"Thanks, Pop. You're right; I can always count on you. Tonight, I'll write what I remember from the dream so I can discuss it with the doctor." I stood up and looked at him. He was warm and kind looking. I wondered if others saw what I did. I noticed a little gray had sprouted in his dark hair, and I realized he was getting older. *Stop—definitely, can't go there tonight.* The thought of losing my dad was something I couldn't survive. I stood and rested my hand on the doorknob.

"Dad?" He turned to face me. "How fast do seniors get sick from those illnesses affecting the mind?"

He looked at me with a bewildered expression. "Am I the senior in this scenario?"

"No, Dad, I'm serious. I chatted with Mr. Hap today before my release. He became confused retelling one of his old stories. It was as if his memories were of someone else's life."

"Ell, honey, you shouldn't encourage Mr. Parsons to reminisce about his past. Remember the rules. Memories are difficult for many people, and for others, they are dangerous."

"But I didn't ask him to tell the stories this time. What he said contradicted what he'd told me before today. I don't want him to be in trouble, but I thought he might be sick. Don't you have medicines to help that kind of thing?"

"I know you didn't mean any harm. Why don't I talk with him to consider whether he's having some issues? Before The End, I sometimes helped seniors with an illness called Alzheimer's. If he shows signs of it, I'll ask him to come for a check-up, and I can learn more about his condition."

"Thanks, Dad. He's my friend—I want him to be okay."

"I'll take care of him," he said. "I'll make a reason to stop and look in on him. Try not to worry."

My Dad was a problem solver. He could find a solution for anything, and I relied on him. I could go to him with a problem, and he had the fix. I never had to worry. How amazing was that? I leaned over and gave him a real hug.

My mother was preparing dinner when I walked into the kitchen.

"Hello, Ellis. Wait," she said, mid-chop of a carrot. I stopped.

"You shouldn't have taken the cookies without asking first. Plus, they will ruin your appetite for dinner."

"The cookies were for Mr. Hap. He told me to thank you."

"Mr. Parsons," she corrected. "I assume you ate at the Fountain with Ana?"

"Nope," I said, to vex her with improper English. "I need to journal for my release homework," I said, walking away. Once in my room, I kicked my sneakers off and threw myself onto the white bed comforter, snuggling into its cool, welcoming embrace. My dataport lay on the desk. I held my hand out to grab it. *If…I…could…just… reach it—nope.* Okay, journal later. I wanted to lay here and take time for myself today that didn't include school, studying, daily chores, release therapy, or cookie theft. Within minutes, I drifted off to sleep, and the dream returned.

I'm outside Horizon and not alone. An ally, in the form of a shadow, is with me, but I don't feel entirely safe. I want to stay with my family, but I feel compelled to go with him. He tells me my mother has gone. I ask about my dad, and there is silence and emptiness. I hear a comforting voice calling me. It's pulling me away from the only home I can remember. If I stay, people will hate me, and if I leave, others will hate me. I run. My legs seem to work despite my psychological resistance. I'm not controlling where I'm going. I am so scared. Where is Dad? My companion pulls me. "Let it go," he says. "Nothing was ever real."

CHAPTER 4

Today, we mourn for Nurahatum. Yesterday, scientists confirmed the SHLE385 asteroid impacted our home planet. This asteroid was larger than any previously recorded in history. Scientists believe the collision resulted in the total annihilation of the planet and every life form, including the remaining Atum not yet transported to Earth.

Evacuations began when I was less than two years old. In school, we have studied the history of the exodus to planet Earth that began over twelve years ago. I am too young to remember Nurahatum, but I join with all Atum as we grieve for our lost citizens.

When scientists discovered we had less than thirty years before the collision, they researched the possibilities for other settlements. Two planets provided suitable solutions for our new home. Our people had a relationship with Earth for five thousand years. The human study had been extensive. Since Earth was our closest neighbor, and we were familiar with its history and cultures, our government thought it the best chance for our survival. We needed a new planet, and Earth was on the brink of eradication. Scientists concluded the planet would soon be destroyed because of its many wars. The proposal to help Earth would save both our civilizations. Scientists and researchers formulated a plan.

—Brauchm Chaulchgluer
The Children's Planetary Memorial Documents

HUMAN STUDIES 101

OUR PROFESSOR SHOCKED US WHEN HE READ THE notice.

"I have extraordinary news. The Habitat project has chosen this class to visit, observe, and research." Most everyone cheered.

"Quiet, please. Habitat researchers have never bestowed this honor upon persons outside the project; therefore, we must obey a strict set of rules. This is not an opportunity to get out of class. You must use this experience to educate yourselves further in the differentiation of human behavior. Now, because the facility operates as a controlled community, we will learn and follow procedures. We will not make mistakes. Listen and understand. Since the war in 2032, researchers have conducted studies without the surviving humans' knowledge. What an amazing achievement that in twenty years, no incident has occurred. Therefore, we will not merrily romp about treating this opportunity as if it were a field trip to Disney World."

Several people laughed; I did not. He meant for us to understand the enormity of this prospect.

"So," Professor Daulchmanu said with an exaggerated pause, "the humans are unaware they are living in a city-sized observatory, and when we are finished with our studies, they will still be unaware. Do I make myself understood?"

No one made a sound.

"Excellent. We understand one another with perfect clarity. The year 2052 will not be the year my research students jeopardized the Habitat project."

"Now, open the guidebook being handed to you. Read every word and afterward, read it again. We must adhere to these rules.

"The majority of species act and react differently when being observed. We have studied humans for thousands of years but never so thoroughly in an authentic, natural, daily environment. The Habitat provides that environment for study purposes. Researchers understand the enormous responsibility to protect humans and help them flourish in their newly created world. So, let us start at the beginning. Shall we? I want you to turn to page three. Bram, will you please read aloud for the class?"

"Yes, Professor," I said, hating the thought of being in the spotlight. "In accordance with the Requirements for the Ethical Treatment of Humans, researchers and caregivers must adhere to very specific guidelines. The following conditions must be provided. 1) Medical and psychological care, 2) Food and other sustenance, 3) Housing and safety, 4) Absence of project knowledge, 5) Adequate simulations of positive human life experiences, and 6) Hope."

"Thank you, Bram. You see..."

"Professor Daulchmanu?" Shuhaln asked, "Were humans so irresponsible they needed confinement?"

"Allow me to share an opinion and not a scientific hypothesis. Before the Atum intervened in the wars creating such destruction on Earth, one human leader ordered nuclear weapons to be used on a massive scale. One human. Within hours, global nuclear war engulfed the planet. That was the degree of power held by an individual. One human began the destruction of their entire world."

"Was their war so horrible?" asked Meziem.

"I haven't always been in a classroom, you realize. My assignment was to help with reconstruction. After determining the immediate danger was over, emergency teams landed here and began rescue efforts. I worked with the bravest Atum ever born. We arrived in the second wave of relief and saw horrors we had never known. My team posed as a surviving United States Military unit whose duty was to transport people to safety."

"The Habitat?" asked Shuhaln.

"No, not yet. Humans went to different locations for medical treatment and after, relocated to the Habitat."

"And the radiation?" she asked.

"We had the same technology the humans utilized to clean the atmosphere of radiation. Their filtration systems were not as advanced as ours were. For months, teams worked to stabilize the planet. Humans filled their world with so many dangerous things. We knew how to disable their nuclear reactors. Other damaged power systems had to be secured while raging firestorms swept across many countries. War, of this magnitude, caused disruptions with weather patterns and made this planet unpredictable."

"Were you scared?"

"I would be a liar or a fool to answer no. Earth and her humans terrified us. We were on an unstable planet with dangers not yet presented. The Atum chose to inhabit one land mass while other areas of the world became wastelands of what humanity destroyed. Those areas, the Wildlands, are healing themselves now. Nature got to reclaim those places."

"Why not tell humans the truth?" I asked. I heard other students mumble to get on with the lesson, but I didn't care.

"Well, Bram, the answer is complex. Humans could not care for themselves. Our leaders placed survivors into the community we constructed for their benefit and our own. By creating this natural habitat for humans, we could care for and protect them from outside dangers and themselves as well. If the humans discovered they were being confined by what they call *aliens*, we would have had an uprising that would lead to war and the total extinction of the human species. No, they must never learn the truth of their world or the existence of us as their captors—captors isn't the right word... we are their protectors. We are not without sensitivity. We *chose* to save the few remaining humans on Earth. However, we will never live together because coexistence between our species is no longer a logical, safe solution."

Deep within, I wondered if we were wrong to treat the humans in this way.

For the next week, documents, official visas, and other identification had to be obtained for admission. Several students thought the Habitat was nothing more than a visit to a human zoo. However, many soon discovered this extreme security was more than precautionary. If a breach occurred, every minor detail must be in place to contain any situation that might cause a significant failure in the entire project. We required physical cosmetic changes in case a face-to-face encounter with a human occurred. We would, at least, *look* human.

Although the Atum race was nearly identical in physical design to humans more than to any other known race of beings, minute differences in our appearance separated us visually. Our race of people didn't have the external diversity found in humans. In our unaltered form, we had subtle shade differences in our black hair, light green eyes with silver-lined, rectangular pupils, and what humans called suntanned skin. The differences in shade variations were visible to us, although humans could not distinguish between them. Because we didn't have as many distinctions in our physical form, it became fashionable to change these colors. Many Atum changed their hair, eye, and skin color weekly. By taking a tiny pill, anyone could change these features within twenty-four hours. Those changes lasted from four to seven days, with no side effects. Because our world knew of Earth for a long time, occasionally Atum copied the looks of famous Earthlings. My mother told me of a famous human woman named Marilyn Monroe. Many of our females copied her style long ago, including my great-grandmother.

Even with our ability to change our looks, our final appearance had to be approved for the trip. On New Earth, humans no longer had access to beauty products from before the war. Hair colors were now natural shades. Vibrant shades of hair were no longer possible in their world. The professor expected us to resemble the same look found in today's earth population. The Habitat advisor offered occupills to change our eyes to human green, blue, brown, and hazel; however, the Atum had a thousand eye color and pupil design choices. Limiting the selections to four human colors was painful for many females in our study group. Dermipills changed the skin color. The advisor showed us various shades of neutrals available for use. The professor warned anyone attempting to join us with pink, purple, or other outrageous skin would stay home. Pilipills changed hair color and texture. The human population limited our choices here again.

"Jdis dimoh sobus," Glairn exclaimed.

"Glairn," began our professor, "I will remove you from this class if you do not speak English."

Although less than eight thousand humans remained in the

world, our human studies course required a mastery of the language. Our schools began teaching English decades ago on Nurahatum when we realized Earth would eventually be our refuge. Our leaders said if we were to seek help from the American government, we should be able to communicate properly in its official language. We continued the use of both languages on New Earth.

The professor insulted Glairn's ego and pride by reprimanding her, but she raised her hand and corrected herself. "How grotesque," she said, now in perfect English. "How could anyone find a human attractive with such bland features?"

Several of her friends laughed with her. I did not. "You like them, Bram?" she asked in my direction, challenging what she assumed to be my answer.

"I don't want to offend anyone here, but the human females are…"

"Chote," called out one of the other guys using our word for hot.

Others in the class added their own descriptions. I smiled, grabbing the opportunity to infuriate Glairn. "I can appreciate an exotic female."

"Exotic…sure," she said.

"Gentlemen, this isn't the type of conversation I encourage when females are present," the professor now reprimanded all of us.

Glairn didn't appreciate someone, in particular, a human, rivaling her position as an alpha female. Atum standards considered her gorgeous. She never admitted to making any physical alterations using pills, but others suspected her hair color not to be natural and her skin to be darker than average. Her conceit was so great she refused to choose any human physical disguises for her outward appearance. The professor threatened her, and she chose an eye color. Most students didn't agree with her opinions about the quality of attraction in humans. Most Atum males shared my views on the mesmerizing human female and referred to their colorful differences as an Earthling rainbow.

In January, I received my list of potential mates. By some cruel fate, Glairn was on my list. The probability of already knowing one of my couplings was minuscule. Scientific tests determined suitable mates for us from every other Atum of the required age. Glairn and I scored high in the physical attraction category. Our brains registered we found each other physically appealing. The next highest scoring category was in genetics. Our blood analysis suggested a high probability of producing a healthy, intelligent child. However, our tests don't consider that psychologically, her demeanor was so unattractive, her outward beauty could not compensate.

Glairn clarified the fact she found me desirable. She acted jealous when I spoke with other females. In a childish way, her reaction brought me pleasure. If it were possible to fabricate the test results to bring us together, I might have accused her of doing so.

"Professor, how is it possible a breach never occurred in the Habitat?" asked Shuhaln.

"If there has been accidental contact with humans, I don't suppose we would be privy to that information," he said. "Human-Atum contact is only allowed after extensive training. Specialty workers, Habitat maintenance, and the Habitat governing committees are the only people authorized to have routine access to humans. They have trained and studied diligently for this privilege."

"Privilege," huffed Glairn, "please."

"Glairn, if you are so anti-human, why are you taking this class?" asked Shuhaln, a smart girl, fortunate to be excluded from Glairn's inner circle.

"I don't see how it is any of your concern, Shuhaln," began Glairn, "but I am taking this course to prove scientifically that preserving the human race is a ridiculous waste of time, energy, and resources. Humans do not differ from other stupid animals existing on this planet. Their evolution has crept along, which proves they are a detriment to civilized advancement. You see how they caused their own demise."

"Shuhaln, what's your problem? Don't you remember how many Atum deaths the humans caused?" asked Meziem.

No one ever spoke of the deaths occurring during the time of the restructure. Glairn's uncle had been a part of an expedition team encountering hostility and died at the hands of a human. The Atum considered him a hero of the rescue efforts.

The conversation ended. No one spoke for a moment. The professor walked to the front of the class and stood as if he was deciding whether he should discuss the issue or continue with our lesson.

He said, "Names. You have chosen your physical changes. You will receive your pills two days before the trip, and we will take them together in class. The medicine will take effect in a timely fashion so our transformations will not unexpectedly reanimate into their natural states. Now, you should choose human names as another layer of your human identity. Open your dataports. I sent you an extensive collection of English human names listed in alphabetical order. Look through them and choose carefully. You will address your classmates for the remainder of the class term with these names. Next, assignments. Write a believable personal history to share with us tomorrow in class. These mini-biographies should contain information you will memorize should you make contact with a human. Please begin and be as thorough as your imaginations will allow." He looked with raised eyebrows at Glairn.

I opened my dataport and looked through the file of names. My mother and father named me for a human who served as a leader of America in the 1800s. My father enjoyed Earth history, and my mother often commented if Abraham Lincoln served as president twenty years ago, war could have been avoided. Although our alphabet spelled my legal name differently, Dad chose the English Earth spelling for my nickname—much to my grandmother's disapproval.

"Professor," I called out, "considering Bram is an English name, do I need to choose another?"

"I suppose there could be no harm in keeping your name. And what of your personal history, are you prepared in that area?"

"I think I should keep my backstory simple," I responded.

"Well, I am astonished," the professor paused. "It is curious you have a believable story so soon. Are you accustomed to making up lies at a moment's notice? If so, your chosen potential mates should be notified at once." He laughed, something rarely done by him during class. The others joined in and looked at Glairn, knowing her to be on my list. I laughed and nodded my head. It was the truth; I loved making up stories. As a child, often I imagined being on pretend adventures read to me at bedtime. My favorite book series featured a boy wizard.

"I am Abraham Potter. Bram for short. I'm twenty-two years old. I lived in South Carolina at the time of The End. My mother and father work in agriculture."

The professor studied me and said, "Which town?"

"Which town?"

"Which town did you live in when The End occurred, Bram Potter?"

"In…in Charlotte," I said.

"Charlotte was not in South Carolina," he said, turning to the rest of the class, "We have a simple example of an accident which could cause complications within the Habitat. Mr. Potter, every detail must be accurate. What date were you born? Who were your birth parents? Did you have brothers and sisters? I don't remember you in school, what year did you get your placement?"

Maybe I wasn't as ready as I thought.

"I will expect you to answer difficult questions in class tomorrow. Young Mr. Potter has come to understand one must be prepared for many possible questions. We have less than one week to prepare for the visit to the Habitat. You must take advantage of this opportunity, for it is unlikely to present itself again. The emphasis is on increasing understanding and awareness of the species. Prepare for your research, complete the paperwork you have received, develop your identities, and print your new name badges. We will use those names tomorrow." He turned to leave, stopped in mid-stride, and said without looking at anyone, "Please address me as Professor Frost from this moment forward." He walked out and left us to stare at each other. We had no idea what fantastic events awaited us in the Habitat known to humans as the community of Horizon.

CHAPTER 5

Studies have proven humans function better when relieved of memories associated with stressful situations (Kirby, 1963, Abducted: New Hampshire), (Lowe, 1999, Post-Traumatic Stress Disorders), (Eisluf, 2017, Wislou Daut Wos). It is a logical conclusion that the loss of loved ones and/or the clinging to pre-war positive memories are detrimental to the overall health and emotional stability of the human psyche. By controlling the feelings associated with these memories, we relieve the sorrow causing humans within the Habitat to produce undesirable results regarding normal functioning. The majority of patients are easier to release from experiences than a minority who require intensive treatments. Those who fail to respond to treatment and those incapable of suppressing emotional distress must be assessed for possible replacement within the project.

—Dr. Ethan Webster
Thesis Research
May 2033

MEMORIES

NOT EVERY CITIZEN OF HORIZON COULD KNOW every other person who lived here. It was impossible to know the other 7,199 people in town, personally. However, when you think of less than eight thousand remaining people left on the planet, the number is minute. Close friends were those who fall within a person's daily path. For me, that means students in my class, those I interacted with at the Hobby Center, my therapist, neighborhood, and people I saw at the Fountain. I estimated having a hundred acquaintances. Ana was my best friend. There was a difference between acquaintances and friends. I chose quality over quantity, and I suppose since I was interested in psychology, I analyzed people more than necessary. I found fault easily although I didn't think myself better than anyone. To be honest, I had more faults than almost everyone did, and that was probably the reason I was drawn to psychology—I wanted to learn about myself.

I was fascinated with life before the war. This subject, however, was forbidden. People wouldn't lose privileges (the equivalent of jail), but instead, be called to meet with the council if they had acted in a way which harmed the progress of another person. Dad said this happened before but shouldn't be discussed either. Consistently, I violated this rule with Mr. Hap. Perhaps my curiosity about the pre-Horizon world outweighed the threat of reprimand. Truthfully, my opinion constantly swayed on the benefit of burying memories. To speak of or not to speak of, that was my question.

I left exhausted from my volunteer duty at the Hobby Center. At thirteen, kids performed volunteer work three times a week. Ana always loved books, so she was perfect for work at the Archives. Today, I taught self-defense to ages fourteen through eighteen. I also taught the nine to the thirteen-year-old group, but those weren't as tiring. At five-years-old, I took my first self-defense lesson from my mother, who had always been interested in ancient martial arts. Her skill was remarkable. At age six, I took two classes each week. Her goal was to keep me healthy and thin. Mom expected me to choose that for one of my two required enrichment classes. I mastered each level and became the youngest instructor on staff when I turned fourteen. I found comfort knowing how to protect myself from danger. In Horizon, crime was nonexistent, so I never had my skill tested realistically. Even if I'd never use it, I was glad to know self-defense. According to my mother, the skills we don't have, we must learn. The skills we do have, we must teach. In this way, our knowledge won't be lost.

Next quarter, Ana and I were organizing a Jane Austen book club and taking a digital media class. Between enrichment activities, volunteering, school, studying, release therapy, and home duties, Horizon's youth stayed busy.

I hoped Mom cooked something tasty; I was starving. Ahead, I saw three official cars at Mr. Hap's house. They looked similar to our transport buses for school during the cold months when biking was suspended. I stopped to check that he was okay. A serious-looking woman was carrying a suitcase from his house. Next, a man with a massive build came out carrying two storage boxes. I laid my bike on his lawn and walked to his door.

"Can I help you, young lady?" said the man, putting items in with other boxes.

"I'm here to visit Mr. Ha…Mr. Parsons," I said politely, trying to hide my growing fear Mr. Hap was moving to the assisted living facility.

"He is not here. He became sick this morning and is at the hospital for treatment."

"But the last time we talked, he was fine."

"I'm sorry, but I have no details," he said.

"Why are you moving his belongings? Won't he come back?"

"I don't have those answers, I'm following orders, but don't worry. The hospital will take care of him."

I rarely visited my Dad at work. He was always busy, and interruptions prevented him from finishing on time, but I needed to check on Mr. Hap.

I arrived at the hospital entrance and walked past the visitors' desk. My friend, Wynn, was volunteering there. She waved and gave me the you-don't-need-to-sign-in-look. I took the elevator to the third floor, where Dad was most likely working.

As the doors of the elevator opened, I ran into my father.

"Hey, you. What are you doing here? I was on my way home early tonight, for a change." He stepped into the elevator, and the doors closed. I stepped forward and stopped them with an upraised hand.

"Dad, we need to talk," I said.

"Junior, are you sick?" He clutched my elbow and looked me over from head to toe for an ailment or injury that brought me to the hospital. He had a worried parent-look on his face that made me love him.

"No, Dad. I'm fine. I need to talk to you. Can we go to your office?"

He let go of me and paused. "I would rather not be late for dinner. Your mother gets vexed when we aren't on time."

I wanted to say something impolite, but those words weren't permitted in public—or in our home. So instead, I said, "Okay, we'll tell her you had an emergency and had to work over your normal time."

"Ellis, honey, I understand your mother can be demanding, but lying is wrong. She wants our life to be structured for our well-being. Lies are born out of fear."

"You think so, Dad? I'd rather lie to her than get chewed out because the cauliflower-rhubarb-dirt casserole has gotten a little cold. Believe me, Dad, it won't taste any better hot. What makes more sense? Lying to keep the peace or having a household war because we were five minutes late?" I took a breath. I was getting loud and angry with him because of my concern for Mr. Hap. "Look, I'm sorry. That's a subject for another time. Please…it will be quick, I promise."

He paused again. He was wondering how long these five minutes might take and if those five minutes would send Mom into meltdown mode, with or without a lie. I put my hand on his shoulder and gave it a squeeze accompanied by a smile. If I could wave a magic wand to make Mom more patient and less—whatever the word was for her, I'd do it. In a perfect world, people didn't fear dinner might be on the table for a whole thirty seconds before eating.

"Okay, Ell," he said with a furrowed brow.

We walked into his office. I sat behind his desk the way I always had since I was a child. Years ago, he let me pretend to be the doctor, and he pretended to be the patient. He loved to tell the story of when I was four. I sat in his chair with a clipboard and a pencil. He told me his symptoms, and I took his stethoscope to listen to his chest and back. I placed my hand on his head to check for fever and made him open his mouth to say "ah." After the exam, I gave him little white mints from his candy dish and said they were medicine. My diagnoses varied. Sometimes it was "sweet tummy" caused by eating too many sweets. Sometimes, he had "veggie-itus" caused by pretending to eat his vegetables when he actually slid them into his napkin. The funniest diagnosis was "the snots" caused by jumping into mud puddles. He roared with laughter at that diagnosis, so I sang, "Daddy has the snots, Daddy has the snots,"—much to the displeasure of my mother.

"Dad, where is Mr. Hap? I rode past his house, and officials were cleaning it out. They said he was here. What happened?"

"Oh, Junior. I'm sorry you found out about Mr. Parsons in that way. I was telling you tonight. You were correct; he was suffering from a memory issue. He is undergoing tests to see if something is causing his brain to malfunction."

"You mean a tumor?" I asked.

"That's one possible cause, but I can't be sure until the tests are completed."

"If he's only having tests, why are they moving his things from his house?"

"I'm not aware of his belongings being moved. I'll check that out tomorrow, but I don't want you to worry. He needs care."

"The moving man used those same words. I want to see him, Dad."

"You can't."

"Why?" I asked impatiently and, to my horror, with the voice of my mother.

"Ellis, Mr. Parsons isn't himself at the moment. He's having issues which prevent visiting."

"A minute."

"I'm sorry. If I could guarantee your safety, I'd allow it, but he is in quarantine until diagnosed. It is possible he might have something contagious. We can't risk anyone having contact with him."

"This makes no sense. He was fine last week…almost. I understand you want to be careful, but I'm sure he is scared and confused. I want him to see a friend."

"No, Ellis." My father seldom spoke in a harsh manner. He turned from me and picked up his briefcase placed in the chair earlier.

"What's on your neck? What happened to you? Are you okay?" I reached to touch a bandage on his neck.

"No, don't touch it," he said, jerking away from me.

"Mr. Hap did this?" I asked.

He paused. His hesitation was confirmation my old friend had done something. "His physical condition is stable, but he is confused. He fought us when we put him to bed. Such aggression is typical of patients with his symptoms, but I can't diagnose him without the test results. I didn't want you to learn how drastically his health deteriorated because I believed you might try to assume responsibility for this," he said, pointing to his neck. "I'll not risk your safety by allowing you to visit him while he's still aggressive. Please try to understand. Mr. Parsons was fortunate you recognized his condition otherwise, he might have hurt himself or someone else."

"I don't feel better about it, Dad."

"I'm sorry, Junior. He won't get well without treatment. Now, you and I need to get home before your mother starts throwing things and we both need bandages. Let's enjoy a nice dinner. I promise to tell you when it's safe to visit your pal."

I allowed him to lead me to the elevators. Along the way, I watched the staff around me, and they watched us with stares that made me question the details of Mr. Hap's condition. My dad thought we were on our way home to battle with my angry mother and a crap casserole, but I sensed the real battle lay ahead of us and would begin somewhere within this hospital.

CHAPTER 6

Mirrored glasses placed in key locations will monitor humans. Designing the Habitat to feel realistic for the test subjects while enabling research teams unobtrusive observation will be the challenge. Underground will serve as the center of operations for the large support staff maintaining the Habitat research facility and will provide many services needed for human survival. The observation galleries will act as the backstage of the Habitat and not be accessible nor made known to the humans. This design will function as an enclosure without appearing restrictive. Humans will be oblivious to being watched, studied, and contained.

—Reece Briggs, Architect,
Classified Doomsday Project Horizon
August 2016

FIELD TRIP

THE ENTIRE GROUP WAS EXCITED. OUR ENTHUSI-
asm for visiting the Habitat was contagious. Even Professor
Frost was lighthearted. We arrived early to school for the first day
of travel. With human makeovers completed and mandatory documents identifying us with new names, we boarded the bus. Glairn's
not-so-secret admirer, Meziem, now named George Washington,
tried to convince the professor being the first president of America
posed no risk since there existed little chance of a human encounter.
After our no-nonsense teacher renamed George Washington to Jim
Sanders, we left. Most everyone changed his or her appearance to
some degree. Glairn now had blue eyes. I chose the same. Did our
choosing alike confirm we were compatible?

Our school campus was three hundred miles from the center of
the Habitat. We first traveled to the Habitat Transit Line Station. At
the station, three methods of rail travel were available. Our group
would transfer from our bus to a passenger pod designed to take
many travelers at one time. Some workers inside the Habitat used
vehicle pods to transport their cars. The third type was a storage pod
used to carry large quantities of equipment and supplies to the Habitat. This method of transportation allowed us to travel the additional
150 miles underground at a speed of over two hundred miles per
hour. At the end of each day, we would return in the same manner
and be taken to our hotel outside of the Habitat not far from the
Transit Station.

Humans believed the government built this town in case of an
apocalyptic event. If a human escaped the above ground enclosure
of Horizon, 150 miles of rugged, mountainous terrain surrounded
by barren desert-like land lay between the town and the outer wall.
Even if they survived that trek undetected, a thirty-foot wall was

the next obstacle to their freedom. Because no exit gates existed, a human would have to scale the impenetrable walls made of smooth stone with no grooves. No living creature could touch this wall without severe injury because it conducted an electrical current via a mineral from our planet layered beneath its foundation. A similar wall surrounded the outer perimeter of Horizon. The humans thought it protected them from dangers outside the town. The design for the Habitat was perfect.

Soon, we were on our way, and students discussed the what-if scenarios of meeting humans. Others slept, while a few memorized their fake character profiles last minute in case a what-if became a reality. Frankly, most of us were hoping for an accidental encounter. Few Atum had met or interacted with humans. Many citizens demanded the Habitat become a reality series created for entertainment. Humans, in general, were a source of curiosity for our people.

I was looking over my notes when Glairn moved into the seat beside me. *Why didn't I sleep?* She wanted to discuss the coupling results. I wasn't ready to have that conversation, and the reason for it was my fault. No matter the other choices, I couldn't see myself happy with her for the rest of my life. I understood the tests we took were scientific, but I wasn't convinced an algorithm could know my heart. My father told me true love wasn't determined by science and testing. True feelings within the heart couldn't be measured, and love shouldn't be based on chemicals or brain waves. I wanted to find the one person designed for no one else but me. Glairn wasn't it, and I was positive I could never make her happy. I faked exhaustion saying I needed a nap before arriving at the Habitat Interior Station. She grabbed her bag and left, making as much noise as possible, without concern for disturbing anyone else. Her spoiled and selfish ways could be someone else's joy but not mine.

I closed my eyes to fake sleep and imagined what adventure

might lie in wait for me behind the walls of the Habitat. I had an inexplicable sensation as if I were being pulled by one of those Earth magnets causing me to cling instantly to something inside that town.

I wondered how many accidental meetings had occurred. The law of averages suggested at least one mishap. Our trip coordinators told us this was impossible if we followed the rules. Fortunately, rules often got broken when I was around.

"Ellis, remember why we are here," said Ana.

I shot her a glance with wide eyes and nodded my head. Last night, after dinner, we discussed the mysterious way Mr. Hap left his home. I told her the conversation we had and how his sweet stories had changed. I also told her what happened at the hospital with my father. During our conversation, she said something that gave me chills. 'It sounds as if someone is trying to erase not only Mr. Hap's memories but erase him as well.' Why should anyone want to erase people? Didn't the war cause enough loss? Release therapy shouldn't rewrite feelings. Something, however, changed Mr. Hap's stories. Ana was adamant that information inside the Archives could solve this mysterious behavior. Her logical mind was perfect for solving mysteries. Ana was Sherlock Holmes, ready to uncover the truth, and I was Watson, supporter, and protector. She loved a mission.

"Hello, girls. Ana, you aren't scheduled for duty today," said Mrs. Croft, stepping away to get her clipboard.

As she walked back to the desk, Ana said, "No, we're here to get prepared for our Jane Austen book club in the fall."

"Oh, I love her work," she said, shuffling papers with no real purpose than to look busy. "You can find what you need; I have so much work to do. Besides, you are familiar with everything, so I'll let you two get going. Have fun."

As we walked away, Ana gestured for me to glance back toward the jovial Mrs. Croft. She pushed away papers and pulled what appeared to be an old magazine from under the counter after looking for anyone nearby.

"What is she doing?" I asked.

"It's called People Magazine. They were entertainment documents from the antiquities' department. They have pictures and stories describing the lives of celebrities from long ago. She isn't supposed to have them out of the case. She's in love with an actor named George Clooney."

I snuck another peek at the woman who was nibbling on cookies and engrossed in whichever story gave her such delight.

"Ellis, let's stay alert," she said, as if we might be spies. "There aren't many people here today; it's slowest during this time, so Mrs. Croft risks reading her magazines. We don't we want anyone to see us, so we will go to the second floor and browse in the fiction department for books."

"Why can't anyone see us looking for books?" I asked. She didn't respond. We made our way up the staircase. Everywhere stood heaving bookshelves with volumes as old as three hundred years. Ana said how lucky we were government officials included a book collection in the bunker for a purpose such as this.

I spent a few minutes looking at different books. The halls were quiet and spooky with no others walking around, and I started to say this to Ana until she motioned for me to follow her.

"Where?" I asked.

"You're the lookout. Stand at the door," she said.

"What? I'm sorry, I'm the what? Ana, this section is restricted. We can't—it's off-limits to us."

This part of the Archives was only accessible with a particular identification badge that also acted as a key card. Ana handed me a stack of books she gathered. I watched as she pulled one of those badges from her pocket with the name Louisa Croft printed in bold letters across it.

"Ana!" I whisper-shouted, "When did you get her badge?"

"Slick, huh?" She smiled. "I was hoping she'd be preoccupied with a magazine. Let's hope our luck continues."

"Wait, what do you mean?"

With a mischievous smile, Ana said, "I read once desperate times call for desperate measures. I can't imagine a circumstance more desperate than a massive government cover-up forcing us to choose between being sent away or forgetting the details of our lives. Can you?"

I stared dumbfounded. "Who are you, and what have you done to Ana?" This was my fault. By telling her the story of Mr. Hap, I poured fuel onto the fiery rage she had been struggling with for the last few months and unknowingly provided a direction for all of that anger. We needed a lie, if we were caught.

Ana swiped the card. A heavy metallic clunk sounded. The door's lock had been turned. I'm sure I heard her release a massive exhale. "Thank goodness."

"What? You weren't sure it would work?" I was amazed she took such a crazy chance.

"Nope," she said bluntly, "I didn't know if she had clearance." She pushed, and the door flew open.

The books I carried as a ruse hurled into the air, and I hit the floor with an enormous thud.

"Ja mau...I...I am so sorry," he began as he bent over to pick up books. He stopped abruptly and gave me his hand to help me stand. "I…I didn't see you. Are you…harmed, I…I mean hurt, are you hurt?"

I looked up at his face, my muscles went weak, and I slumped back to the floor. He dropped the books and used both hands to help me. No doubt, my face turned red, "I'm sorry, I…am fine," *so eloquent*, "are *you* all right?"

"Yes," he said with a laugh. "You're sure you aren't hurt?" he asked again.

I realized I was staring, mouth open, looking ridiculous. *What was my lie? I forgot my lie.* Since my trance had taken away my ability to speak beyond two-syllable words, this man leaned closer as if to examine me for a concussion-like state and put his hand under my elbow to lead me to a nearby chair. Without words, I followed his lead and sat.

"Ellis," said Ana.

Her voice brought me back to reality. A flush of heat from the top of my head tore through my body down to my toes.

"Can I get help for you, Ellis?" he asked.

His voice was so calming I wanted to close my eyes and melt into it. His words poured over me like a pitcher of warm bath water. *He said my name.* The sound was…velvety. *Ellissss.* I realized I had, for an unknown amount of time, been staring with a blank expression in a daydream state. Was it one minute? Was it five minutes?

"I'm…not hurt." *Great, now one-syllable words.* I paused again in this slow-motion moment. "I had the breath knocked out of me," I said finally.

"Thank you for your help," Ana said to him. "Ellis, we will be late." She pulled at my arm showing we had to leave.

"Late?" I said stupidly. I stood. "Oh, late, yes, late for the…thing. Right, well, I…thank you again and sorry…again…" *Snap out of it. Think…think.*

"Bram," he said. "My friends call me Bram." I wasn't asking his name; I was trying to think of words to say.

"Bram," I repeated. *I am an idiot.* Ana pulled me toward downstairs.

"Wait," he said. *Oh no, this is it, we are in trouble.* As he walked closer, he smiled, and I waited for my chest to explode. "I love her."

"What…I'm sorry, what?"

"Jane Austen," he handed me one of the books I carried in my arms when we collided. "She was a great writer. My mother made sure I read her books."

"Why?" I said, before thinking it might have sounded rude.

His smile could have melted an iceberg. "She wanted to make sure I understood how a perfect gentleman should act. She said Jane Austen's books were full of men who knew the proper way to treat a woman."

I'm not entirely sure, but at that very moment, I possibly suffered a small heart attack. My lungs heaved for breath and found only heated air. I tugged at my collar to fan myself. "Ana and I are organizing a book club featuring her work. Which one is your favorite?" I asked, oblivious to the titles of her books, even the one he just handed me. Ana continued to fidget, and I continued to ignore her.

"Sense and Sensibility," he said. "How can you not admire the agonizing love story between Edward and Elinor? Or the intense passion between Marianne and Willoughby?"

Is the room spinning? Waves of heat…

"You've never known another man who was a fan of Jane Austen?"

"I…" *come on words* "am sure it's a girl thing," I said. *Oh no, stupid, stupid, stupid. I think I just called him a girl.*

"Well, I suppose I'm different." *Yes, you are.* "In fact, I'm glad because I might not have met you otherwise," he said. *Definite impending stroke alert. I think I have lost the ability to move.* Ana grabbed me by the hand. "Wait," he paused. "I thought you were entering here," he said, motioning to the restricted entrance door.

"Umm, I believe we might have the wrong door," Ana said. She pulled me along further until I yanked away and stood still.

"Thanks for your help, Bram." I took a large breath. "I hope we didn't take up too much of your time. It was nice to meet you. Come join us in the fall." *Wow, all rational statements without offending him. Way to go, me.* I smiled and turned. I walked away, now leaving Ana to stare dumbfounded.

As we descended the stairs, I looked up to see if he was watching us leave. He wasn't. My heart sank. I hoped we'd have that fairy tale last look and…

"Ellis? Hello?" Ana pointed to where we should put our unneeded books on the return cart. We walked through the front doors. Mrs. Croft was nowhere to be seen. The moment we were outside, Ana shot me a look, which needed no words, but I thought I'd make her work for the answers she so terribly wanted.

"Yes?" I said.

"Come on. What was that?" she asked while fluttering her eyelashes and looking doe-eyed.

"What?" I asked, misunderstanding her tone. I thought she wanted to discuss how awesome he was.

"Really?" she persisted. "My God, you act as if you'd never seen a guy. We could have been in huge trouble, and you are having a discussion on Jane Austen and the men who love her."

"Oh, don't give me that," I quipped, "the time to worry about being in trouble is before you actually are in trouble. You didn't worry when you were planning this crime spree. Besides, admit it, he was incredible."

"He had nice eyes, but I mean…" she responded.

"Ana, he was beautiful."

"I don't think guys want to be beautiful," she said, wrangling her bike from the rack.

"Whatever, he was fantastic. How old do you guess he was? I've never seen him at school. Have you ever seen him at the Archives before?"

"No, and I hope I never see him again," she added.

"What if he were John?"

"Please, Ellis, be serious. He caught us sneaking into the restricted part of the building. Remember? What if he tells someone? And stop teasing about John. He's just a friend."

"Oh, really?" I said, bursting into a riot of laughter. "Look, I don't think he suspected anything. He didn't act as if we were in the wrong place. By the way, you're an excellent spy and thief."

"What did I steal?"

"Hmm, Mrs. Croft's security badge?"

"Technically, I *borrowed* Mrs. Croft's badge—which I intend to return…eventually. So, I'm *not* a thief," she replied.

"Okay, *not a thief*, then you are a *really* lousy borrower."

"Uh, whatever. And about being a spy, I'm hiring a better sidekick. I can't have you melting every time a guy flirts with you."

"Don't be crazy. He wasn't flirting with me. And I didn't melt, although it was getting a little warm for a moment."

"If you don't believe he was flirting, you're the crazy one," she responded.

"Great. My partner-in-crime is delusional, so, I need you to move back into Realityville. I'm not the type of girl he'd find interesting."

"When did you go blind?" she asked with a laugh.

"When did you get so brave? I didn't know you were such a rule-breaker," I said. "Next, you'll be running down little old ladies with your bike and taking candy from babies."

"Ha, ha, you're so amusing. Therapy is helping me assert myself. Dr. Webster loaned me a book about finding inner strength. I read something last week I can't forget. 'It is better to live one day as a lion than a hundred years as a lamb.' I have to stop living my life as a lamb, Ellis. I can channel my anger and frustration to create something positive. We *all* need to stop being lambs."

I heard what she was telling me. I understood she had found something to help herself cope, but I didn't *think* I lived a weak life.

I watched her pedal in front of me, and I realized she was changing. She found a part of herself she considered defective, and now she was taking steps to change. Was that the act of maturing?

"Hey," I yelled to her, "Sorry for being an idiot."

"That's okay. It'll be my turn tomorrow," she yelled back.

If our government manipulated us and stole our memories, we had to make a stand, and we would do it together.

CHAPTER 7

The Coupling Laws ensure the survival of a successful and strong species. Scientific tests will determine ideal matches based on acknowledged criteria. During their twenty-second year, citizens will receive a list of three suitable mates. This list allows Atum a practical degree of choice. Citizens may choose a coupling they believe assures the greatest chance of success, felicity, and natural attraction. Those unchosen will be labeled as Discarded. These citizens can continue to serve society through alternate means but may not reproduce or couple. The law forbids couplings not included on official results. Citizens who break these laws will receive punishment and be forbidden to enter into any future coupling.

—Nurahatum Coupling Decree
243 A.D.

OBSERVATION

A HUMAN. HER NAME WAS ELLIS. MY MIND WAS REEL-ing. *Did that really just happen?*

Now backtracking, I found the corridor where I first became separated from the group. I didn't understand how my wrong turn—several wrong turns—might take me into the Habitat. When I walked back through the same door, I noticed a large sign that read RESTRICTED. Was it possible she had clearance allowing her to be there? Her demeanor said otherwise. I was lucky the identification badge allowed me to gain access to and from the backstage. Being away from the group was horror enough, but becoming lost within the Habitat could have been disastrous. I entered a restroom and stood before the mirror, leaning on the lavatory. Why was I grinning? An involuntary laughed escaped, and I slapped my hand to my mouth, trying to muffle the sound. *How old am I? Twelve? She's just a girl. A human girl.* I couldn't stop smiling. *I am in so much trouble.* It was worth it.

Focus, you idiot. No one saw me except the two girls. *Why did I use my real name? Her eyes.* If anyone asks, I'll say I was sick and in the restroom the entire time. *Her smile.* I hadn't upset the balance of the Habitat. Both of the girls assumed I was human. *She was gorgeous. And her...*

"Bram, where have you been?" Chaolo raced to a cubicle.

"Shalid, you scared me," I cursed. His sudden burst through the door ripped me from my thoughts of Ellis. "Here, I've...been here, sick."

After he came out, he stood beside me, washing his hands.

"You look like shalid," he laughed. "What's wrong? You need me to get the professor? Or that Habitat guide, Nya? I'd let her help *me* feel better."

"You're an idiot, and no, I'm okay," I said splashing water on my face. He handed me a towel. "Thanks, I'm better now."

I followed Chaolo to where the group was listening to a guide give history on the Habitat construction, including its effectiveness of keeping humans from escaping. Professor Frost had not noticed when I slipped back in with the others. Glairn had.

I sat, ignoring the speaker, trying to understand what happened. My mind kept returning to Ellis. I couldn't forget her. She was unlike anyone I had ever met—and not in the sense she was the first human. I didn't care I broke the rules or entered the Habitat. The thought of Ellis looped through my head—shy, kind, natural, smart, funny, gorgeous, and interesting. What was it? Five minutes? Can you know someone so soon? Was that instant attraction?

I looked up and saw Glairn motioning for me to sit beside her. She and my mother would choke up an organ when I announced my decision. Mom considered Glairn a spectacular match. On the first day of our twenty-first year, Atum took the Coupling Test. Researchers studied and processed the results. One year from the test date, each Atum received a list of three possible companions most suitable. Packets with detailed information and pictures of their potential mates were included with meeting times for the introductions. I remembered the ultra-luxurious hotel where my convention was held. The males visited the females, who stayed in their rooms. Parents were present to chaperone and help in the interview. Glairn was on my list, and of the three females, Mom liked her most. She had Atum beauty, and she was smart, but she acted conceited, spoiled, and opinionated. She wasn't the one for me.

We had no time limit in which we must couple. My mother and father married nine months after they first met. It had been three months since our official meeting at the Coupling Convention. My mom ambushed me into a weeklong date with her. Glairn's parents, wealthy and politically connected, planned an impromptu vacation, with help from my mother, at the same resort in June. It was torture to be in such a tropical paradise and not enjoy it in the way I intended. Glairn determined to confirm our coupling in any way possible.

She looked at me again and squinted her eyes. Was she desperate? Her parents made a point of telling me that she had offers from both her other matches. What awesome news! They assumed that information worried me, but I'd have given either of those two idiots a million credits to relieve me of the burden. Now, I was paying for mistakes I made on vacation—ones I might pay for the rest of my life. No matter when I told her, she'd explode. I looked away from her. Frustrated, she turned back to the speaker.

"So, in the event your path crosses with a human, you should retreat with no communication and inform a guide so damage control can be considered. Now, I will turn you over to Nya, who will escort you to the Orchard building for observations."

Everyone stood and Glairn, who had a badge with the name Angel on it, *yeah right*, walked over to me. "And where have you been, Bram?"

"Ja gidlsi shalid," I said. I used the vulgar term meaning to use the restroom. "Is that okay with you, Angel?" She spun away from me, causing her ponytail to smack my face.

We boarded the underground tram taking us to the basement or "backstage" of the Orchard building. While in route, the guide told us we could roam the observation halls. Accidental meetings were impossible without security clearance badges. Here, my identification would not allow me to pass between the human side and the non-human side. Most students, including Glairn, began their observations at the ground floor offices. I hustled to the second level hoping to escape the others.

Two-way mirrors lined the hallways. Therapists decided when or if to activate them for viewing release sessions held inside each office. The first window was open, so I pressed the volume switch and listened to the conversation. I watched a male patient who lay on the sofa. He was crying.

"Reverend Wilson, why not consider marrying again? It has been a long time since you arrived in Horizon."

"Dr. Adler, she was my everything, and I was everything to her. We weren't blessed with any little ones running around, so we just had each other. On Sunday mornings, Doreen fixed pancakes before church. I never figured out how she made little hearts inside mine. She said it was her secret way to tell me how much she loved me." The oversized man raised a hand to shield his face.

"Reverend Wilson, let us begin one of your relaxation techniques. Close your eyes and count backward from ten," she said, tapping on her dataport. Reverend Wilson continued his countdown until he reached one.

"Reverend Wilson, on Sunday mornings, you love to fix eggs for yourself. They are scrambled and delicious." She took a long pause before beginning. "Do you eat eggs, Reverend?"

Reverend Wilson opened his mouth and closed it again. His forehead creased and then relaxed. "You ever had farm-fresh eggs, Doc? They're wonderful. I scramble them up with crumbled bacon. My wife loved bacon."

"Reverend Wilson, you never ate breakfast with your wife." More typing on the dataport. "Reverend Wilson, describe a typical breakfast."

"I love breakfast, best meal of the day, my mama used to say. I cook eggs; they're good for you; lots of protein."

"And pancakes?" she asked.

"I love pancakes," he said. "My wife…"

"Reverend Wilson," she interrupted, "your wife never cooked breakfast nor ate breakfast with you. You hate the taste of pancakes." This treatment didn't appear successful. "Let's count from one to ten." The man counted like a child performing for a proud parent.

"Reverend, are you relaxed?"

"I sure am."

"Are you eating well?"

"Like a horse." He sat upright on the sofa. "In fact, I could eat the hind legs off a billy goat right now," he said, rubbing his stomach.

"Do you ever eat pancakes?" she asked.

"Nope, never much cared for them; I'm more of a meat and potatoes man."

"Wonderful, I am glad you have a healthy appetite. We will stop here. I'll see you next week."

"Alrighty then. Maybe I'll have a report on that little lady I been thinking of asking out. Wish me luck, Doc." Reverend Wilson stood, shook the therapist's hand with a hearty motion, walked to the door, and left with no sign of sadness.

On my miniport, I tapped a quick message to my mother. I watched as she picked up her miniport and read. She looked at the mirror and smiled. She walked to the door opposite the one Reverend Wilson had taken and, in a moment, she was standing in the hallway with me.

"Hello, son," she said as she placed her hand on my cheek. "Have you time for a quick chat?"

"Do you have time to see me?" I asked.

"Always."

"I forgot my dataport this morning when I left home. I can't make notes on my miniport. Can I borrow yours tonight to type my daily research assignment? You could bring mine from home, and I'll get it tomorrow."

"And I thought you came just to see me healing the Habitat," my mom said.

We walked through the door and were inside the office. I looked at the colossal mirror hung behind her desk. No one would guess the mirror was two-way. Researchers watched patients from the other side without their knowing.

"Come, sit." She pointed to the sofa.

"Are you tapping a button on your dataport and asking me to count?"

"Funny. You know we're immune to the chemical that releases memories."

"Show me how it works," I asked.

"Alright," she said, picking up her port. "When I get ready to alter memory, I press this icon on my dataport and the chemical is released through those vents." She pointed to three circular vents on the ceiling of her office. "To humans, it smells similar to fruit or flowers they prefer. They're not aware, and no danger exists for them or us. Were you watching when Reverend Wilson mentioned his wife and the pancakes?" she asked. I nodded. "After the chemical entered his body, I could suggest different opinions. Sometimes it works, and sometimes the process is much harder. It depends on the person and the intensity of the memory. Today was a breakthrough for the reverend. He still struggles releasing the memories of his wife, who died during The End."

"I see," I paused. "I think it's sad." Wanting to change the subject before she preached on the virtues of release, I spied a photo on her bookshelf. The photo was one I'd never seen. "What's this?" I asked, walking towards it.

"It is my fake family," she said. "When I had my review last week, the department supervisor suggested I personalize my office. Rather than use a real photo, I had this made."

"Why not use a real photo? Are you ashamed of me, Mom?"

"Yes," she said, laughing. "No, I'm only joking. I need to maintain a distance. Is it not enough I know everything about my patients' lives? The personal relationship I have with them must include some boundaries. Work and personal life should be kept separate, so I use fake pictures. This is your fake dad," she said, pointing to the photo. "He's very chote, isn't that the word your pals use?"

"Great, there goes my appetite," I said.

She laughed. "I've been practicing Atum slang. So, sit and tell me what you have experienced today. Was it everything you'd hoped for?"

"Better than I thought. But I'm not sure research is right for me. Hey, you do have the mirror off, right? I wouldn't want some of my classmates to come through for observation and listen to our conversation." She laughed. She knew my statement was a way of diverting her attention from my waning interest in the field of research.

"Yes, the mirror is off." She sighed, "Oh Bram, son...you must find something. I want to support you, but you are floating through life."

"Mom, don't start. I'm trying. I have mixed feelings concerning humans and research, and Glairn..."

"Bram, I am your mother, and I love you. I acknowledge life has been difficult since your father..." she stopped. She looked away and returned her gaze with a weary sigh. "He wanted you to be happy. I want you to be happy. What you choose does not matter, but you must choose. You wanted to play professional drichsc, you wanted to join the Guard, and then, you decided on human studies. Now, you tell me you're unsure. As for Glairn, I want you to marry and have a child. I understand it's tempting at your age to want to…try out…as many females as possible."

"Oh, Mom, alstch, no, do not go down that road today. We are *not* having *the talk*."

"Son, what I mean is this—you may think marriage is stifling when instead, you have so many…"

"Stop. Don't say it again, please."

"Bram, marriage will fulfill your needs. You will be an amazing father. If not Glairn, contact Malah or Hilia. They were nice, and I am sure potential for happiness could be found with one of them. If you don't choose soon, they may couple with another. I don't wish a lonely life for you."

"Why?" I asked when she finished.

My tone clearly startled her.

"Why should I do what's expected? Maybe I don't want marriage because *none* of them suit me…"

"You don't want to be married?" Her face had a look of horror I thought was a complete overreaction. She sat beside me.

I escaped to the bookshelf to see her fake family picture again. I understood what she was saying. "Mom, I'm not convinced my mate should come from one of three women chosen for me. I need to find the perfect person for me."

"Son, we have laws and traditions. If you choose not to marry, you can never have a child." She came to where I stood and put an arm around me. "Are you telling me you would prefer a barren relationship with a Discarded? Your father and I wanted your life to be happy."

"I'm leaving. I'll be late." I walked to the inner door.

"Bram, wait," she said, handing me her dataport. "I love you. You have had enough psychology to see why you can't commit. I understand giving your love to people risks hurt when you lose them.

I grieve for you and with you. However, you're an adult and must choose a path. Stay with human studies. You have a caring heart. Call one of the other girls and ask her family for dinner. Possibly, they've changed more to your liking since May. Please try, for me...and your father.

I left without saying a word, angry she would use my father's memory to coerce me into a coupling.

I returned to the group. Most were watching sessions being conducted in other parts of the Orchard building. Many doctors used the same techniques for controlling memories, and I felt sympathy, and even guilt being associated with this practice. Regular debates questioned whether the Habitat program was humane. I believed we needed to define what humane meant. They were well kept, but they were also kept in the dark. Their lives were being erased, and although that method resulted in less stress, was it fair to take away the memories of happier times spent with their loved ones?

By the end of the day, I couldn't keep my eyes open. I was on sensory overload. They told us we might experience mixed emotions. The Habitat project was a delicate and complex undertaking. I struggled with my allegiance. Humans should be protected, but they should be free. My body wanted to collapse, but my mind wouldn't cooperate. I wanted to please my mother, but I wanted to please myself. These battles had no end in sight.

Although I was hungry, I skipped the evening meal to avoid Glairn. Once inside the hotel room, I lay in bed, hoping when dreams came, they were filled with images of Ellis.

I see the asteroid glowing brighter and brighter as it nears our atmosphere. The object grows larger with each minute that passes. Why didn't I go to Earth? I fall to the ground and curl into a ball. I try to close my eyes, but I am captivated. It's closer now. The heat doesn't burn me. Instead, I feel warm and safe. Reaching for the impact and void that will follow, I prepare for the end, but instead, a soft hand takes mine and lifts me. She is glowing, and she wraps herself around me so I am protected. The collision does not affect me, and I am unharmed. She is my savior.

I jolted awake wanting to hold on to the dream and make sense of its meaning. In seconds, I had lost it but not its basic connotation. I wanted and needed Ellis in my life.

My roommate, Chaolo, snored like a hovercraft in his bed. I got up to pace and sort my thoughts. The dream was melting away faster than I could decipher its meaning. It was useless to try. I felt like a caged animal trapped in this cramped hotel room. From the auto dispenser, I got a glass of water and took a seat at the worktable trying to pull stubborn remnants of my dissolving dream. Absentmindedly, I spilled water on top of my mother's dataport. I wiped it away with my nightshirt. I opened the port to see if water had seeped inside. Using the driest portion of my shirt, I cleaned the remaining water droplets hoping I had not ruined any of my mother's research documents. The action of my hand rubbing against the screen opened a half-dozen files.

"Shalid! Her files," I said aloud.

The volume of my voice was loud enough to wake a normal

person. Luckily, Chaolo didn't move. Without considering the consequences, I scanned the open documents, and there, before me, was the file marked patients. Why hadn't I thought of this? Inside the folder, I found a patient file list meant for no one but my mother. I clicked the file marked patient database, and I typed in the name Ellis. In less than a second, her full name and Habitat identification number appeared. Yes! I clicked on Ellis Bauer while thinking how pleasing it sounded and I realized a huge smile had spread across my face. *Bauer, Bauer, Ellis Bauer.* My actions betrayed my mother's trust, and yet, I didn't care. What were the chances of Ellis being my mother's patient?

I slipped back into bed with the dataport as if I might be caught, but nothing would stop me from learning everything about Ellis Bauer. The photo files from each year of her life displayed images available only to the researchers. The first photo showed Ellis as a newly rescued baby and a member of the Horizon 5000. After, came the photos from toddler to the awkward years, even our species experiences. The recent pictures were the Ellis I met. I had never been more physically attracted to a female. It was a mixture of agony and obsession. Whether this feeling was real or the result of human fascination, I didn't know, and I didn't care.

Her hair fell in long, loose waves and reminded me of the reddish-brown color some leaves turn in the autumn of the year on Earth. I imagined it silky and soft. Her eyes were a mix of gold and green. It was the color I thought of as the sun's rays splashed across the forest surrounding my parents' lake house. She was everything that reminded me of warmth and tenderness. But I saw more. I saw her…humanity. I saw laughter and sincerity. She had girlish innocence coupled with an unintentional sensuality. She was womanly and voluptuous with curves and muscles, something Atum females tried to avoid. In our brief conversation, could she have suspected the effect she had on me? I wanted to discover everything. I memorized her home address and her dataport address, although as I did, I said aloud, "Why am I doing this?" This time the sound of my voice startled me and caused Chaolo to roll over.

"Go to sleep, you geek. Enough with the studying," he said, speaking while yawning.

This one accidental meeting had so changed my world I couldn't stop. I clicked on the tab marked therapy and read notes my mother compiled.

> *The subject has exhibited an increased immunity to drug therapy. Attempts to change certain memories have failed. Given she was a baby at the time of The End, I can see no reason to continue trying to re-image memories. The prognosis for this patient suggests she may be predisposed to times of depression because she has no memories of biological parents. Although the subject describes a loving, bonded relationship with her father, I suspect she longs for a mother figure with whom she feels a similar closeness. She may mourn for her unknown biological mother, and this action could cause depressive tendencies. This issue should be noted for further developments in her therapy.*

Her memories could not be altered easily. My mind raced with concern for her welfare. I could ask my mother how often humans are resistant to treatment and the long-term effects of their continual suffering.

> *Because the subject has an extreme devotion to her father and not the mother, I believe this may have caused several anxieties about self-worth. I suspect the patient manages parental expectations with deceit. Her avoidance of conflict is a primary motivation for her. Her best option will be to move from the parental home after placement. She exhibits signs of being*

subjected to oppressive control by the mother that causes the patient to search for ways to rebel in secret.

I clicked on the highlighted word mother, and a picture of an ordinary human came onto the screen. Harsh was the word that came to mind. Her name was Greta Bauer. I clicked on the personal information tab, and a security screen presented itself, not allowing me access. Possibly, my mother wasn't her therapist and therefore, did not have access to her files. I backtracked and clicked on the word father. Alex Bauer's face appeared. I'd be closer to him than the mother. Sometimes, people's faces draw in or repel. His was a face that encouraged happiness. He was nice looking for an older guy and reminded me of my dad in a way. I remember Mom telling me Dad had been a real charmer and his other two coupling matches had pursued him relentlessly. I had a taste of that myself with Glairn. But Ellis's dad could have done better. The Habitat must have had other women survivors who'd have loved to pair with him. Checking further, I found he, too, was not my mother's patient.

I returned to Ellis's file and read every detail. *Am I a human stalker?* I separated myself from that notion. My head spun, thinking of the rules I had broken. I wished the most serious had been contacting a human without authorization. The most severe rule-breaking lay ahead of me. Our society would never permit relationships between Atum and humans, but I couldn't possibly forget her. This was a dangerous path, and I didn't care.

I had to talk to my mom, so I grabbed my miniport and walked into the bathroom, tapping her number.

She answered after a few beeps. "Bram, is everything fine?"

"Yes, I've been thinking of our conversation today. Did I wake you?"

"I wasn't asleep. Son, are we okay?"

"Yes, Mom. I understand what you meant today, and I am trying, but I need you to back off for the present. Okay? Give me time."

"I can do that," she said.

"Mom, do you ever think about Dad?"

"Yes," she replied. "What drove you to ask that question?"

"Mother, I'm not a patient. Tell me you miss him. Talk about him with emotion and affection." I wanted her to be Mom. I understood her nature to resort to a therapist in times of stress, but it infuriated me.

There was nothing except silence for a few seconds. "He was the most patient person I've ever known. Your dad was good and saw good in everyone else. He would sit and peel oranges for you and me. It was your favorite earth food when you were young. We'd sit on the floor in front of the fire with a small basketful. He took his time peeling and cutting and making sure your slices didn't have any seeds. And he never ate any until we were finished. He couldn't have thought we would eat every orange, so I always wondered why he waited to eat. It was one of the last conversations we had. He said his pleasure came from watching us enjoy them. So yes, I miss him. I never doubted his love for me. When you came into our lives, our family was complete. He was so proud of you and loved you so much. Now, tell me why you thought of him."

I couldn't speak for a moment because I remembered those times with the oranges. "If he were here, I could talk to him." I looked into the lit mirror and realized for the first time how much I resembled my dad. He would walk around in pajama pants with no shirt. Mom would giggle and tell him to put on clothes. He'd pat her on the butt, and she'd giggle more. At the time, I thought that gesture was sickening, but it showed me how much he loved her. I wanted that life.

"Bram? Son? Are you still there?" She brought me back from where my mind had drifted.

"Yes, I'm listening."

"I understand I'm not a man, but I can help if you…"

"It's a Dad day. I miss hearing his stories and playing drichsc together, and I miss him because…he isn't here."

"I understand you've been without him for a long time, but we will never lose the memory of him. That is what we hold on to—his memory. I love you, Bram," she said.

"You, too," I said.

We ended our call. The last words Mom said were we would never lose the memory of him because that is what we hold on to. But the humans were losing their memories, and right then, I decided it was wrong.

I slept a dreamless sleep. Occasionally, I awoke to reposition myself, and I'd smile as I let her face drift into my thoughts.

CHAPTER 8

I am descended from a line of proud Preservation-ists. Those who want to share this planet with the human species as equals threaten our way of life. Those same people would risk our race being tainted by interbreeding, thus putting our evolutionary superiority at stake.

We ask for everyone's support to protect the path for our survival. While I focus my education and career plans in human studies, I am not inclined to promote conservation. I intend to establish that human existence is a menace to our society. History has proven them a species destined for self-destruction. Human-caused extinctions of numerous animal and plant life-forms attest to their merciless nature. If we consider, alone, what they did to cause environmental havoc on their own planet, our mission is justified.

Our organization will forever be anti-human and stands firm in its goal to see the human population exterminated. We believe that as long as one human survives on Earth, our people are in danger. Until we have eradicated all humans, the future of the Atum will not be secure.

—Glairn Nirgal
New Earth Post Editorial
September 2050

THE MEETING

WE ARRIVED AT THE HABITAT AT TEN O'CLOCK for our second day of observation. I was first in line to exit the bus. I should have felt tired, but instead, was thrilled I might see her again. Today, the human teenager was the focus. My focus was Ellis. This part of the human population was near our age, so our professor assigned us a compare and contrast paper to present in class. The goal of this assignment was to consider how we Atum were similar and different from the humans nearest our age group. We traveled to a section of the Habitat to view school-aged humans from the observation halls. Of the seven thousand inhabitants of Horizon, three thousand ranged in age from three to twenty. This was the last week of their term before the four-week late-summer break. On Nurahatum, children attended school year-round with four weeklong breaks every year. The Habitat school calendar was created with a similar schedule allowing students sixteen weeks of vacation throughout the school year.

The course work changed drastically after The End. Neither the Atum nor the human teachers in the Habitat supported a regular curriculum. Students learned information that helped them in the current world. The minute details of who invented what or what day an insignificant battle occurred no longer mattered. The survivors who became teachers designed a curriculum that taught basic history, math, English, health, and science. Students interested in physical education, art, foreign languages, or music enrolled in those classes at the Hobby Center.

From ages three to five, children were in a pre-school environment where they learned socialization and behavior skills. After, they entered school at age six and graduated fourteen years later. The oldest level of education was Year 14. During that year, humans took placement tests to establish what abilities they possessed that might be useful for Horizon's growth. After placement, they entered apprenticeships to learn the finer aspects needed to perform their jobs.

At our leisure, we could free-view any classes of interest. I chose the oldest grade Ellis likely attended. By 11:30, I found her. There were six of us viewing the same group, including Glairn.

"They get uglier as they get older," she said, as she pointed to different humans. Shuhaln was making notes on her dataport as she studied them.

"Look at the red-faced one in the green blouse. Others flock to her as if she holds authority," said Glairn. She wasn't speaking of Ellis, for she sat off to the side with the same girl from yesterday. I was careful not to stare at Ellis, for fear Glairn may notice and wage her verbal war.

"Can anyone hear what those outcasts in the corner are saying?" Meziem said. He was pointing to Ellis and her friend, no doubt to please Glairn. I tried to separate the noisy chatter from what she was saying but couldn't. Her eyes danced when she talked. Her laugh was infectious, and I caught myself smiling.

"And who are you studying?" asked Glairn.

"No one, why do you ask?"

"Are you interested in that large, ugly one over there?" She pointed in Ellis's direction. Vicious thoughts raced through my mind. I could have destroyed Glairn's reputation right then and taken great pleasure in thinking how she might have reacted if I exposed her secrets. I should have humiliated her. I seethed, and I'm sure she must have noticed. However, if I lost my temper, I might reveal my feelings for Ellis and jeopardize the chance to stay in the class.

"No one here interests me," I said, "*absolutely* no one." I emphasized the last statement so she would understand my true meaning. I turned toward the exit without another word. As I walked out, I heard her ask to join me, but I didn't stop. I no longer cared what Glairn or anyone thought.

The Atum debated whether humans deserved the title of "higher life form." Many scientists argued humans were marginally more intelligent than their closest relative, the chimpanzee. Others agreed, citing the gorilla, dolphin, elephant, and pan paniscus medius (a dwarf chimpanzee, discovered in the Amazon Rainforest in 2030) as being near to the evolutionary levels at which humans perform. "It is ironic," a leading scientist noted, "humans consider apes inferior in the same way Atum consider humans inferior." Nevermore than the moment I met Ellis, did I realize humans were not an ignorant species.

I left the school observation halls and walked to the underground for lunch. Below were researchers, mechanics, and others responsible for maintaining the Habitat.

I bought nlashfid—roasted meat skewered with vegetables from a food vendor. Tables nearby gave me an opportunity to sit and people-watch. There were many Atum. Workers moved human foods on rolling carts. Technicians worked on lights. At the next table, therapists had been observing the youngest humans in the school setting.

"I find interesting their fascination with the crayon. Their imaginations are complex," one said.

"With some of the humans, I agree, but among them are those who prefer instead to break, throw, or eat the crayon. One tiny male put the crayon in his nose and got it stuck. They needed the school medic," said another, laughing at the child's misfortune. The youngest therapist at the table chimed in, "I don't care. They are adorable, and I wish I had one for my daughter. She talks about them nonstop. The poor human would be bathed, dressed, and fed to death most likely."

My stomach churned as I listened. At first, I admired how the young therapist spoke of the little humans until she expressed wanting one as a pet for her own offspring. Why was everyone blind to the fact they were our equals? The DNA of the Atum is ninety-nine percent identical to humans. They weren't as advanced in their sciences and technologies as we were, but was that the only hallmark of an intelligent society?

As I watched the heavy traffic of workers, I wondered how humans believed the story of their government's doomsday plan. So many of our people helped to operate the Habitat. Did the citizens of Horizon think they were making this happen on their own?

I looked at my watch and realized I should get back to the viewings. I walked to the observation hall I left earlier, hoping to be alone. The viewing corridor and the classroom were empty.

"Hello, can I help you?" I jumped. It was our guide, Nya. "Sorry," she said.

"I'm viewing the students but can't find El...the group I was looking for," I said.

"Let's check," said the red-haired woman as she tapped on her dataport. "That group is at lunch. I can send directions to your port." She tapped a few more times and held up her port. I lifted mine to hers, and we tapped them together. "There you are. Enjoy your viewing." I thanked her and activated my port. There, waiting on the screen was her message with the directions. When I looked at them, I realized why she didn't simply tell me what route to take. After a ten-minute walk, I arrived at the cafeteria-viewing gallery. At least a hundred students of different age groups sat eating their lunches. I had to find Ellis. She was wearing a shade of violet, which caused her green eyes to sparkle, and I hoped that color might help her stand out from the other humans. No luck. I looked at my port and saw an attached outdoor eating area.

I navigated to another hall and looked out onto a narrow court-yard filled with tables. There were a few students sitting here. At the far end was Ellis alone. I walked along another hall to get closer. I switched on the monitor even though I was sure she wouldn't talk to herself. She sat looking content. Hair fell across her face each time a small wind blew. She laughed to herself at the third time of putting it back into place. She had a bag I assumed held her food. She placed the contents before her on the table, and when she had finished, she sat without taking as much as one bite. What was this ritual? She closed her eyes and bowed her head. I had read about religion and prayer. She opened her eyes and took a band from her wrist to tie back her hair. In the distance, her friend approached.

"Konnichiwa, Ellis," she said. I wasn't familiar with that word. "Did you forget the last sushi day before summer vacation?" Her friend held up a multi-colored piece of food in the shape of a circle with two sticks. She dipped it into a brown liquid. "Mrs. Jones told me this was the last of the tuna harvest for the entire year." I had never heard of that food. "She said I could have the leftovers." Ana twirled the tuna harvest close to Ellis's face. "Hmm, spicy tuna, your favorite."

"Get your spicy tuna away from me," Ellis laughed. "Dad made my lunch."

"It's burnt again...*yummy*," said Ana whose laughter caused her to spit food into Ellis's plate.

"Eww, Ana," said Ellis. "Yuck, I didn't want my own sushi, nevertheless what you've half-chewed. Don't make fun—Dad can't help it. He's still trying to master the art of the barbecue, but all he can manage is to burn the outside. The inside is sometimes raw. Cooking isn't his forte, but he loves it. It's not too bad if you dip it in lots of sauce. Besides, he enjoys making special meals for me."

"Yeah, that's *really* special. Your teeth are black, gross."

Ellis opened her mouth to smile and show how the burnt char of the meat had blackened her teeth. "Have I got something in my teeth, Ana?" Ellis asked, flashing a comical smile. They both roared with laughter.

"Oh, that's gorgeous, Ellis. Wait until Bram sees your beautiful smile." They continued to laugh. *Did she say my name?* Ellis wiped her teeth with a napkin.

"I'd die if he saw me," she said, continuing to use the napkin to remove the stains from her teeth. "Ana, he was being nice, nothing more."

Ellis was thinking of me, and she was oblivious to the fact I was interested in her. How could she not know? I had never met a girl who attracted me this much.

"Ellis, if he didn't like you, he's an idiot. You are fun and cute except when your teeth are black. He was flirting with you at the library."

"It wasn't flirting, and I looked horrible," she said as she searched for another napkin.

A tall male was walking toward their table. I didn't remember him from the classroom before. "Hello, beautiful ladies," he said with a deep voice. I hated him immediately.

"Hi, John. How was your interview?" asked Ana.

He sat between them. "Nailed it. No probs." The board had a lot of questions about technical stuff. Try to control yourselves, but I think you're talking to the next communications apprentice." *I really hate him.*

"Goof-ball," said Ana, offering up a piece of tuna harvest for him to try. He smiled and popped it into his mouth.

"Thanks. Gotta love the last sushi day of the year. Listen, Ana, are you working at the Archives today? I need books that Dr. Williams suggested."

"Sure, I'll be there," Ana replied. They liked each other. Maybe I didn't hate him so much. Ellis didn't join in the conversation but sat quietly wrestling with what remained of her burnt sandwich. She kept glancing at the two of them talking.

"Great, it's a date," he said, not taking his eyes off Ana, who blushed. Ellis turned her head away from them, in my direction with a huge smile on her face.

A bell chimed, and the girls packed their leftovers. John said goodbye and walked away, leaving Ana staring at him.

"Date, huh? You beautiful lady." Ellis teased. "I think you need a chaperone. We should go to the Archives together."

"You don't fool me Ellis Bauer; you hope to see Bram again." Both girls laughed.

"Ana, say you'll meet me after your release at four. Don't make me tell John you think he's cute with his new haircut."

"Ugh…yes, I will. But it's not a real date with John. He was teasing. I hope you won't be disappointed if Bram doesn't show up again. What are the chances he'll be there?"

Both girls turned away from me. I smiled, thinking the chances were outstanding.

I was getting back inside Horizon. But how? I needed a plan and soon. Our next group meeting was at Brook Haven, the assisted living building. We were studying the older humans in this setting. I had to catch the underground tram, so I left the school. The tram ride should have been my time to devise a plan, but the different Atum workers that kept the Habitat running distracted me. On the color-coded walls were the names of the buildings directly aboveground. This must help workers distinguish the different locations. We passed a gray-striped wall with the words Horizon Hospital in large gray letters. Those stripes gave way to lavender stripes reading Brook Haven in matching, colored letters. I had arrived.

The tram slowed and ahead I saw my professor. I wanted to avoid him until my plan was complete, but he saw me.

"Mr. Potter, how are you today? Are you enjoying your observations?" He walked toward me, his arms heavy with books.

"Yes. Thank you, Professor Dau...Frost. May I help you?" I took half of his books. "Professor, I am glad we met now. I need to ask your permission to stay with my mother tonight. She became ill, and I don't want to leave her alone. If she isn't better tomorrow, I'll call the infirmary, but she's stubborn and doesn't think it will last long. I worked through lunch and can finish my reports at her apartment." It sounded excellent when I said it. But I wasn't sure he believed me.

"Your mother still keeps an apartment here? I thought she and your father chose a vacation lake home nearer the Habitat."

"Yes, they have a place, but she likes to save time rather than commute every day. Sometimes, she overbooks her daily schedule so she can take a three-day weekend from work instead of two. She likes the convenience of having an apartment."

"Well, I will need to speak to her. I know the Habitat rules differ for family members, but she must accept responsibility if you are to stay separate from the school group tonight. He pulled his miniport from his jacket and waited for me to give him the number. I did, but the number I gave connected to her dataport tucked in my school satchel.

"Dr. Adler, this is Professor Fro…excuse me, Jdochleur Daulchmanu. I am with Bram, and he has told me of his plans to stay over tonight. I wanted to contact you for your assurance his presence within the Habitat would be with your authorization. Please call when you are able."

"When I spoke with her, she was planning to go straight to bed. I am sorry for the extra trouble," I said.

He looked at me for a few seconds longer than felt comfortable. "I hope she is well. Tomorrow, we meet at Horizon Hospital for our first observation at eight o'clock in the morning. Contact me if you cannot attend. Now, we will be late for this session if we don't hurry."

That was it. Perhaps no one had broken out of the Habitat, but I had just broken in. I walked to the next session, arms full of the professor's books, and a wonderful scheme growing in my mind.

I thought the final observation would never finish. The Orchard building was far, so I took the underground tram instead of walk. How could I get from the patient's exit door in my mother's office out into the Habitat? When I thought through the system of doors and locks, I realized Ellis and Ana had been the ones to unlock the door at the Archives. Humans *couldn't* have that type of access. The moment before they opened the door, I tried my student badge and found it did not work from the backstage, but it had worked to unlock the door from *within* the Habitat. I would ask my mother how this worked, but I was sure no explanation existed for a human being able to enter that part of the Habitat.

I arrived at the Orchard building and raced to the second floor. My mother had her observation window closed, so she may have been without a patient. If the window was closed, the volume wouldn't work, but I thought I heard voices within. I sent a message to her miniport, and within a few moments, she opened the inner door of her office.

"I've finished for the day. Instead of taking a lunch break, I worked. I felt sick, so I asked Professor Daulchmanu for permission to come to your office instead of going back to the hotel. I can't live through another night of craziness. The students act as if they've never been away from home."

"Oh, I see. I thought I left you a message earlier saying I was staying tonight in the apartment. You didn't get it?" she asked.

"No, do you have a late meeting?" I asked.

"Well, yes I did, I mean I do, but I'll cancel so we can go home." She was holding back something.

"No, we should both stay in the apartment," I said, seeing a window of chance for time with Ellis.

"Bram, this is risky because you might come in contact with humans. I'm not sure." Her brow creased, and she kept checking her clock. I knew my mother, and something was happening she didn't want to discuss with me. Mom never kept secrets, but she acted strangely.

"Mother, give me directions and a key card, and I'll go to the apartment. You can have your meeting, see your patients, and when you finish, you come there." My case was getting stronger. I was winning her over, or either her important meeting was convincing her this idea would work.

"Okay," she said, breathing out deeply and looking at the clock again. "Here are the rules. You will go straight to the apartment. You don't have to enter the actual Habitat, out there." She pointed, as if I might get confused. "I'll give you the directions to get to the apartment entrance via the underground." She grabbed her miniport and typed. "Let me have your port," she said.

I handed it to her and began, "I could get to the apartment easier if I go through the Habitat."

"Nice try, but no. You're aware it's against the rules." She took our two ports and tapped them against one another. "There. You have the directions. Stop and get something for your dinner. I doubt the food dispensary is loaded at the apartment. Don't wander into the Habitat and don't answer the door."

"Yes, Mother. I understand. I'll go straight there." She walked to her desk and laid down her port, eyeing me the entire time.

"I'm not sure what time I'll come home. I should be there by nine, but if my meeting runs late, I'll message you." She walked toward me with an unusual look. "Are you sure, son?"

"Mom, I'm an adult, okay? The big, bad humans won't kidnap me and take me to Area 61." I leaned in for a hug and snuck a peek at the clock.

"Area 51. I'm more worried you might harm the Habitat than the humans harm you."

It was 3:30. I wanted to catch Ellis before Ana arrived. I had to travel underground to the apartment, exit into the Habitat, and travel back to the outside of this building. If my mother saw me strolling across the street inside Horizon, I would be in more trouble than ever before.

"Do you remember the details of your character profile if you cross paths with a human?"

"Yes, Mother. Bram Potter, twenty-two, apprentice to release therapist, Dr. Smith. My mother and father both work in the animal husbandry division. I live at 216 Magnolia Court."

"Cute name. I work with animals? No one would ever connect us with that story. But you won't need to use it, right?"

"Yes, Amadjir." She loved when I called her 'Mommy' in our language.

"Please, I've already agreed, you can stop being so cute. Message me when you have arrived. Oh my, remember you cannot cross into the Habitat door of my building or enter the apartment without my security key card." She reached into her document case and pulled out a card. "This will also act as a form of payment. It works below or above ground in case I am out on a visit." She gave me the card and then took her hand and ruffled my hair like always. It was her display of affection.

"Don't worry, I'll manage; I'm not five anymore. You'll get a message when I get to the apartment." I walked toward the patient exit. This was more than thrilling. I reached for the door handle.

"Bram. The other door." She pointed. "Don't make me regret this decision."

In moments, I would break every promise I just made. She opened the inner office door, and I walked out with a gigantic smile I was glad she couldn't see.

CHAPTER 9

Therapists require parents within the Habitat to attend child-rearing classes. After orphaned children were assigned to couples in Horizon, weekly sessions discussed the most successful parenting methods. Therapists monitored progress with information gathered during release sessions to determine the efficacy of the training program. If adults proved ineffective at child-rearing, children were removed and placed with another family. Scientists agreed that if the Habitat was to be successful, the overall health of children must be a priority.

Researchers have completed the twenty-year Adolescent Human Study comparing two groups of humans aged ten to twenty years old. The first group, studied from 2020 to 2030 (pre-war), was compared to the second group, studied from 2040 to 2050 (post-war).

Finding:

Habitat adolescents are healthier than adolescents living prior to 2030.

1. Increased physical exercise (mandatory participation in hobby activities)
2. Absence of unhealthy/processed foods
3. Absence of drug, alcohol, and tobacco products
4. Routine medical assessments and care
5. Improved environmental conditions (absence of pollutants, chemicals)

Finding:

Habitat adolescents are more emotionally well-adjusted than adolescents living prior to 2030.

1. Mandatory release sessions
2. Safe and loving home environments (routinely monitored for efficacy)
3. Reduced stress in school
4. Stable and positive community support (absence of violence, crime, gang-related activity, etc.)

Finding:

Habitat adolescents are more socially/psychologically mature than adolescents living prior to 2030.

1. Absence of divertive interests (video gaming, excessive television, social media, and internet)
2. Increased social activities within the community
3. Required volunteer work (providing a sense of contribution and self-worth)
4. Placement Program apprenticeships

Finding:

Habitat adolescents showed significant sexual immaturity (physical and psychological) compared to adolescents living prior to 2030.

1. Absence of explicit material found in

music, literature, movies, television, social media, and other entertainment media

2. Familial ban on teaching or discussing sexual education (coupled with required educational classes beginning at age sixteen)

3. Dating restrictions (chaperoned dating beginning at age eighteen and unchaperoned dating beginning at age twenty)

4. Absence of hormones in animal products

5. Absence of environmental contaminants

Conclusion:

The Adolescent Human Study suggests with careful parenting, children will grow into successful adults, and thereafter, successful parents of the next generation.

—Faris Kirosh
Habitat Human Development Report
June 2050

E L L I S

AS SOON AS I WAS A SAFE DISTANCE FROM MY MOTHer's office, I broke into a half-run-half-jog so I could arrive in front of the Orchard building at the same time as Ellis. I boarded the underground tram bound for Mom's neighborhood. The tram crawled and arrived at the apartment building after what felt like an eternity. I jumped off and ran to the underground entrance of this building. The door opened and closed behind me. A staircase lay before me, and my adrenaline pumped as I made my way to the top. The second security door required my mother's card. The unbolting sound sent a rush through me. I pulled the door open and walked through to the lobby, which was empty and quiet. Snippets of memories as a child being in this place with my parents flooded my head. The port directions led me to the apartment but not my true destination. I tapped a message to my mother and stopped. It was too soon. At this moment, I should be buying my food from a vendor below ground. I finished tapping the note and set the message to send in fifteen minutes.

Twenty feet ahead of me stood an ordinary door. I took slow and unsteady baby steps forward intending to use the ten-second journey to scour my mind for reasons not to open the door. When I reached it, I counted the reasons. There were many. I gripped the warm, metal handle and stood motionless. Was it possible this two-inch-thick wood and glass panel separated their world from ours? Could I step through this portal? Did the fate of two civilizations depend on what I did within the Habitat? I didn't want to shoulder so much responsibility. It wasn't fair. This one door stood as a bridge between two worlds. I wasn't trying to break the rules or upset some cosmic balance. I just wanted to spend time with Ellis. I tightened my grip and took a breath.

The warmth of the sun spread across my face, and I realized this same warmth spread across the faces of everyone. There were no differences between the Atum and the humans. We breathed the same air and now basked in this same sun. Atum viewpoints had concocted an immense distinction between the two species. We understood the reality of what this world was, and they were oblivious. Deepening pity gnawed at my gut. For a moment, I considered stepping back, disobeying what fate chose for me long ago. I couldn't let this be a playful diversion on my part, and I couldn't be the boy who never grew up. That wasn't a fictional story from my childhood. This was real, and humans were intelligent beings with feelings—with minds and souls. I couldn't choose this path unless it was for the right reason. I paused at the top of the steps looking out over Horizon. This wasn't like me. I had never allowed emotion and sentimentality to rule my actions. My life guides until now had been pleasure and recklessness. I didn't know if a higher being presided over everything and he or she or they planned this moment a million years ago. This speck in time might be accidental. No matter the explanation, an all-consuming pull drew me to her. If I wanted to retreat, something would have stopped me. This was uncompromising destiny.

I took an unwavering step toward the future and…nothing. No fireworks, no earth-shattering explosions, no sirens. It was a drumroll followed by silence. However, joy and anticipation filled every part of my soul.

On my way, I passed several humans. We exchanged smiles. I was moving among them unnoticed. I strolled through the park into downtown as if I had lived here my whole life. I neared the Orchard building and searched for Ellis. There, I saw people shopping along one of the streets. I quit the role of researcher and instead become an active participant in this world we created for them. The feeling was different as a student. At the Archives, I accidentally entered the Habitat. Now, I was entering deliberately to make contact.

Alongside the building, nestled under flowering trees was a bench sitting near a bicycle rack. Here, I would wait. I attempted smoothing my wrinkled clothes and noticed my student identification badge still attached at my waistband. I snatched it off, shoved it into my pocket, ran my fingers through my hair, and tried to look nonchalant. Within moments, I saw her peddling in my direction. I had no story, and I panicked.

"Bram?" she called a few yards from me. She beamed.

What do I do? What do I say? She is glowing. What excuse do I have? "Hi, wow, what a coincidence." *I am an idiot.* I stood. She rolled her bike into the rack. "How are you? Have you recovered from our crash?"

"No," she said, "I'm pretty sure I'll have permanent damage."

We both laughed. "So, why are you here? Have you just had therapy?" she asked, taking one side of her hair and pushing it back behind her ear.

"Yes, I decided to sit and soak up the sun," I said. *So lame, I sound like a grandfather.*

"You sound like my dad." *Great.*

"Are you here for therapy?" I asked.

"No, I was meeting my friend." She looked over my shoulder, and for a moment, I was disappointed Ana would join us. I turned to see nothing. "You met her in the Archives. She's late, but she should be here soon. I swear she told me she'd be out by four o'clock... wait, unless she meant her appointment was at four o'clock. I'm so confused. Was it an extended session?" She put her palm to her head as if to jar her memory.

Everything she said and every movement she made was charming—I had a flashback to the therapist calling the little human child adorable and thinking of it as a pet for her own child. Was I trying to turn Ellis into a pet? Was she my latest plaything I'd soon tire of and put away? No, no, that can't be. I won't be that Bram again.

"Oh well, when she gets out, we meet at the Fountain. Want to go with me? I mean, if you don't have plans. Have you eaten?" She stopped her nervous chatter and looked up at me with a kind smile and a look that told me she wasn't sure I wanted to spend time with her.

"No, I'm starving. I'd love to go with you," I said. One of the few truths I had told her.

"Great, I'm sure Ana will come as soon as her session is finished," she said.

What have I done? "Hey, should I trust you? I hardly know you," I said, trying to be funny. "You should tell me something about yourself. I don't want you to think I go off anywhere with perfect strangers." *I hope I didn't sound like a complete srumof.*

She laughed. I breathed easier. "I promise you're safe with me, I don't bite," she said. "Besides, we aren't complete strangers. Remember, we have literally run into each other before."

"Have we? I don't remember," I said. *Please let it work. Where is cool Bram? I sound stupid.*

She laughed but ended with a little snort. She swiped her hand at me as if she would hit me but delivered only a playful tap.

"Ow—so violent and angry, are you sure you don't need a quick therapy session before we go?" I asked, pointing to the Orchard building. More laughing and fake fighting followed. This had to be what my mom called "love taps," and I thought it felt awesome.

In Atum culture, men aren't concerned with proving masculinity or behaving in ways humans consider manly. For Atum, providing a successful family dynamic was vital. Atum females considered an attentive husband, gentle father, and competent worker, an attractive mate. However, it didn't hurt to be handsome. Our compatibility and genetics testing confirmed our ability to function as valuable mates. For us, there were other ways in our culture to prove ourselves. My father doted on my mother. He treated her as if she were his reason for living. His goal was solely to please her, and females desired that type of Atum mate. My virility wouldn't be questioned by admitting I felt this way toward Ellis. The only problem I faced was her not being on my coupling list, and furthermore, she was a human. That was a major problem.

We walked together, with me letting her lead the way. Of course, I had never eaten at the Fountain or any other restaurant in Horizon, so I needed to be careful. I didn't have the choice of telling the truth, so my lies had to be perfect.

We stopped at a shiny, one-story building with many windows.

Outside was a large, advertisement with glowing colored lights. The sign simulated the motion of a fountain spewing water, in multiple shades of blue. "Have you been here before?" Quick thinking told me it must be possible *not* to have eaten here.

"No, I haven't. I'm hungry, and it smells delicious," I said. It was fortunate, my mother exposed me to human foods. Otherwise, I would have been apprehensive about what I might be forced to eat. Humans enjoyed many foods for which our people had not developed a taste. Fried skins of a pig, an underground nut made into a thick paste, a grit that looked much like sand, and a slimy, green vegetable called an okra. My mother had taken great pleasure in introducing these 'human-alien' food items into our Atum household.

We reached the door, and she grabbed for the handle. Like lightning, I remembered to open it for her. We had this custom in our culture. Males performed acts to shelter and protect females. Automated doors executed this task in our buildings, but there were other ways to show this courtesy to females. I grabbed the door handle and pulled, it caught. I pulled again, and it didn't budge.

She laughed. "Push," she said.

Great…and now, I am officially an idiot.

I pushed the door, and I joined her in laughing. "Oh, I'm so smooth. Let me warn you—it will be hard to resist my obvious charm." More laughing on her part. *Maybe I'm not too bad at this wooing business.*

"Hey there, precious. Who you got with ya today?" asked a cheery woman with enormous hair. I was glad I didn't lie about eating at this restaurant before.

"Hello, Mrs. McCoy," said Ellis, "This is Bram."

"Hello, Bram. Have we met before? Nope, I'd remember you. Ellis, he's just cute as a bug in a rug," said Mrs. McCoy. "Y'all take a seat, and I'll be right with you."

"Cool, huh?" said Ellis, looking around the restaurant. "I keep telling myself to try other places to eat, but Ana and I keep coming here because it's close to the Orchard. Where do you eat?"

Mrs. McCoy delivered menus. "Here you are, darlings. What can I get you to drink?"

Luckily, she kept me from having to answer Ellis about which restaurant was my favorite. "So, what do you recommend?" I said, before she asked me the same question again.

"I love everything, but the fries and burgers are incredible. What are your favorite foods?" she asked.

"In our house, eating is a science experiment. You never know how the results will be," I said, telling the truth this time.

"My dad loves to cook. His effort makes up for his lack of culinary discipline concerning those insignificant rules about cooking times and temperatures." She laughed again.

Mrs. McCoy took our order and left.

"So, I'll go first," I said. "Tell me everything about you, Ellis."

She smiled. "I hate to point this out, but that isn't you going first, that's you telling *me* to go first."

I returned a smile and said nothing.

"Okay," she began, "I'm twenty. I'll be twenty-one next February. I finished my placement tests last week and can't wait to get the results. My dad is a doctor, and Mom was in the healthcare field before coming to Horizon. They met here, married, and adopted me. Within two weeks, I became Ellis Bauer. I guess I never told you my last name."

I hesitated. "No." I smiled. "It's a beautiful name."

"How old are you?" she asked.

"I'll be twenty-two in September."

"Oh," Ellis began, "wait, why don't I remember you in school? You graduated in '50?"

"Oh…I moved ahead," I said. I surprised myself thinking of it so quickly.

"You're kidding me. Oh…so you're one of *those* kids."

"What kids?" I asked.

"The brainiacs. That's what you are. You're a nerd." She laughed.

"Okay, you got me. I'm a nerd. I love to study. Have you always been a bully?" I asked, hoping I was funny.

She play-slapped my hand, "I'm not a bully."

"What do you call that?" I said, rubbing my hand. "You're so vicious. I can help with your anger problem. You need to learn to control your outbursts," I said, teasing. "That's part of my job."

"What? I want to be a release therapist," she said. "Is your job related to release therapy?"

"I…" I paused to think of something. "am interested in researching human psychology."

"Isn't that a release therapist?"

"Not technically, I don't practice in the office doing sessions with patients. Instead, I study case files to determine needs created by the Ha…Horizon…by the town. Huma…people are changing because of what's happened on Earth, and many psychological changes will continue to result."

"You really do sound like my dad. And, by the way, he is king of the nerds." She laughed. "Do you know him? Alex Bauer? You must study at the hospital."

"No, I don't think so. I haven't begun my work there. I'm in the last phase of my training."

Mrs. McCoy returned with our food. "Chili fries, grilled cheese, and chocolate cake. Enjoy."

"Thank you, Mrs. McCoy. This looks incredible," I said.

"Well, I declare, Ellis, I could just sop your fella up with a biscuit," said Mrs. McCoy, giving us a wink. Ellis giggled. I didn't understand what Mrs. McCoy meant, but it sounded painful and not pleasurable at all.

I looked at my sandwich and dessert. They looked delicious. So did Ellis's chili fries.

"You must have a sweet tooth," she said. I wasn't sure what that meant either, so I laughed. She did too. I thought I would rather have a tooth that was sweet than let Mrs. McCoy sop me.

"Your fries look great. I've never tried them with chili."

"I'll trade you fries for a bite of your cake. What do you say?" She pushed her plate toward mine and picked up her fork, letting it hover over my dessert. In our culture, sharing food from our serving dishes was an intimate act, and people did this only with family or spouses. I felt strange seeing her enthusiasm over this nonchalant human practice. She smiled at me as she lifted cake into her plate. I scooped fries over into my plate and returned the smile.

I was unsure about everything I said, but being with Ellis felt easy and right. I wanted to tell her everything and skip to the part where she knew the real me, and I knew her completely, and we were…

"You're putting way too much thought into whether chili fries were worth the sacrifice of cake," she said. She was clever and quick.

"I think I might be in love," I said. She turned a gorgeous shade of pink. "These chili fries are fantastic," I added. I noticed she had chocolate on the corner of her mouth. I wanted to reach out and wipe it away, but instead, I took a napkin and held it in front of her. She looked confused. I pointed to my mouth, and she looked embarrassed. I remembered when she had lunch earlier with Ana and said she would be embarrassed if I had seen her with the burnt sandwich stuck in her teeth. I wished I hadn't told her the chocolate was on her lip, so I picked up a chili fry and purposely let the chili graze my mouth. She laughed and started to wipe at the frosting on her mouth. "No," I said, "leave it. We should start a new trend."

She leaned across the table and took her napkin to wipe away my chili. "Sorry, the world isn't ready for that fashion statement." This was the second time she touched me, not counting the time we collided. I understood, to her, this was not intimate. But for me, it was electric.

According to my research on human behavioral history, in American societies, touching wasn't forbidden. Handshaking was a form of greeting and taking leave. The practice of greetings called high fives was absent of intimate connotation. Humans made more general physical contact with one another than my race. What were we thinking?

"You never had chili on your fries? Where have you been living, Mars?"

"No, not quite." *If you only knew.* "Mom is more into health food."

"Eww, yuck, so is my mom. And your dad?" she asked.

Without thinking, I said, "He died not long after The End." I forgot to use my bio story; fake Dad was alive.

"You mean your biological dad?" she asked, amazed I still had a member of my own blood survive with me. No family had more than one member survive The End.

"No, my Horizon dad; it's only my mom and me, now."

I cringed and felt guilty every time I told her another lie. Was I fooling myself into thinking we could have a happy ending? *Oh, yeah, by the way, Ellis, I am Atum, what you call alien, and Horizon isn't real. You are living in a giant science experiment. I thought you were my ideal mate, so I faked a whole life story, and now I want to confess. My mother is your therapist, and I've read your private files. Oh, since you aren't supposed to know this, we can't date because my government has a ban on human-Atum relationships, so we are breaking one of the worst laws ever.* I couldn't do this to her because she didn't deserve to be hurt. I had to leave.

"I need to go," I said. "Ellis, I can't do this." I slid from the seat of the booth to stand.

She looked at me, her face full of surprise. She reached across the table and took my hand. "Stop. I miss my real parents, too." My every thought and feeling spiraled and fixated on our joined hands. "Even though they died when I was a baby and I don't remember them, my heart misses them. I have no mementos and no pictures, but I believe you can love someone without knowing them."

I stared at her for a moment and let my thoughts swim in the words she spoke. Did she truly believe that? I was taking a chance and hoping she was sure of her feelings. She didn't know the real me yet, but I wanted her to love me. Our hands still lay intertwined. I smiled and slid back into the booth.

"How about another bite of cake?" I said. She looked at me and smiled. There was no turning back. I committed myself to her at that moment for the rest of my life.

CHAPTER 10

My husband was a good person and a good father. He was intelligent and dedicated to his work. I didn't want to hurt him, so I never confessed he wasn't my first choice. When I received my three matches, I was ecstatic to see a familiar name. It was someone I had loved for two years. To complicate matters, he was my best friend. When the Habitat Human Studies department chose his team for the earth expedition, I was miserable. He promised me when he returned to Nurahatum, we would make our declaration, so I said no to the other matches. However, when he did return, he told me he'd fallen in love with another person. I was sure I would die of a broken heart and a broken promise. Two weeks later, I buried my pain and married another match still hopeful for our alliance. I never told my husband I longed for someone else, and in time, I came to love him.

—Dr. Claire Adler
Private Journal Entry
2040

THE LAKE

I CONVINCED MY MOTHER TO LET US BOTH STAY AT the Horizon apartment for the rest of the weekend. I argued the Habitat setting inspired the writing for my research paper. She believed I was taking life seriously because the plight of humans interested me more than ever before. Surprisingly, it didn't take my full arsenal of reasons. She said she needed time to finish bookwork in the office. She agreed, provided I promised to stay in the apartment only going backstage for meals. I planned most definitely to break that promise. On Thursday, when Ellis and I ate at the Fountain, I asked to see her the next afternoon. She told me no because of her volunteer duty at the Hobby Center. I asked for that night, but she was having Ana for a sleepover. I questioned if she had any feelings for me, but then she suggested Saturday at five o'clock. I was orchestrating something that could destroy our families, the Habitat, and all humans. I didn't care—I should have, but I didn't. I felt addicted to her and couldn't stop thinking of her. She would come.

And there I was, waiting.

The sun was setting—the time of the day I loved best. Earth was so colorful. Although I had no real memories of my home planet, I had seen pictures. There was a time of day when our suns hung low in the sky. They cast an aqua glow upon everything. The pictures were fascinating, but it couldn't compare to the warmth of oranges, reds, and pinks that lay before me from the earth's single, gigantic sun. It was gorgeous, but nothing equaled what now appeared in the distance.

I'd been thinking of a loveless future with an Atum woman chosen for me, and when I lifted my eyes, Ellis was walking from the other side of the lake toward me. The exquisite splendor of that moment progressed in slow motion. As she walked, the air swirled around her, bringing with it bits of dust and seedlings from nearby plants. They stirred with her every movement, corresponding with my own feelings. A pale-yellow dress hung to the top of her knees. She had put her hair up loosely so wavy strands cascaded at random. I wanted to drink in every hypnotic step she took toward me. Her smile was natural and easy. Was she blind to how exquisite she was? Did my face not express how I felt? I etched each part of her into my memory, but I wanted everything—her favorite flower, her favorite color, what made her laugh, and what made her cry. I'd love every facet of her. She walked closer, and my chest tightened with breath. The passion I felt was unparalleled. Fire ripped through my body, and I wondered if she saw me with the same intensity. I could have walked toward her, but I wanted to savor every second of her movement.

"Hello," she said, lowering her head to the ground, no doubt embarrassed because I had been staring at her.

I gently put my fingers to her chin and lifted her face to mine. "You are so beautiful."

She lowered her head again, avoiding my gaze.

Was this indifference? Was this insecurity? I had to know. Again, I cupped her chin and tilted her head upward. I didn't let go until she returned my smile. I held my hand out, and she grasped it gently. We looked at our hands joined and then looked at each other. That was how it happened. A connection—not of common interests, shallow physical attraction, or intellectual admiration—it was just "knowing".

"Tell me something…anything," I said. She took a misstep and lost her balance. I had her firmly, and she did not fall. "Are you okay?"

Her cheeks flushed. I had seen that look several times, and although she was embarrassed, it made her even more desirable.

"I'm fine. Tell me something about you first. Are you as graceful as I am?" she laughed.

"I have my moments, too. Tell me more about you, Ellis."

"I thought it was your turn," she said.

I wanted her to have the truth—it suffocated me. I didn't want to wait any longer. With every new lie, I would be taking the same knife which stabbed me in the gut and use it to slash any trust she might ever have in me. I risked the chance she could love me—the real me. My only relief was hearing her speak and look at me and smile. I talked; I lied. Misery and exhilaration took turns in my head. I kept waiting for whatever brought us together to give me a sign when I should tell her the truth. Searching for an opportunity that never appeared was torture.

The sun began to disappear. I wished for more time with her, but we were already breaking the rules.

"I don't want to say goodnight, but it's getting late, and I wouldn't want you to get into any trouble with your parents," I said. She smiled. My heart fluttered. This is how love should feel. For my world, questions and mathematical probability determined compatibility. Did the Atum know what passion they were missing? Had anyone been so in love with a calculated companion? I must be the first Atum in the world to understand we didn't comprehend the power of such human emotions. I took her hand again; it felt soft, warm, and fragile. I brought it up to my mouth, opened it to reveal her palm, and kissed it. I didn't think; I simply did it. Words didn't exist in any language to describe how that moment felt.

I forced myself to let her hand leave my lips. I looked at her, wanting so much more and knowing it wasn't possible.

"Can I see you tomorrow?" I asked, letting her hand fall back to her side.

"Yes, but you should meet my parents first. I wouldn't want us to get into trouble."

What could I say? If her father searched my name in the official database, he would discover Bram Potter didn't exist.

"I want to meet them, but my mom has a tight schedule. Why don't we plan to introduce our parents at The Beginning Celebration picnic?"

"Oh," she said frowning, "not until Thursday?" I heard the disappointment in her voice, and it gave me hope.

"We could meet tomorrow outside the Orchard building. We can go to the Fountain."

"I can't tomorrow. There is the project I'm doing with Ana. How about Monday?" she asked.

Mom would demand to go home Sunday or Monday. I was off from school the entire week, but I didn't know how long she would let me stay inside the Habitat. I took a chance, "I can't meet on Monday. Are you free Tuesday to meet at the Archives? We can run into one another in the fiction section again. I'll be there at three." I was trying to calculate the timing in my head.

She stepped closer. "Yes."

That single word of response from her lips sent warmth through me. It was like bees' honey on hot bread. Thick and slow and sweet. I wanted to take her in my arms and not let her leave me. I used every bit of restraint I had to keep from kissing her. In a blinding halt, I considered where this relationship could go. Eventually, she must learn the truth, and I would be the one to tell her. My heart had bound me in this relationship, but Ellis needed the whole truth before I let her give away her heart. When she learned everything, would she forgive me? And could I forgive myself if I ever hurt her?

CHAPTER 11

Habitat Security Department

(1) Chief Inspector (Atum) will assume executive responsibility within the Department of Security. The position will report to the Director of Human Affairs headquartered in New Earth City.

(1) Horizon Inspector (Atum) will oversee the duties of security officers and handle final decisions about non-threat-related issues in Horizon. The Horizon Inspector will report to the Chief Inspector.

(24) Horizon Officers (Atum) will manage general community welfare daily. These officers will report to the Horizon Inspector.

(1) Habitat Inspector (Atum) will manage the containment and control of the Habitat. The Habitat Inspector will report to the Chief Inspector.

(60) Habitat Officers (Atum) will manage the bor-

ders surrounding the Habitat. The main purpose of this office is to protect the Habitat from being breached. These officers will report to the Habitat Inspector. Officers will not have contact with humans, (unless a breach occurs) and will work only in the backstage region of the Habitat.

Five-Year Annual Incident Report
for the Habitat Security Department

36 Detentions:
    (2) vandalism
    (7) attempted escapes
    (6) assaults
    (6) disturbing the peace
    (3) thefts
    (12) miscellaneous violations

68 Arranged Releases:
    (10) socially impaired patients
    (19) emotionally/mentally impaired patients
    (23) medically/physically impaired patients
    (16) emergency releases

6 Accidental Deaths:
    (2) drownings
    (1) electrocution
    (1) fall
    (2) farm-related accidents

32 Suicides
52 Natural Deaths

—Inspector Thomas Ryder
Habitat Security Department
August 1, 2037

THE FOUNTAIN

I WAITED FOR ANA TO FINISH HER RELEASE. WE hadn't discussed my date with Bram at the park. Mrs. McCoy had taken my order, and only one other customer sat in the Fountain. Here, we could talk without being overheard.

"Cherry pie and coffee, dear," said Mrs. Young, who must have been near seventy-five or eighty. She was still an elegant woman. Mrs. McCoy told me she had been something called a beauty queen as a young girl. It sounded shallow, but many things in that world were different.

"Okay, coming up, sweetie," said Mrs. McCoy. She hurried away to get coffee while I heard Phil in back whistling and singing an unknown song in Spanish.

Mrs. McCoy dropped off my hot tea and delivered coffee to Mrs. Young. I wished Ana would hurry; I felt odd and thought maybe that I was coming down with something.

Finally, Ana walked through the door. "Sorry I'm late," she said. "What have I missed?"

"I'm having hot tea, Mrs. Young is having pie, and Mrs. McCoy is fussing at Phil because she can't understand the lyrics to his song. Other than that—nothing."

"Hello, darling," said Mrs. McCoy. "What can I get today for you, hon?"

"Tea and fried pickles, please," said Ana. Mrs. McCoy hurried off, and Ana turned to face me. "I've so much to tell you. You are not going to believe what Dr. Webster and I talked about. But you go first. You aren't eating? Are you sick?"

"I'm fine, Mother," I said. "Maybe I'm taking a cold."

"Get to the juicy parts and stop stalling, Grandma…with your hot tea." She grinned and made kissing noises.

"How old are you again?" I asked. Ana laughed and made a kissy-face. "Okay, it was incredible," I said, "and we talked about everything. He's studying to be a type of therapist, and he's almost twenty-two."

"Did he kiss you?" she asked.

"Ana," I said, "You get right to the"—a shriek and crash ripped through the restaurant.

We both whipped around to see Mrs. Young standing in the middle of her shattered coffee cup. She screamed an ear-piercing cry. When she stopped, Mrs. McCoy was first to step toward her. "Stop," Mrs. Young commanded, pointing at the confused waitress. "You won't take them."

Mrs. McCoy froze with bewilderment. "I…I want to help you, Mrs. Young."

"I know what you want. You want memories of him, and you can't have them. I remember. I remember everything and you want to take it away." She looked down at the spilled coffee and fragments of pottery. "I loved Curtis. We married fifty years ago today. Everyone thought I wanted him for his money. His family didn't understand I loved him…despite his faults. When it happened, they left him behind and took me. I refuse to forget him. That's why they want him now. But I won't let go. Those memories are all I have of the good times, and I won't let you take them."

Mrs. McCoy, perhaps for the first time in her life, could not speak. She looked at us as if we might understand what Mrs. Young was saying. "Phil, call Assistance." Assistance was our emergency office. Phil, who had come from the kitchen, moved faster than usual but stopped and tiptoed for fear he might upset the already upset

Mrs. Young. Had this been a different situation, it would've been comical to see Phil tiptoeing.

Mrs. McCoy turned back to the elderly lady, desperate to help in any way. "Honey, can I get you another cup of coffee?" There was no answer. Mrs. Young continued to look downward.

She and I talked a few times before, but I didn't have a close relationship with her. I wanted to help, so I made a lightning decision. I stood and took a deep breath to make sure my voice sounded soft and monotone.

"I want to hear about Curtis. Tell me what you remember, Mrs. Young."

She raised her head, and tears streamed amid the aged lines of her face. She was, however, smiling. "We drank coffee every morning in our sunroom. We might have been drinking this coffee together, but he wasn't taken. They took *me* from him, and now, they want to take *his memory* from me. But I won't let them," she said as she stooped forward.

"Let me help you clean that, Mrs. Young. I can do it for you," I said. I stepped closer.

"Stop." She held up a withered hand. I did as ordered. She allowed herself to crouch until she was sitting on the floor. Her beige skirt soaked in the dark brown liquid. She touched the stain now spreading on the fabric. When she raised her head, I could tell an idea sparked clearly in her mind. Her wrinkled mouth curled upward and stretched to reveal an unnatural smile. Her eyes grew wide and wild.

"Stop them, Ellis. They aren't what they appear to be." She picked up the largest shard of the broken coffee cup and sliced along the underside of her wrist, and then changing hands, with greater speed, slashed the other. Her expression never changed. If she was in pain, her face showed no sign, but it must have been excruciating. She looked at me with that eerie smile again, "Habitat," she muttered, as the color faded from her lined face, "Habitat." Her skirt soaked in a different liquid of dark red. Still looking at me, she stopped smiling and fell to the floor with a dull thump. Within seconds, Mrs. McCoy followed to the floor with a similar sound, only much louder.

Ana rushed by, elbowing me out of her way. I was still trying to sort out what happened. Her words kept repeating in my head—stop them, stop them, stop them. "Stop who?" I said aloud, to no one listening except myself.

Ana leaned over Mrs. Young, but I couldn't understand why. She was screaming something, but I couldn't hear. I'd gone deaf. The sound roared back into my world as plates crashed in the kitchen, and I came back from wherever I had been.

Phil screamed my name, and I stumbled to Mrs. McCoy, who sat up and screamed again. I wished, for a moment, she hadn't regained consciousness. Phil and I helped her into a booth. I watched him cradle her, rocking back and forth, and I realized I had joined in the rocking motion. Time had stopped. How long had it been?

Ana stood and walked toward me, covered in Mrs. Young's blood. "She's dead," she yelled over the waitress's screams that began again after seeing Ana blood-soaked.

I looked over my friend's shoulder at Mrs. Young's body lying in an unnatural heap. Her eyes were closed, and I was thankful. That unnerving smile had faded, and her face now looked peaceful. The agony had vanished.

The door burst open, and three officials raced into the restaurant. That action helped to break through the haze into which I'd fallen again. I shook my head, hoping to wake from this nightmare. Was I in the middle of having one of my horrible dreams? Could I be in Ana's bed safe and secure right now? I couldn't clear my mind. This moment was the same as waking from a dream and being unsure of anything—where you were, what day it was, or if you were even awake. I raised my head after a few moments and saw a man turn the open sign to read closed. He took out his miniport and walked through the door to stand outside the entrance. Another official, a tall woman with a thin, chiseled face, walked toward Ana and me. The room spun. If Mrs. McCoy would shut up, I could focus. I shook my head again, and I pinched my leg as hard as possible. It was useless. There was no waking from this.

"Please follow me so we can help the lady," said the woman official.

I wanted to say I thought she was beyond help, but I had no words. I recovered my hearing only, to have now lost my ability to speak. The official nearest Mrs. Young stood over her body staring, with an angry expression.

The female, whose nametag said Nicole, ushered us into the kitchen. My legs carried me, but I felt unsteady and numb. She asked us to wait while she looked for chairs. I looked at Ana. Thank goodness Mrs. McCoy's screams subsided into a much quieter sob.

Ana leaned over and whispered into my ear. "Why did she do it? What did she mean when she told you to stop them?" I shrugged my shoulders, the only response I could manage.

"This is what we've been trying to find, Ellis. Why did she say Habitat?"

Nicole returned with two chairs. Ana straightened up and spoke no more. Mrs. McCoy sat, now silent, but tears and eyeliner still flowed. Nicole left again. Almost unintelligible, Mrs. McCoy asked, "Why'd she do that, Phil?"

Phil began to speak but stopped when Nicole brought other chairs.

"Please sit. You have had a great shock," Nicole said. We obeyed.

A new official, another woman, appeared and walked toward us.

She had not come in at first. She carried a small case with her. "Hello," she said. "I'm Taylor. You have suffered a stressful event. I will check your physical condition."

No one spoke at first. Phil sat up in his chair and leaned forward. "What was that out there?" He gestured to the dining room where Mrs. Young, no doubt, still lay.

"I don't have those answers," replied Taylor. Phil looked to Nicole for an explanation, but she was silent.

After we had our pulse, blood pressure, and eyes checked, Taylor stood and walked to the other room without a word. She returned with the male official. He was the one who stood over Mrs. Young. His name badge read, Thomas Ryder.

"Hello, my name is Inspector Thomas Ryder," he said while pointing to his badge. "I am here to help." His voice was so calm it frightened me; it seemed unnatural to show such little emotion. "According to your physical exams, you all are experiencing shock. We have medicine which will relieve you of stress and make you feel better." He turned to Taylor. She opened her case and searched for something.

"You each will receive a medipen injection," began the inspector. "This medicine will help you to relax, so you don't put excess strain on your body. Excess anxiety can make you ill. You should not suffer because of this unfortunate situation."

"No man, I'm not having a shot, dude," announced Phil. "I don't like those things."

"I see," said Inspector Ryder. "Follow me, and we will find a solution. Taylor, please proceed."

"Roll up your sleeves, please. You won't experience any discomfort except a slight warm feeling which will disappear within seconds." Taylor leaned forward to us and whispered, "Men can be such babies about these things."

Each of us complied before Phil and the inspector returned. I wanted to ask what happened but knew to keep quiet. Phil did not receive a shot in front of us. I wondered if he convinced the inspector or the inspector convinced him.

The official named Nicole typed our names, addresses, and H numbers into her dataport. Our H number was our Horizon number. It identified us along with our name. "Ana?" said the inspector, "Please go with Nicole and change clothes."

Ana, without a word, stood up and looked at me. *Don't go, don't go.* Fear seized me, wondering if she might not come back. She turned to Nicole, and they walked away. I realized I was silly; I didn't want her to stay in those clothes. Mrs. Young's blood had covered her entirely from when she had propped Mrs. Young against herself. When Ana looked at me, I noticed she even had blood on her silver hoop earring plus all over her hands. I would have welcomed scrubbing in a hot shower.

Taylor, apparently a nurse, walked to the sink and filled four glasses of water from the tap. She placed them on the counter near her case. Inspector Ryder walked to the front of the restaurant again without a word. I heard a commotion and then the sound of the broken cup being swept. I could imagine a mounded sludge of jagged shards and blood. The sound of the ceramic pieces scraping against the tile reminded me of fingernails clawing a rough surface, and a painful shiver bored through my spine.

Ana returned wearing a hospital gown. She didn't look embarrassed, but I wanted to show support, so when she sat beside me, I took her hand in mine. She had washed because I saw no sign of blood on her. I didn't notice her sneakers when she came back, but I was glad the visible signs of Mrs. Young's suicide no longer covered her. When I took her hand, she looked at me and smiled. She was tough, and for that, I was thankful.

The inspector returned, but this time, he had a chair. He placed the chair, so it faced us. As he sat, he smiled for the first time and began in a different tone, almost cheery, "I hope you are feeling calmer." He was a different person. His manner was friendly and gentle; he wasn't acting in the stiff official way. "I now want you to take this tablet," he motioned to Taylor, who produced four tiny yellow pills. "This medicine works with the medipen injection to help reverse aftereffects of shock."

While he talked, Taylor gave each of us a glass of water. Phil made no objection this time, so I assumed he understood these were not requests, but instead, direct orders. After we had our water, Taylor handed each of us a tablet. Everyone, including Ana, had taken theirs by the time I received mine. I hesitated.

"Ellis?" Inspector Ryder began, "Take yours now, please." I did. "Thank you," he said. "Let us begin. I want to ask you a few questions." He paused as if we needed time to process what he said.

"You are Juan Felipe Lopez, thirty-nine, cook at the Fountain?" Phil nodded without speaking. "You are Josephine Katherine Andrews McCoy, forty-nine, a waitress at the Fountain?" Mrs. McCoy nodded, her tears no longer flowing. Inspector Ryder looked at Ana. "You are Ana Gracia Hamilton, twenty, a student at Horizon Academy, volunteer at the Archives?" Ana agreed without saying a word. I was next in line. "You are Ellis Elizabeth Bauer, twenty, a student at Horizon Academy, volunteer at the Hobby Center?" I began to say the information was correct but remembered everyone else had been quiet, so I did the same and nodded. "Perfect. The information is correct."

Didn't you already have these facts? This information must be on his dataport.

Inspector Ryder took a deep breath. "Today, you have witnessed something distressing."

No kidding, you are one sharp tack, Mister.

"Mrs. Young has had a massive heart attack."

What?

"She was a customer here at the Fountain today. She had been ill because she did not take her medicines correctly. Unfortunately, this did not have to happen. Her heart could not function properly without her medication."

Wait a minute. Are we talking about the same Mrs. Young who is probably still lying in a puddle of blood?

"When she rose to leave the restaurant, she fell into the table. She died instantly without a word. She was fortunate not to have suffered."

I opened my mouth to ask what in the world Inspector Ryder was talking about when he looked at Phil.

"Juan?" he asked.

He doesn't go by the name, Juan. But he can at least tell you the real story.

"Yes?" Phil responded.

"Did you see what happened to Mrs. Young?"

"I...was in the kitchen," he said, "but when I came out, she was sitting on the floor."

"No," corrected the inspector. "Mrs. Young fell to the floor after her heart attack. She was dead instantly. That was sad, wasn't it?"

He paused, staring at nothing. "I do feel sad. Mrs. Young was nice. She liked my pies. I didn't know she had heart problems."

Wait, a minute...

"Josephine," he began, "Do you recall what happened to Mrs. Young?"

Before she spoke, the seconds ticked by like hours. *Tell him...go ahead...*

"She...poor Mrs. Young had an attack...I can't believe she died.

I think it was her heart." Mrs. McCoy put her own hand over her heart and shook her head. "I sure will miss her."

"You are correct, Josephine, she had a heart attack," he said.

What? Why are they agreeing with this? They saw her. Am I going insane?

"So, Ana," continued the inspector, "You were kind to try helping Mrs. Young."

At last, the truth.

"I tried to help, but I…" began Ana.

Tell them, Ana.

"I got dirty."

What?

"You got your clothes soiled, Ana," said the official. "When Mrs. Young fell into the table, she knocked a cup onto the floor spilling her coffee."

This is insane. My heart raced. What was wrong with the others? They acted like…robots. I looked at Ana and then looked away. I had to act normal. I had to control my breathing.

"Coffee?" asked Ana, furrowing her brow.

"You had to change out of your clothes. You are now wearing a hospital gown because your clothes are covered in coffee."

"Oh," she said. "Yes, a hospital gown. I put it on because my clothes were covered in…"

Blood. In Blood! Your clothes were covered in Mrs. Young's bl…

"…coffee," Ana finished.

"Excellent."

What is happening? This is crazy.

He slid his chair closer. My heart was pounding so fast I couldn't be sure I might not have a real heart attack. *Think Ellis, think. What happens when I tell him the truth? Wait, this man doesn't want the truth; he wants the same lie he has planted in their minds. The pill and the shot—that was it. They must be drugged.* It was affecting their memory recall. Mrs.

Young's words struck me, "Memories are all I have…I won't let you take them." Someone tried to take Mrs. Young's memories of her husband and Mr. Hap's memories of his wife. They have taken the memories of Phil, Mrs. McCoy, and Ana. They want my memory of this, too.

"Ellis…Ellis, can you hear me?" A switch flipped, and I felt pulled back into reality with the others. He was calling my name, but I had been in such deep thought, I zoned out. "Is she having problems?" he asked the nurse. She stepped forward and again shined a light in my eyes. I blinked several times.

"What? What did you say?" *Careful. I must be careful…and convincing.*

"I said, can you tell us what happened today?" He inched closer and put his hand on my hand. My skin changed into bumpy flesh.

"The drugs may be too strong for her," said the nurse. "You should hurry in case the sedative is also too strong. She may be getting sleepy."

I must hurry. What do I say? "It was awful. Mrs. Young…had a heart attack and died. I think she made a mistake with her medicine." I couldn't stop tears streaming down my face. I was positive they knew I was lying.

"Yes," he exhaled and released my hand. I inhaled the stench of his breath as it blew against my face, and nausea wrenched my stomach. He sat back in his chair and said, "You are absolutely right." I dropped my head, thinking I was going to be sick. Hot saliva filled my mouth. My head spun with the images of Mrs. Young and Ana, covered in her blood. Mrs. Young said 'Habitat.' What was Habitat? Blackness was closing in around me.

"Ellis, Ellis." The woman was holding me by the shoulders.

"Is this a problem?" I heard a man's voice.

I opened my eyes. Taylor was looking at me. "Shock."

My heart was racing. My throat was tight, and breathing now came in exaggerated gasps. The woman now had a wet cloth to my face. *Maybe I am in shock.*

"She will recover. She was last to receive the injection; perhaps shock had already begun its course." She bent down to me with a smile. "Relax Ellis," she whispered, "don't speak. Just breathe."

Inspector Ryder stood. "Does anyone have questions?"

Something told me asking questions would get a private audience with the inspector like Phil when he refused the medipen injection. I sat staring, only at him, and tried to concentrate on slowing my breathing. My nausea seemed to pass.

"Someone will take you home now. You have experienced a stressful day. The medicine you have taken will allow you to go home and sleep well through the night. When you wake, you won't stress over Mrs. Young's heart attack. Mrs. Young forgot to take her heart medicine. While sitting in the restaurant, she became unwell. She stood and suffered a heart attack. She fell to the floor knocking, her coffee cup off the table. It broke after hitting the floor. Ana Hamilton tried to help her. Her clothes became covered in coffee. Ana could do nothing to save Mrs. Young. She is no longer sick and no longer in pain. You will remember exactly how this story happened."

Yes, I will remember exactly how this story happened.

CHAPTER 12

Horizon Citizen Council

The Horizon Citizen Council (HCC) will comprise nine elected officials whose duty will be the administration and management of a specific department within the city organization. Each member, known as a Councilor, will present a departmental management report during council meetings. Members will vote on issues with the majority having the power to declare final decisions.

The nine departments are:
Education
Finance (Give and Take system)
Horizon Factory
Horizon Farm
Maintenance and Energy*
Security*
Technology*

Therapy and Health*
Work Placement and Volunteer Program*

* Atum transplants will fill these positions.

—Habitat Planning Commission
August 2031

DECEIT

FOUR OFFICIAL CARS WERE WAITING FOR US OUT-side the restaurant. People gathered on the sidewalk. Inspec-tor Ryder led us from the kitchen through the seating area of the diner. The restaurant looked spotless and ready for customers. Mrs. Young wasn't there, nor was any of the blood and mess. Someone had cleaned our tables. No sign of the event existed. Officials led us to separate cars, each with an escort and driver. I watched the others walk out of the restaurant as if they were catatonic. I had done the same. There were no words exchanged between us, nor did anyone in the gathered crowd speak to us. Before my car pulled away, In-spector Ryder stood at the restaurant entrance and addressed the onlookers. I imagined he was telling everyone how poor Mrs. Young died of a heart attack. No doubt, they would believe him.

As we drove through town, I tried not to show much emotion and act as the others had. I saw this town, my town, with different eyes. Instead of a picturesque hamlet, I now saw something artificial and misleading. Something dark and ugly. My stomach rolled and not because of the gruesome scene I witnessed earlier. I leaned my face closer to the window, looking at this illusion of utopia until I was touching the glass. The coolness of it brought little relief from the inevitable sickness rising within me. What they did to us wasn't a community service to help four bystanders of a tragedy avoid post-traumatic stress. What they did to us felt sinister.

As we pulled into my driveway, I panicked. The medicine wasn't only to help me forget the incident but make me calm. The moment I saw my Dad, I feared bursting into tears, and that wasn't the expected way to act. I tried to think of any happy memory so I wouldn't become hysterical with my father. I thought about my Cinderella birthday party when Dad dressed as the Prince. I thought about the first time Ana and I jumped from the high dive at the Hobby Center pool. I thought about being with Bram at the lake. Nothing worked. I was literally devoid of any happiness. As the car came to a stop, my mother, followed by my father, came from the front door. Officials, no doubt, had informed them I was coming home.

I reached for the handle and stopped. I am helpless. Remember. My mother reached the door first and opened it as she talked with the escort. I stepped one foot out of the car and threw up right at her feet.

"Oh, Ellis," said my mother.

"I have her Greta, you speak to the official, and I'll take her inside," my father said. He wrapped me in his arms and led me to the house. "Shh, you're safe, Junior, I have you," he said. Hot tears flowed. My back was now to the escort and my mother.

My father took me to the bathroom and sat me on the edge of the tub. "Sit here and don't speak. You have received a shock to your body, and I understand they have given medicines to calm you."

He sounded exactly like the nurse.

"These medicines will prevent you from being able to talk much or show great emotion." He had a warm cloth and wiped my face gently. I took massive gasps of air, but I couldn't get enough. I struggled to control the rush of emotion. The bathroom spun out of control. My father shushed me as he pulled me close to him in an embrace.

"You must be calm. Look at me. You…must…be…calm. It is expected. Nod, if you understand," he said. I nodded. "It can be explained why you're crying. Tears are a reflex of severe nausea. If we are visited by officials, I'll tell them this." He gave me a glass of water. "Rinse." I did. He spoke rapidly. "After we are finished, your mother will need to come in and help you change into your night-clothes. You will be sleepy, and she won't be expecting you to talk nor manage to undress by yourself. Open your mouth. I want you to swallow this medicine. Hurry. This will calm you, and it will help you to act as they will be expecting."

From his pocket, he produced an incredibly small tablet and held it to my lips. I panicked thinking back to the nurse in the Fountain. My father sensed my thoughts immediately.

"Ellis, you are the most important person in my world, and I could never hurt you." There was the sound of our front door open-ing and closing. My father turned his head toward the sound and back to me. He bent and whispered, "Quick, take it."

I opened my mouth without hesitation. He spoke the truth. My father was incapable of harming me. I swallowed it with a sip of water.

"You will get sleepy. I'll check on you in the night and if you need me and I'm not by your bed, call me; I'll come. You're safe, I promise," he continued to talk softly. I nodded.

"Alex, the official asked to speak with you," interrupted my mother. "Did you not hear me call you? He is waiting." She stood at the doorway of the bathroom.

"I'm sorry, Greta. Ellis became sick again, and I know how you feel about those things. I wanted to get her cleaned up so you could help her dress for bed. She can't manage herself. Ellis, you must be sleepy, so you should go to bed. I want you to rest the entire night, and I will see you in the morning. I love you so much." My dad helped me to stand, which wasn't necessary and kissed me on my forehead before hugging me.

He allowed my mother and me to walk out first. Muffled sound came from the other room while I let her dress me. I sat on the bed while she pulled the curtains shut and the remaining light of day was instantly gone. She tucked me into bed without a word, cut off the side table light, and walked to the door. She stopped and stood with her back to me for a moment. Her still silhouette lit from the hall light frightened me. She turned, walked toward the bed, and leaned over me.

"Ellis, I do love you," she said, and not in her usual manner. She kissed my forehead and walked away, closing the door behind her.

The room lay still in darkness. That's what happened here in Horizon. They shut the curtains on those memories they considered unwanted. They blacked out the events they considered dangerous. Everything in my life had become a mystery to me. Quiet tears flowed until sleep relieved me of the day.

CHAPTER 13

The final preparation for removal took three years, and the rescue was done in three hours. No one on the collection teams knew when they might receive the command. All units were expected to be moving on the ground within thirty minutes of receiving orders. Failure was not acceptable; so many lives depended on their performance. Our most elite soldiers trained to survive the danger and possible complications.

We practiced, sometimes with actual human removals. We stopped doing that midway through the preparation; returning them was too complicated. We learned that particular lesson from over a half-century before. Returns were most likely damaged, if not physically, certainly mentally.

We thought we were ready, but there were obstacles we had not considered. Teams collected as many humans as possible with losses resulting on both sides. Chaos engulfed the planet during the last hour, and countries used several methods of deadly warfare. These extreme tactics left the rescue mission vulnerable to the madness of these warring Earth nations. Most casualties could be explained, but others were speculation. We have verified that some humans killed Atum attempting rescues. Those humans were released, being unsuitable specimens for the program.

These instances were not the first time our people had been victims of humans' murderous tendencies. Throughout history, we've suffered many acts of cruelty from governments of Earth who knew of our existence.

However, no matter the past, we look toward the future. We risked Atum lives, securing our safety and civilization. For those who side with the human realm, we give them this analogy. Does human man regret destroying an anthill when he builds a house where a colony has settled? An ant is insignificant to a human. Man does not consider its feelings or welfare because they do not exist on the same evolutionary level. So what is our deterrent? A human represents the same insignificance to us as the ant does to him. Why should we not take this planet? We are far more evolved than humans. No, we cannot consider their feelings or well-being because, in the universe, humans are unimportant.

We are not barbaric. In the interest of science, we will preserve the species. We will live on this planet, but it will be their colony we step on and destroy. It will be their lives we control at our discretion.

However, we will show more mercy for humans than they have ever shown their inferiors.

—Urbara Izzau, Director General
New Earth Acquisition Public Hearing
November 2032

D E S P E R A T I O N

"ELLIS? ARE YOU AWAKE? HONEY, INSPECTOR RYDER is here to talk with you."

I opened my eyes to see Dad standing over me.

"You can't remember much because of the medicines given to you at the Fountain. They helped to calm you, but the official might need to ask you questions. It's acceptable if you don't remember the events at the restaurant."

In a flood of memory, the whole of yesterday's events came crashing down. My father looked at me, detecting my thoughts.

"You may feel sad because of her death, or you may feel no emotions concerning yesterday, but you are calm," he said. "Understand? You can do this." I nodded. He walked out of the room after kissing my forehead and squeezing my hand.

Tears welled up; I had to pull myself together. It was 10:30 and I should have been awake by now. I sat up in bed, trying to remember what my father said last night. He talked in such a strange way as if he suspected the medicine didn't work for me as it had the others. He couldn't know they tried to manipulate my memory, so why had he told me how I should act this morning? No matter what manipulation the official attempted, I should have suffered at least a little emotional or physical shock. Perhaps I had imagined the way my father treated me.

I grabbed a T-shirt and jeans along with slippers and carried them into the bathroom. After dressing and brushing my teeth, I stood in front of the mirror, trying to practice a happy, non-stressed demeanor. It wasn't easy. I splashed water on my face and pulled my hair back into a neat ponytail. I stared into the mirror; I looked too normal. I grabbed a wrinkled shirt from the hamper and changed. I pulled my hair out of the band, bent my head forward and tied it into an off-centered, sloppy bun. Next, I splashed more water on my face and allowed it to splatter my shirt.

"Ellis?" my mother called.

I darted from the bathroom but slowed my pace to the kitchen where I found my mom, dad, and the official from the Fountain. *Be calm.*

"Morning, everyone," I yawned. "Excuse me. Good morning Mr....I'm sorry your name has slipped my memory."

He looked pleased. "Inspector Ryder," he said. "Good morning, Ellis. I hope you slept well last night."

"I think I ate something that didn't sit well with my stomach; I was sick last night." Another fake yawn. I rubbed my eyes and wiped away real tears—hoping they'd look like sleepy tears. He narrowed his eyes, and I forced myself not to break my return stare.

Dad walked over and hugged me. "Morning, Junior." He patted my crazy hair bun and let out a chuckle. I walked to the refrigerator.

"I am here to ask if you needed to discuss yesterday's event." He tapped his port and stopped, eyeing me, waiting for my response.

"Yes," I leaned my head around the fridge door and looked at the three adults. "Did I leave my bike?" It didn't happen, but in my imagination, Mom and Dad breathed huge sighs of relief. I stuck my head back into the refrigerator and cringed out of their line of view. I needed just a second to compose myself; this man suspected me.

"No, Ellis. Officials brought your bike home with you yesterday," he said, picking up his dataport from the kitchen table. I closed the door after choosing a container of juice.

"Wow. Weird. I didn't remember. Thank you," I said while getting a glass from the cabinet. "Juice, anyone?"

"No. Are there questions concerning Mrs. Young?" he asked.

I paused pouring and hoped I looked sincere. My mind was

screaming the words I wanted to say; *SHE KILLED HERSELF, YOU MORON!* "Well, I suppose we need to go to her Farewell, do you have those details?"

"No." He paused with a dead stare as if he were summing up my reactions one last time. "Well, this will be enough unless we learn other information. If you have questions, contact me," he said to my parents. "Goodbye, Ellis."

"Goodbye, Inspector Ryder," I said, holding my glass up to him as if sending him a cheer for his health and then taking a drink. I almost buckled because my mother and father looked at me with wide-eyed horrific stares. *Why did I do that?* The rest of my performance was normal. I turned my back to my parents before I lost my game face.

They returned to the kitchen after taking Inspector Ryder to the door.

"Ellis, what was that? Are we in an Old West saloon slugging back alcohol? Are you out of your mind?" she asked with a blazing stare.

I looked at my father and said, "I'm okay, why?" I wanted to roll on the floor and laugh until I peed because I never saw my mother react or speak that way.

"Why did you…" she began.

"What have you planned for today?" My father interrupted; something he rarely did.

"Ana and I are doing research for the autumn book club, so we're going to the Archives." My mother looked at my father but said nothing. She still stung from being interrupted by Dad.

"Dr. Adler called and wants to meet with you today," said my father.

"Oh, because of yesterday?" I asked. *What horrible acting.*

"Ellis, what happened at the Fountain?" asked my mother. My

father dropped his teacup into the sink. It might have been an accident, but I wondered if he was giving me a signal.

"Ellis?" she asked again. "Do you hear me?" I hurried to put my glass into the sink where my father was still standing. He stared as if trying to caution me.

"Sorry," I said, turning towards her now, "I remember Mrs. Young was standing and fell to the floor. She dropped her cup of coffee. The officials said she had a heart problem, and she hadn't taken her medicines correctly. She was so nice. Had you met her?" I needed her to stop asking me questions because I feared my lying was becoming apparent.

"Yes, once. You said she had a..."

"Oh, what time is my session?" I now interrupted.

"Dr. Adler wants to meet at one o'clock," said my father, taking over the conversation. "I want to eat lunch with you and take you to therapy."

"Oh, okay," I said. "That'll be fun. You aren't working today?"

"Yes, this afternoon. Let's leave in thirty minutes and take our time. Are you hungry?" asked my dad.

"I'll be ready; I'm starving," I said, walking toward my room. I shut the door behind me and leaned back against it taking slow, deep breaths. Something enormous was coming. Whether what I felt was intuition or common sense, my life was taking a serious change in direction. Nothing would be the same again.

My father was waiting in the cart outside for me. "Want to drive us?" he asked.

I got little driving time since my Dad had the cart most of the day, so when given the opportunity, I jumped at it. This time, I shook my head and climbed into the passenger seat.

"Okay, then. Are you ready for this? Can you handle the speed?" he teased. I realized my mood had better perk up, so I laughed, and it sounded fake.

"No spin-outs. I'm sure Mom is watching," I said.

Off we set with a jerky start. Cruising at thirty-five miles per hour, we zoomed through the neighborhood and found ourselves headed toward town.

"Where are we eating?" I asked. I wasn't going to the Fountain anytime soon.

"Sorry, can't tell…top-secret," he said, stopping in front of the Market.

"We're going grocery shopping?" I asked.

"No, you wait here. I'll be five minutes."

I nodded my head and sat looking around town. The Market was our shop that stocked groceries and household necessities. We had depleted many emergency supplies the government stockpiled for us, so we made many things. Horizon Factory made bath products and cleaning supplies along with other necessities in bulk. We brought empty containers to fill. Horizon Kitchen made and delivered foods to the Market and restaurants. For me, this was the way we lived our lives. For others, the change had been difficult.

Dad came out later than he had promised, carrying a reusable food bag. I slid over into the driver's seat.

"Taxi," he shouted.

"Taxi? What's that?" I asked.

He laughed. "It's when someone drives you where you want to go."

"Well then, I guess I'm a taxi. Get in."

He laughed again. "I sometimes forget how much you'll never experience."

"What is this?" I said, looking in the bag. "You said we weren't grocery shopping."

"These aren't groceries; this is a picnic masterpiece."

"Okay, still looks like groceries, but whatever. Where are we going?"

"The park."

"The park? Okay, hang on," I said, taking off and making sure the tires made noise. He laugh-snorted like I did.

"I thought we could have privacy at the park," he said.

I breathed easier because I had to tell him the truth—I couldn't pretend much longer. He had the answers I needed. We got to the park in under five minutes. The whole way he teased about my driving technique. He said my cart should have a siren to alert people when I was nearby.

Dad opened the back seat and pulled out an old quilted blanket.

"I can't remember the last picnic we had," I said.

"I am glad you approve," he replied, tossing me the blanket. "Follow me, please."

Winding through a maze of twists and turns, we ended at a grassy, little knoll overlooking the lake. There was a tree, heavy with draping white blossoms and an amazing scent. I threw the blanket hard until it snapped and fell to the ground. We both sat. I took foods from the bag and laid them on the blanket between us. I looked over to Dad. He had his face in his hands.

"Hey, what is it?" I shuffled over beside him on the blanket. "Dad, what is it?"

"Ellis, I don't know where to begin. I've made mistakes, and they will hurt you," he said. I pulled back to look at him. My once rugged, handsome daddy looked aged, worn-down, and miserable. Now, nothing mattered in my crazy life except our family finding happiness. Not my conspiracy theories, not Bram, not Mrs. Young; the only thing that mattered was what changed my father into the person sitting before me.

"Ellis," he began again, "your mother isn't…"

"I knew it. You're getting divorced. You aren't happy, and she never has been. Well, I'm living with you. You can start over again. You're still young…"

"Ellis, wait…what makes you suspect we aren't happy?" he asked.

"Dad, please. Are you serious? Come on," I said. I realized I said it in a hurtful way. "Wait. I didn't mean to sound harsh, but Mom has never acted happy."

"Ellis, you are mistaken. We need to discuss what happened yesterday first, and we can come back to this later." He spoke sharply, which signaled he needed my full attention.

"What happened? The truth."

I looked around us. I was unsure whether I should tell him the truth, even if he had asked for it. "Something happened to Mrs. Young." Maybe he didn't want little details.

"What happened to Mrs. Young?" he continued.

"She…had…a…type of attack," I said. He wanted me to elaborate, but I was still unsure I wanted to say the words aloud.

"What type of attack?" he pushed.

"Inspector Ryder said it was her heart," I offered.

"Was it?"

Now, came the decision. I paused.

"Was it her heart, Ellis? Was it?"

"No."

My father pulled his gaze away from me and looked out over the water. I took a breath. I had no idea what he was thinking.

"Tell me what you saw."

The whole truth gushed from my brain even before my lips parted. It was a dam running over with water desperate to be released, and when I spoke, my story lasted for thirty minutes at least. Uninterrupted, I told every detail I remembered from start to finish. Dad never showed great emotion, but that wasn't foremost on my mind. I was desperate to purge the horror from my head. Someone had to tell me I'd not gone crazy. I finished by telling him I hadn't told the real story to anyone. When at last I stopped speaking, we sat staring, at one another.

Dad clenched his hands together and wrung them as if exercising the tendons and joints. He ended with rubbing his face. This was his stress relief, and I had seen him do it a hundred times.

"I am so sorry you had to experience that, and I am so proud you kept your senses. You were lucky to realize you had to pretend the effects of the medicines. Never tell this story to another person. Don't tell your mother, Dr. Adler, or anyone. Do you understand what I am saying to you? I've seen patients unable to accept realities they'd experienced; they can become confused and angry. Sometimes patients succumbed to madness that causes them to become a danger to themselves and others. When this happens, doctors institutionalize them for their own protection. These are the reasons we must be protected from our memories. I don't want to give anyone the impression you are resistant to treatment. I worry Inspector Ryder may discover the medicine didn't work on you and will force you to be tested. He couldn't allow you to walk around, knowing the truth of what happened."

"Wait. What do you mean he couldn't allow me to walk around? Are you saying I'm on the path to insanity?"

"No, of course not. I've known of others who didn't respond to medicines. You aren't the first. However, Horizon has determined memories should be released, so you must consider your predicament seriously."

"The reason the medicine doesn't work for some people isn't the main question. The important question for me is why Mrs. Young chose to kill herself rather than continue to live in Horizon. And why someone went to so much trouble hiding her suicide? Don't you see? First, Mr. Hap became confused, and next, Mrs. Young said people took her memories. Dad, something's not right. The release doctors must be aware of this manipulation, and I don't want Mr. Hap to end his life in the same way as Mrs. Young."

"Ellis, try to understand, older people have endured so much trauma and loss. Many people can't live healthy lives without giving up memories of their old lives. I don't mean to sound insensitive, but Mrs. Young was one of these people. Suicide was her answer. If her release treatments had been successful, I don't believe she could have become so disturbed. Think of the pain she carried every day, remembering everyone she loved being killed in the war. Your memories have been created here in Horizon because you were taken as a baby. I am grateful you don't have reminders of your first family to give you heartache."

"And you, Dad? Were you able to release your memories from life before the war? You refuse to discuss that time. Don't you miss your family?"

When I spoke, Dad lowered his head into one hand. I found a subject too painful, and I brought it up to make my point.

"I'm sorry, Dad. But I wonder how healthy is it to bury our feelings, or worse yet, be forced to forget people we loved, so we don't drown in sorrow. Aren't you tired of lies or hiding your true feelings or whatever you call what's going on here? Let me ask you this question—if something happened to me, would you want me erased from your memory?" My dad turned away. My words had scored painful reflection. He stood and looked into the distance.

"Ell, this lake is beautiful; I can almost forget we're confined here. I wish I could offer you other lakes and other views and other experiences."

A small breeze stirred and caused a much-needed distraction. I hopped up to chase a few papers, and a bag caught in a tiny whirlwind. I didn't want to disturb it, but I didn't want our litter to be taken away.

"Dad, look at it." As I turned, I saw my father trying to wipe tears away without my seeing. "Talk to me. What is it?" I walked to where he stood.

"Nothing," he said. "We must be careful, so we don't make a mess."

I wondered if he meant the mess caused by the whirlwind or the situation we were in now.

I gathered the scattered debris left behind by the now absent whirlwind and replayed what Dad said. He felt pulled between telling me what I should do and telling me how proud he was I disagreed with keeping quiet. I returned to the blanket where he now sat and placed the trash in our grocery bag.

"Promise me you will keep this to yourself," he said.

"I'll try. I don't want to cause you any more pain, but I can't promise I'll forget what's happening. It's not right. Now, can we discuss you and Mom?"

"Ellis, I won't leave your mother. She has many wonderful qualities. She struggles with the past and has issues with forgetting troubling memories. In that manner, you two are alike."

"Having wonderful qualities isn't the definition of true love. Once upon a time, there lived a fairy princess who had many wonderful qualities. Dad, come on, let's be honest. Both of you deserve to be happy."

"Your mother and I tried to be outstanding parents. We have made mistakes; it's what people do. You have made mistakes, and you will make more, but the important part of being human is to learn from your errors. We must strive to be better."

The more he spoke of his life, the less I understood. I *needed* a therapy session because I didn't want the trauma of yesterday to confuse my reasoning. I looked at him; he seemed fascinated with that small body of water. Dad was the one person I'd never doubted in my life. He knew my secret now and provided a somewhat logical explanation. Whether my experience at the Fountain, his relationship with Mom, or something that had yet to be revealed, I was certain he was trying to teach me a life lesson for whatever he was battling.

"Ellis, you often ask about my past, so let me assure you. Nothing from before is better than being your father now. I can't imagine the world without you in it, and I want you to be safe and happy. So, I need your promise to never discuss the actual events at the Fountain."

"Okay," I responded.

"No, I need you to swear to it," he pressed. "Solemnly swear you will never tell another person."

"Okay, I swear on everything I love."

"Come in. There you are," said Dr. Adler. "I am so happy you came today. Hello, Dr. Bauer."

My dad smiled, "Hello, Dr. Adler." They shook hands.

"Dr. Bauer, will you be joining us?"

"No, I wanted to come to apologize for being late. I took Ellis to the lake knoll for a picnic, and I'm afraid we lost track of time," he said. The way he spoke caused me to think he wanted to stay. Dad and I didn't get many of these father-daughter outings, and when we did, Mom caused them to be cut short.

"That's understandable. I imagine a picnic was a positive way to release stress. How are you today, Ellis?"

"I'm fine." We stood smiling as happy as possible when I suspected each of us knew some amount of the truth.

"Well, I'll leave you two alone." Dad walked to the door. "Ellis, I'll wait for you outside on the bench. I brought a book and thought I might…"

"Vitamin D. Yes, Dad. But it isn't necessary; I don't mind walking. I might go to Ana's and ask if she wants to work on the book club."

"I want to wait. After your session, we'll go home together. You can get your bike and study materials, and then take off to be with Ana. Agreed?"

"Okay, I'll see you soon." I walked over to where he stood and gave him a squeeze.

He squeezed back. "Goodbye, Dr. Adler, nice to see you again." Dr. Adler smiled without saying a word, and my father left.

"So, Ellis, let's sit, shall we?" Dr. Adler pointed to the patient seating. I had a choice of the sofa or chair. Today was a sofa day, but I'd taken Inspector Ryder's happy pills, so I chose the chair.

"I received a few details of what happened yesterday. I hoped you could fill in some gaps for me. Will you start or shall I?"

"Well," I began, "It wasn't the best day, but I'm feeling better. Mrs. Young and I talked occasionally. She was kind and personable. I suppose she reminds me of what a grandmother might have been. She's at peace now, I imagine." Did she suspect I was lying?

"I am glad you aren't worried, Ellis. Mrs. Young is no longer in pain. It was her heart, is that correct?"

"Yes, a heart attack. You're right. She was in pain, and now, she isn't. So her death is a happy event?" I said half-question-half-statement toned.

"Ellis, we have life and death. When life is torturous, death is a relief."

I needed bunches of time to think through that philosophy. I nodded my head silently rather than challenge her statement because I didn't want to commit the time it would take to debate the point.

"Ana and I haven't talked today," I said, "but I hope to see her later." We had been planning another trip to the restricted section of the Archives. Now, we had to find information that might explain the mounting questions. First, I must find out if Ana knew the truth about yesterday at the Fountain. Possibly, she was pretending, in the same way, I had done. Otherwise, I would have to tell her what actually happened.

"You mentioned your project a few times. You seem very motivated. Tell me the details."

"What?" I said, surprised.

"Your book club project. What is it?"

"Well," I hesitated with my mind racing, "Ana and I are hosting a book club for people who want to read novels by Jane Austen."

"Oh, I see. I love her work. Which is your favorite of her books?" she asked.

I panicked. I had never read a Jane Austen book in my life. My father had given me an ancient copy for my sixteenth birthday, but I never read it, and now couldn't even remember the title. Which book did Bram mention? Seconds were ticking away since she asked, and I had to talk, or she might suspect the club was nonexistent.

"Well, let me see..." My brain searched at lightning speed, trying to come up with a title or an excuse for not giving an answer. "I love every one of them, but I don't know my favorite." She knows I'm lying. I fidgeted in my chair.

"Name one you prefer over others," she said with a slight smile developing.

"I…am lying," I confessed. "I met a boy last week at the Archives, and I hoped to see him again. We are preparing for our book club, but I want the chance to talk to him. I'm sorry I lied."

She looked satisfied with my answer. I had to make sure she didn't suspect my going to the Archives for information about Horizon.

"Thank you for being honest," she began. "This is normal. You're beginning your career, and a husband will be your next major life choice."

"I chose not to have a date for the graduate dance to avoid the discomfort caused by Mom and Dad acting as parent-chaperones. I guess I'm not ready to tell my dad I'm interested in this boy because I'm still his little girl, and I don't want him to worry."

"Ellis, your father loves you. Yes, he may see you as his little girl, but he is intelligent and realistic. He knows you will develop other interests that will take your focus away from family. It is the natural process of maturing. Your father may surprise you. He wants the best for you and will want someone who will treat you well and love you." She waited for me to respond, but I didn't.

"Keep me posted on your potential boyfriend. As for Ana, I think it best not to mention the incident at the Fountain. I suspect she doesn't have the strength you do. Her anxiety would intensify by discussing Mrs. Young. Don't you agree?"

"Yes, I do." *Lie.* "I believe discussing the events of yesterday can't possibly bring about any positive feelings." *But I do believe it would bring out the truth.*

I found my dad sitting on the same bench I found Bram sitting a few days before when we accidentally met. He sat engrossed in his book. "Boo," I said. He jumped and laughed.

"Hey, I'm an old man. Don't scare me," he said. "How was your session?"

"It was fine. I said nothing…do you think she knows?"

"No. She is a caring doctor; I've trusted her with your well-being for many years. It's best not to discuss this issue with anyone. If you had told her the real story of Mrs. Young, she would require more information from officials about the discrepancy."

"Dad, was Mr. Hap going to kill himself?"

"I don't know. I understand your concern, but he is safer at the facility. He can socialize with others his age and not be alone. Don't think he will be friendless." He put his arm around me and led me to the cart. "There are wonderful celebrations to anticipate. You are getting your placement test results at The Beginning Celebration, and you will start your new career in September. You'll be getting your own cart. What color will it be?"

"Color? I don't know; I guess my mind is full of other matters." We stopped walking, and he turned to grip my shoulders.

"I'm sorry. You're right. I am trying to divert your thoughts to silly, insignificant matters. I suppose I'm a big supporter of trying to forget bad memories."

"Maybe if you shared them, they wouldn't hurt as much," I said.

"Spoken like a future therapist," he laughed.

"I hope so. I want to heal the mind, not hide the bad." We drove away, speaking on trivial subjects. Intuition told me I would never be a therapist. I suspected the last thing the officials needed or wanted was someone to sweep in and try changing standard memory protocol. But, it was more than that. My future was here—living and dying. That was a certainty; the Horizon 5000 and her descendants had no alternative. However, deep within, I couldn't see a future here. Perhaps I was being pessimistic, but I felt my life would never be ordinary.

As soon as we arrived home, I picked up my notebook for my fake book club project. Before leaving, Dad asked me to remember our agreement. Considering he was talking in code, he must not have shared his suspicions with my mother.

I made my way to Ana's neighborhood. Since I had not talked to her, I wasn't sure how she felt. I glided into her driveway. Her mother was watering flowerbeds.

"Buenos días, Elleees," said Mrs. Hamilton, throwing her hand in the air. I loved the way she said my name. "Tell me how you are, honey." She walked toward me while taking off her gardening gloves.

"I'm fine, thank you, Mrs. Hamilton," I said, walking to meet her.

"Yes? You feel better after your terrible day?" she asked, putting an arm around me.

"Yes, ma'am. Mrs. Young isn't sick anymore."

"Muy bien. Ana is better, too. She is reading. Go see her."

I walked toward the house after thanking Ana's mother and wondered how she might have reacted if she had known the truth. When I opened the front door, I called for Ana.

"In my room," she yelled back. I walked to the bedroom and found her with a book. "Hola, chica."

Ana adopted her mother's Hispanic heritage and along with it, her language. We didn't learn foreign languages in school. We didn't need them anymore, according to school officials. Ana loved them and often studied foreign language textbooks at the Archives. Through the years, she learned pieces of different languages, and I picked up a few words. I teased about her language du jour. "Bonjour, I came to take you for a little getaway. Let's go."

"Go where?" she asked, sitting up in bed.

"It's a surprise. Come on, vamos." I pulled her by the arm.

"Jeez, what's the hurry?"

When we were on our bikes, I told her to follow me.

"This is pretty. Why haven't we come here before?" she asked.

We walked to the same spot I had been with my dad. "I didn't know about it until today," I said. I plopped on the ground, this time without a picnic blanket. "Sit, Ana. We need to talk."

"I know; you have to tell me about Bram. I never got to hear details from the date," she said, her smile widening.

"No," I said. "This is something…bigger." I patted the ground beside me. She gave in and sat. When she settled, she looked at me quizzically. "Yesterday, at the Fountain…"

"That was crazy," Ana broke in, "One minute, Mrs. Young was drinking coffee, and the next moment, dead. Life is unpredictable. If she was feeling sick, why come to the restaurant? She should have stayed at home to rest or see a doctor."

"Ana, wait. Why did she die?"

"What do you mean? You were there, crazy. A heart attack." She looked more puzzled. "Are you okay, Ellis? Should I take *you* to the doctor?" Her laughter hurt, and not because she was teasing me. It was cruel someone could separate us from such devastating occurrences, and we have no clue. I thought about Dad. What if he died, but someone made me forget him? Being lighthearted over Mrs. Young's death was an insult to her life. Ana didn't know the actual events because if she had, she would have acted differently.

I grabbed her by the arms. "Look at me, Ana. You need to hear what happened and not interrupt. Can you do that?" Her behavior changed. She pulled away from me, drew her knees up to her chest, and hugged them. She rocked slowly. "Can you?" I asked louder. She nodded, and she looked stunned by my tone. Fear would keep us sharp and motivated.

"Yesterday, you and I were at the Fountain, along with Mrs. Young. Phil and Mrs. McCoy were working. Mrs. Young stood up, screamed, and mumbled something about her dead husband. Her coffee cup shattered on the floor."

"I don't…"

"No. Let me finish. She said someone wanted her memories, and she wasn't giving them up. Then, she mentioned her husband, Curtis. Ana, she sat on the floor surrounded by the broken cup pieces while she talked to me. She said to stop them because they were not what they appeared to be." I paused to take a breath. "Ana, she took a sharp piece of the cup and made cuts on both of her wrists." As I spoke, I re-enacted Mrs. Young's deed by pretending to slash each of my wrists. When I did this, her expression transformed from confusion to sheer terror.

"Ellis!"

"No. Wait. You tried to help her, Ana, but couldn't. You were covered in so much blood. She killed herself, Ana. You don't remember this because we were given drugs to make us forget. They didn't want us to remember what she had done and said. I need you to think and remember. I'm clueless why the medicine didn't work on me. But Mrs. Young and Mr. Hap have tried to warn me their memories were being taken, and someone needs to find out why. We owe both of them that." I stopped. My heart was racing. Retelling this story was similar to reliving it. I waited. Ana was silent. She didn't move. I paused and then said, "Now, I need you to tell me if you remember any of it." More silence.

"Ellis," she leaned toward me, "why are you saying this? I was there. I saw Mrs. Young with my own eyes. That's not what happened." She put her hand on top of mine. "It was a heart attack."

I suspected the truth wouldn't come easy to her, but I had hoped to see a spark of memory. "You were covered in blood from head to toe. You had to wear a hospital gown home from the Fountain."

"I was covered in coffee. Remember, you said yourself she dropped her coffee cup. Coffee was everywhere." She looked sympathetically at me. Now, she had taken on role reversal and was trying to convince me of her truth. I wanted to start the story over again, but something told me it wouldn't trigger her memory. I had to prove her memory was wrong.

"Ana, did they give you your clothes?"

"Oh, I...don't think so." She looked confused.

"If you were covered in coffee, why did you need to change clothes?" I said.

"It was all over me," she replied.

"Ana, why was coffee on the floor?"

"Because Mrs. Young dropped her cup. You said yourself, Ellis, she dropped her coffee cup."

"Yes, you're right. She dropped her coffee cup. Her cup, Ana. That's all. A cup." This had to be the explanation she needed to believe the real story. I was on fire now trying to make her see the logic in my story. "Why change clothes for one cup of liquid at most? We don't know how much coffee was left in her cup. But at most, would one cup require you to change clothes?"

"It…seemed like more than a cup because…my clothes were saturated," she said, using her hands to show me all the places her clothes were stained. She acted confused and looked away.

"Ana, you said she dropped her cup. The most coffee you could have on your clothes if you had managed to soak all of it on yourself, was one cup. Remember, Mrs. Young sat on the floor. Don't you suppose she soaked some of the coffee into her own clothes?" She didn't speak. She was trying to rationalize this fact in her head. I pushed forward. "You would have had less than a cup of liquid on your clothes. Even if they didn't want you to sit with your clothes soaked, why not allow you to take them home?"

"They…forgot?" She stood now. I had to press her to remember.

"They brought your bike home." She looked even more dazed.

"Give me a minute to think." She paced back and forth in a pattern, stopped, looked at me, and opened her mouth, only to close it and pace once more. I could see she was taking this whole matter seriously. She stopped pacing. "Okay. Fact number one, you wouldn't joke about something this serious. So, that means *you* believe what you're saying. Yet, I don't understand why you would have a completely different version of what happened. How can you confuse blood and coffee?" She held her hands as if she were balancing blood against coffee on a scale. "Fact number two, how can you confuse having a heart attack with someone cutting their wrists. I don't believe your version of what happened, but…because you *do* have a different version of the story, something isn't right."

She now spoke as if she was voicing the thoughts running through her mind rather than speaking to me.

"I trust you not to make up a cruel lie. Fact—you and I are positive about what we saw. Fact—only one version of her death can be correct. So, if only *one* of us can be right…" *Come on, Ana.* "One of us has had some sort of fake memory implanted. I can't be wrong because the pictures in my mind of Mrs. Young clutching her chest and falling over are so vivid." She knelt beside me.

"We need concrete proof either your memory or mine is correct. You are so methodical, Ana. You should be a detective," I said.

"So, we have to find evidence. It's mind-shattering I wouldn't remember being covered from head to toe in blood and not remem…"

I jumped up and grabbed Ana by the arm.

"What is it, Ellis?"

"Head to toe," I said. "We have to go." I now half-dragged her to a standing position making her stumble because I was pulling faster than her legs could carry her. "Hurry, we have to hurry."

"What is it?" she said.

"Let's get back to your house. Say nothing in front of your mom. Hurry," I said. If the proof still existed, I could convince Ana.

We sped to her house. This time, her mom wasn't in the yard. We rushed straight to her bedroom. I heard the shower running, so I knew we wouldn't be disturbed.

"Where are they?" I asked, moving things around on her desk.

"Where are what?" Ana replied.

"Your earrings," I half shouted.

"A little box in my top drawer…"

Because I was the closest, I opened the drawer, and I flung underthings everywhere.

"Hey," Ana protested, "I'll have to clean this mess. Why do you want my earrings?"

"Here, look at it," I said, dangling one in front of her face.

Ana took it from me. "What's wrong with my…" She stopped. The silence seemed to run on for minutes. "What is this?" she asked.

"When you left to change, I saw blood on your earring. You must have gotten it from your hands to there. It's blood, Ana. It's Mrs. Young's blood."

She continued to stare at the earring in her palm. Without speaking, she let herself collapse into a sitting position on the bed, still looking at the jewelry in her hand. She looked from me back to the earring.

"It was on your earring and…"

"Everywhere," she said.

"Yes," I responded. I eased down beside her. I didn't want to break her concentration. She *had* to be on the verge of the truth.

"Try, Ana. Please, remember. You went to help Mrs. Young and…"

"Blood was everywhere." She dropped the earring and sobbed.

CHAPTER 14

We have a duty to our own intelligent species to speak out against the Habitat Project and call for the release and repopulation of humans into this new world. Regardless of our part in helping to save the people of Earth, we are not given complete supremacy to direct their lives for our own purposes. We must see they, having a certain degree of evolutionary advancement, are entitled to live as freely as our own race. Let not history see the Atum as a destructive band of warriors combing the galaxy and taking whatever desired. We must allow survivors of Earth's war to become, once again, her free citizens. We shall live as one people—a veritable, universal melting pot learning from each other and working together to survive as a new race.

—Human Liberation League
May 2033

THE TRUTH

THREE O'CLOCK WOULD NEVER ARRIVE BECAUSE I needed Bram more than ever. I had no way of contacting him to discuss what happened at the Fountain, and I was nervous. It was hard enough getting Ana to remember what happened, and she was there. I could wait no longer. I didn't want to lie to Bram anymore. I'd tell him why Ana and I attempted to enter the restricted section of the Archives. He also deserved the truth about what we suspected was happening in Horizon. Technically, I hadn't broken my promise to Dad about keeping the secret. So far, I'd only told Ana. She already knew and just needed help to remember, so that couldn't count as telling someone. I cared for Bram, and I didn't want our relationship to begin with so many lies. If the Archives was empty, we could talk secretly and be undisturbed.

At 2:45, I arrived, hoping he might have come early as well. I passed by Mrs. Croft's desk expecting her to be hiding another issue of her celebrity magazine, but she wasn't there. No one was in the Archives. I climbed the stairs and rounded the corner where I first met Bram a week ago. I was different now from then. So little time, yet so much change.

"Hey, you…"

I spun around to see him standing at the same spot where we first collided. He wore dark pants and a black shirt. His clothes always looked new and perfect. I felt a shiver looking at him. This guy was more than cute. In the old world, he would have been one of those celebrities in Mrs. Croft's magazines. His jet-black hair and piercing ice-blue eyes were gorgeous. He stared at me as he had in the park. How many of my faults did he see? His concentrated gaze made me insecure and yet euphoric because I could fool myself into thinking his lingering smile was more than simple politeness, but instead, desire.

Behind him was the door Ana and I had attempted to enter on the day we met. With Bram's access to this restricted place, we could find information to explain the strange happenings in Horizon.

"You're early," he said. "I wanted to surprise *you* by being early." He took my hand in his. "How are you?"

How do I answer that question? The heated sting of oncoming tears told me I had to pull myself together. "Bram, I need to tell you something that's happened. It's serious, and we need to be in a place where we can talk in private."

"Are you okay? What's wrong?" he asked.

I looked around to be sure this spot was safe for our conversation.

"What is it, Ellis? Are you upset with me?" His smile gave way to concern. He pulled me to a table nestled within the fiction section. "Come and sit. What's wrong?"

I sat at the large, sturdy wooden table, and he took a seat beside me. We were still hand in hand and sitting so close our knees were touching. Had life not dealt the blow of Mrs. Young's death, this closeness to Bram might have been exciting. I tried speaking, but the words weren't there. I tried again, "I…have something to tell you. It's possible you'll call me crazy."

He tried to protest, but I held up my hand to stop his words.

"Please listen. Yesterday, I had to convince someone of the unimaginable. Two days ago, something happened while—no, let me start farther back," I said. I reorganized my thoughts. I explained how Mr. Hap told me a different memory from the one he'd told me long ago. Next, I told him how Mr. Hap was taken away and put into the hospital. I continued through the whole story with Mrs. Young up to where Ana had regained the actual memory of our ordeal. When I stopped talking, I felt psychologically and emotionally out of breath. He said nothing.

"Please say something because I have no idea what you're thinking."

He took a deep breath and swallowed, never looking at me. Why won't he look at me? It didn't matter, I'd gone this far and couldn't stop now. "There is more. The day we met here, Ana and I were breaking into the restricted section hoping to find some proof. I suspect a huge cover-up in our town. It must sound irrational, but there is a reason we are made to forget our memories. My father told me once sometimes bad memories need to be forgotten so we can fill our lives with good memories. The Officials expected Ana and me to forget the memory of Mrs. Young's death because of the stress and sadness it could add to our lives. But who is dictating which of our memories we must surrender? Who has the authority to decide which memories are unhealthy? The Horizon 5000 lost everything and now are being robbed of more. Mrs. Young and Mr. Hap were right. Someone is controlling us, and I want answers. You have access to the restricted zone, I suppose, because of your career placement. You can help us, Bram. We can work together to discover the truth. We can learn why it's happening and reveal those truths so we can take back control of our own minds. I have no idea why I was resistant to the suggestions and medicines from the official, but I wonder—have I ever been forced to forget something else? If I have, how will I ever know my true past? What if I've been made to forget someone I love? What if I were made to forget...?" I stopped before I said the word 'you.' I took a breath. "Bram, how many memories have they stolen from me, you, or anyone? Our paths crossed for a reason. It's been the best part of my life, and I don't want someone to have the power to wipe you out of my mind. Please...please tell me what you're thinking."

"I..." He put both of his hands over his face and ran them through his hair. He took another deep breath, "Ellis, meeting you has been like finding a lost piece of a puzzle you thought you could never complete. Do you understand what I mean? At last, the puzzle is whole. I never realized something was missing from my life. *You are what has been missing.*"

As unbelievable as his words sounded, I waited for him to say the word 'but.' I took a deep breath and fell forward into his arms. He put his arms around me for a moment. He believes me. Then, he pushed me away, his face was tight, and the muscles of his jaw clenched.

"Ellis, I care for you more than anyone ever in my life."

Emotions washed over me—I was confused and scared and thrilled. I leaned into him wanting to be kissed; I closed my eyes. We could make everything right. His hands gripped me; this was the moment. I wanted to melt into his embrace, and then, he pushed me away.

I opened my eyes. He bowed his head. Without looking up, he said, "Ellis, I need to tell…" His miniport chimed. He picked it up and read something. "We must go."

"What? Why?" He stood and took my hand, leading me to the restricted door. He looked around and then slid a card through the security latch; the door opened. He didn't move for a moment until he stepped back and closed the door. "How do we get outside the building?" He took me by the arm. "We must leave now. Lead the way."

"What's wrong?" I asked.

"Ellis, we don't have time to discuss this now. Someone is coming here. You and I must leave this building. Show me the way to get out."

This wasn't part of the fairy tale from two minutes ago. I looked at him and knew if we didn't leave, something awful might happen. I didn't say another word. This time, I was the one who grabbed him by the arm half dragging him along a path he'd obviously never taken. Why wasn't he familiar with the Archives? Students were required to visit this place every week for studies. He was lost. I turned an unexpected corner, and he anticipated a different route. We stumbled over each other's feet. We raced down the stairs into the open vaulted entrance past Mrs. Croft's desk and straight for the front doors. As we reached them, Mrs. Croft called out; we ignored her. By the time we hit the outdoors, we were running.

"Now you come with me." He looked around the town. "The Orchard building is this way, right?" I nodded.

We walked at a brisk pace but didn't run. I tried to ask questions, but he only said we needed to wait until it was safe. I gave in and asked nothing else, but I racked up a hundred additional questions to ask when the time came. Nothing made sense. I tried to imagine any excuse for him not being familiar with Horizon.

We crossed into the neighborhood behind the Orchard building. I was unfamiliar with this neighborhood. I may have trick-or-treated here for Halloween a long time ago, but these were townhouses for single people and adults without children. I couldn't understand why we came to this part of Horizon, but I trusted Bram.

He slowed his step as we came to a block of narrow, three-story buildings. We walked up the front steps, and again, he pulled from his pocket a card to scan through the door latch. The glass door opened, but he looked around before entering. We walked straight back to an elevator. These were uncommon in Horizon. Most buildings used stairs except the hospital. Bram pressed the button, and the doors opened. We stepped inside, and he pressed the number two. The elevator lifted us in seconds and opened to the second floor. There were two doors opposite one another. We walked to the left, and again Bram swiped the card through a door latch. He turned around and mouthed the words—wait.

"Hello?" he called out. He stopped to listen. "Come inside; it's okay."

"Where are we? Is this where you live?" I looked around the room. Things were different from our house. This home was more modern and had odd gadgets and machines. I stopped walking and turned in a circle.

"Come and sit. I'm getting water for us."

"Bram, what is this place? Is this your house?"

He handed me a glass of water, sat, and paused before starting.

"Ellis, I will answer your questions, but let me tell you a story first." He paused. I wanted to speak but changed my mind. He began again. "When you were telling me the story of Mrs. Young, what was the thing you were most afraid could happen?"

I paused for a moment. "I…I guess I was afraid you wouldn't believe me."

"Right. Now, I want to tell you something you may not believe. Will you keep an open mind?"

"Of course, I will," I said.

"Good. Please remember one thing while I explain. I lied when I said I cared for you."

I'm going to be sick.

"It is much more than that," he quickly added. "I've loved you from the first moment I saw you. I can't explain my feelings. It may not make sense, and it may sound ridiculous, but I love you."

There was a relief but not entirely. His words thrilled me, however; they were ominous, like an earth-shattering 'BUT' would be added onto the end of his sentence, for the second time today. *Stop it.* I wouldn't allow this moment to be ruined by thinking everything was too good to be true. I leaned forward into his embrace. His arms wrapped around me. For an instant, I didn't care about Mr. Hap, Mrs. Young, rules, memories, or anything.

He pulled away from me and cupped the side of my face with his hand. He brushed away a loose strand of my hair and looked so deeply into my eyes, I thought I'd catch fire.

"This moment right now is perfect. We are together and understand each other's feelings. I don't want anything to change," he whispered.

He leaned closer. My heart sped, and my face heated. I closed my eyes. His lips brushed mine lightly, and I hoped he wouldn't pull away this time. He kissed me again, but more firmly. Desire and agony raged inside me. The third time our lips pressed together, I knew nothing could keep us apart. Our connection was passionate and intense. Nothing else mattered but being with him. His skin was warm, and he smelled like cedar wood and fresh linen. The scratch of his beard stubble felt wild and raw. He held my face and leaned in until our foreheads touched.

"I had to kiss you before we talked because you may never let me near you again," he said in a hushed tone.

"That's crazy," I added, leaning away from him. I tried to understand his meaning.

He moved toward me and caressed my face again. This time, I kissed him with brazen eagerness.

He pulled away. "I don't want to, but we have to stop. Before I tell you this, please remember I love you. I never want to hurt you, and from this moment forward, I will never lie to you again."

CHAPTER 15

The Road Not Taken

Two roads diverged in a yellow wood
And sorry I could not travel both
And be one traveler, long I stood
And looked down one as far as I could
To where it bent in the undergrowth;

Then took the other, as just as fair
And having perhaps the better claim,
Because it was grassy and wanted wear;
Though as for that, the passing there
Had worn them really about the same,

And both that morning equally lay
In leaves no step had trodden black.
Oh, I kept the first for another day!

Yet knowing how way leads on to way,
I doubted if I should ever come back.

I shall be telling this with a sigh
Somewhere ages and ages hence:
Two roads diverged in a wood and I—
I took the one less traveled by,
And that has made all the difference.

—Robert Frost, 1916
Archives Control
Forbidden Literature Department
Document Destruction Date: September 2032

WAR

I WANTED TO SPARE ELLIS THE STORY OF WHAT HAP-
pened to her world, and I had two choices. If I told her the truth,
I'd destroy everything she knew to be real. The division this information would cause might destroy any future with her. She may asso-
ciate me with those who keep her inside the Habitat, making *me* the
enemy. I worried she'd tell others. Ellis was incapable of forgetting
and living a lie. If she tried to expose the Habitat, she'd be a threat
to the entire project. The government removed humans who created
problems for the experiment, and no place existed for humans outside the Habitat. The worst possible outcome was endangering her
life and causing her to hate me.

I could tell her a lie. I wanted to be the kind of man who was
unselfish and would protect her from hurt. This choice involved me
walking away and never seeing her again. She might be safe, and if
she truly cared for me, broken hearts heal. Maybe she could forget
looking for answers to the mysteries she'd uncovered.

Each choice ended with me losing her. If I walked away, I lost her. If I told her the truth, perhaps she could love me, but I still might lose her. I had learned one of my greatest faults was selfishness. I devoted my entire life to pleasing me. Even now, I wanted Ellis more than I wanted her happiness. The pain after learning the truth would be temporary, and I could convince her to be patient until we thought of a solution that allowed us to be together.

I realized I was trying to justify my actions. My conscience screamed what I didn't want to hear—Ellis had found her cause to fight for and nothing would stop her.

I considered the possible scenarios and stories to tell; I knew what I must do. It was the decision I hoped kept her safest.

I began telling the history of The End.

I took a deep breath.

"Ellis, please listen to the entire story. This won't be easy to tell, and it won't be easy to hear." I took another breath. Her face showed fear of the unknown words I would speak. I had to be strong.

"On February 20, 2032, the war began. Direct nuclear warfare and extreme levels of radiation killed most of the world's population within twenty-four hours. Once it started, it couldn't be stopped. At the twenty-four-hour point, the missiles stopped launching. However, a group watched from space as this occurred on Earth."

"You mean from one of those space stations? How do you know this?" she asked.

"I'll get to that, but yes, something similar to a space station. This group sent emergency teams to earth to rescue survivors."

"I don't understand. We've been told something completely different," she said.

"You have, and that story wasn't correct. But remember the situation with Mrs. Young? My story will involve telling you facts different from what you have learned.

This group in space had experience with nuclear capability and the equipment to enter the atmosphere without harm. After arriving, they rescued many people and took them to safety for medical treatment."

"The Horizon 5000?" Ellis asked. "American military rescued us and put us into the government bunkers underground. I don't understand. How do you know this?" she asked.

"I'm sorry, I know this is so much information, but I should finish the whole story first. After, I will answer questions, if I can."

"Bram, how do you know this information?" she asked.

"I promise I'll tell you."

I took her hand and kissed it, knowing I might never have the opportunity again. What I had yet to tell her might drive us apart, but she deserved the truth. She didn't appear to be worried any longer. Her face softened. I released her hand back into her lap. The affection I had for her reflected back toward me—she cared. For an instant, I considered not telling her or maneuvering the story, so I didn't have to tell the entire truth. I didn't want her to hate me. My decision could affect everything. To choose the wrong way might mean losing her forever, but true love couldn't be based on lies.

"The people on the space station sent teams to Earth with the equipment to clean radiation from the planet. Earth began healing. A group of rescuers tended the people who needed medical care while other teams tried to stabilize disaster areas and begin reconstruction. They made the planet safe again."

"Where are those people who came here to clean the radiation?"

"They are here," I said.

"In Horizon?"

"No, not every person," I stopped. "Other people live outside Horizon."

Her eyes widened, and her mouth opened slightly. "But there *are* no other cities. The Horizon 5000 and their descendants are the only people on Earth to survive."

"No, Ellis. Others live in cities outside Horizon."

"That isn't possible, we'd know. The military told us *we* were the only survivors on Earth. There are dangerous things out..."

I held up my hand. "You are the only survivors of the war." I had until this point tried to tiptoe around the details, but I was at the place in the story where I needed to give difficult answers.

"Ellis, Horizon...Horizon contains the only surviving humans."

She stared as if she was trying to replay my words in her head and make sense of them.

"I...I don't understand. That's right. We *are* the only survivors. So, why did you say others live outside Horizon?" She searched my face for clarity.

Now, the shock. I took her hand in mine and put my other on her shoulder.

"Ellis, Earth was rescued by a race of people humans call aliens."

She sat frozen. If I had known what she was thinking, I could have said the right thing to ease her mind. Toward the last few moments of her silence, I worried she had slipped into a state of shock.

She slapped me on the arm. "Bram, please...are you really trying to convince me aliens saved the Horizon 5000? Aliens are those ridiculous creations in movies from before The End. You're not funny." She gave a nervous half-laugh followed with an uneasy smile.

I had hoped she could understand without disbelief and accept what I was saying to her.

"This isn't a joke. It's hard to comprehend, but remember when you told the story of Mrs. Young? You worried I might not believe you. You were not joking, and I'm not joking either."

Her smile disappeared. "There is a huge difference between my story and yours. I was with Mrs. Young, and I saw her die before my eyes. This is crazy because you expect me to believe little green spacemen rescued us." Her voice became stronger and louder.

"No, Ellis. The aliens saved *you* and the Horizon 5000."

"Wait, what do you mean *me* and the Horizon 5000? Look, this isn't funny anymore. You're horrible with pranks. Your idea of funny is…"

"I…wasn't saved because I was *with* the aliens." I swallowed hard and said, "Ellis, I'm not human. I am Atum."

She went pale and just when I thought I might be slapped or punched, she laughed. Not her normal laugh, but a hysterical laugh that caused her to seem emotionally unhinged for a moment. When she quieted, I sat and stared, and waited.

"Bram, don't make jokes. I need you to help me find evidence of a cover-up within the security department." I continued to sit and stare. Gradually, she lost signs of being amused.

When her smile disappeared, I began. "This is not a joke. I wish it were. I'll prove it to you. Open your eyes, Ellis. How can the 5000 manage this town?"

"Bram, do you think I'm so naïve, I'd believe this story?"

I said nothing.

"So, you're saying we live in a refugee camp run by aliens? And you…are one of them?"

"Ellis, the Atum placed you here to prevent your extinction. You were…you are an endangered species. Horizon is a project called the Habitat. Researchers designed a natural habitat so humans might flourish again."

She jumped up and flailed her arms. "Endangered species," she stopped and became still. "Wait…what did you call Horizon?" she asked.

"The Habitat," I replied.

"Where did you hear the word Habitat? Did I tell you that word?" she asked.

"What do you mean? You didn't say Habitat. You couldn't know that word." Now, I was confused.

"I must have told you because Mrs. Young said it at the Fountain. She said 'Habitat.' It was the last thing she said before she died."

"Ellis, I don't know how Mrs. Young could have known, but it's true. You're here to save your species, but also to be researched and studied by my people. Our planet was in danger of being destroyed. Our scientists decided Earth would be the most hospitable planet. When your planet became troubled, we helped you survive and, in the process, we survived. We needed a new home, and Earth was one of two planets similar to our own. Our leaders didn't believe we could survive together, so we live separately."

Ellis began pacing. "Let's say…you're telling the truth. You said your scientists watch us. Why? When?"

"You are protected for research and preservation, and you're always watched." She was not convinced. "Ellis, I will be a researcher, but I want to help humans and Atum come together and live together. I want to take the Horizon 5000 and let them live beyond these walls as free people. We study your social behavior, your likes and dislikes, and everything which defines being human. We aren't supposed to interact with you."

I stood and intercepted her mid-stride.

"You're so smart and beautiful; I had to know you. Ellis, we can find a way to be happy. I want to keep you safe and telling you is dangerous." I reached out to put my arms around her. She stepped back from me.

Great tears fell from her eyes. I hadn't imprisoned her personally inside the Habitat, but I had been the one who told her she was imprisoned.

I reached again for her, "Ellis, please…"

"Stop," she drew away from me. "This is too much. First, I don't know if I should even believe you. You might be a lunatic. It's…too much," she yelled.

"Ellis please, whatever you do, keep your voice low. The neighbors might hear. People don't know the information I've told you. You're the only one—the only human who knows the truth. You can't tell anyone."

"This is crazy," she said lower. "If this story is true, we're being held prisoners."

"Ellis, technically, your people don't live the lives of prisoners," I said.

"Don't we? Are you allowed to leave this town? Because *I've* never been allowed to leave." Her volume increased. "Officials have told us for twenty years dangers exist beyond our borders. They told us nightmarish mutations live out there. If you're telling the truth, everything before has been a lie." She stopped. Her hands covered her face. I pulled them away even though she tried to resist. Tears spilled from her angry eyes. "Have you ever told me the truth?"

"I said I love you, and that's not a lie."

"I can't do this. Stop. I don't even…I don't even know if I can trust the story you're telling me." She realized where she was, looking around to find the exact place we had entered. After getting her bearings, she headed for the door. "This is insanity. I can't handle any of this until I'm sure you're telling the truth."

I cut her path off. She couldn't leave furious and distrusting.

"Stop. Put this on," I said, handing my student identification to her. "Put this around your neck. Turn the picture backward so no one can see." I now led her by the arm toward the door. I felt her momentary hesitation. She gave in but stopped again.

"What are we doing?" she asked, protesting being taken anywhere without explanation.

"I'm proving our people exist. We are going to the underground." I opened the door leading to the hall and checked for others.

"What is the underground?" she asked. I was now pulling her to the entrance of the backstage.

"Wait." She pulled her arm away from me. "What is the underground?" she asked again.

"Shh. We must be quiet. The underground is where the Atum... our people, move around to the areas of the Habitat for different purposes. You'll see many people. They'll look human, except for their eyes. Don't speak to anyone, and if anyone speaks to us, I'll do the talking."

I lifted my hand to her face and brushed away the last of her tears while searching for a sign she still cared for me. I couldn't interpret her expression, I saw no hatred, and that gave me relief. She didn't push my hand away, and I counted that as another positive sign. I wanted to ease her anguish and let her know I'd protect her. I stepped closer, now with my thumb tracing the line of her lips while wondering if I should try to kiss her. She was still too upset, so I stopped myself and stepped back, letting my hand fall away.

"Come," I said. We walked to the underground entrance door. I swiped my mother's card again, and it opened. The gray steeliness of the stairwell was not inviting and was a dull welcome into my world. We walked down the steps to the next door that would reveal what no human had ever seen.

Her eyes looked wild as they darted to everything laid before her.

Had people been studying *us*, they could surmise she was not familiar with these surroundings. She continued to stare at the newness of this secret place, and I wondered what thoughts might be racing in her mind. People moved about, and to her, it may have looked like a normal scene. A food vendor nearby sold sweets, so I walked to the counter and spoke in our language. The Atum who took my order spoke back. I swiped my mother's card again and took our food. We walked to a group of tables where we might watch unnoticed.

"What…?" she began. She stopped. She was confused.

"I ordered abrosh, it's a dessert we eat," I said.

I slid the dish over to her as if this might make everything okay. She ignored it, instead choosing to watch my people moving around. A man and woman stood talking in my language near our table. I thought she was on the verge of believing the story I had told her. A muscular man dressed in a uniform pulled a large cart of refillable containers provided to humans in the Habitat. A woman dressed in a gray coverall suit stood on a ladder and looked to be repairing a light.

Ellis grasped at my arm. "I need to leave; I'm going to be sick."

I hesitated; she repeated herself. She stood and raced to the door of the stairwell. By the time I caught up with her inside, she had bent over and vomited. I had hoped for a different reaction. When she stopped heaving, I slipped her the napkin I had gotten with our food. She grabbed it, wiped her mouth, and climbed the stairs without me. I followed. When she came to the locked Habitat entrance door, she yanked repeatedly with no success. She started crying, still wrestling the bolted door.

"Ellis, Ellis," I repeated. "Stop. Enough. I have to unlock it."

I came from behind her, and she stepped aside with her head hanging. As soon as I swiped my mother's security card and looked inside the hallway of our building, she rushed around me and headed to the front entrance, which led outdoors into the town.

"Stop, Ellis." She did. "Come back inside, and I'll answer your questions," I said.

"You have lied the whole time I've known you. Your people hold my people hostage."

"No, it's not like that. Please come back inside; we'll talk. You must understand if you tell, your life may be in danger. Also, whoever you tell will be in danger. No one can learn this information."

"So, you're saying we aren't prisoners, but if I tell the truth of Horizon…or Habitat or whatever it's called, my life will be in danger. Yeah, that sounds *nothing* like being held captive," she said. "And you may not think we're prisoners, but you're lying to yourself."

"Ellis, if you aren't concerned about your own safety, think of your family. I told you because I didn't want you to be caught in the restricted section with Ana. I swear to you, I don't agree with the way things are, but…it's the way things are. One person can't make a change—at least not alone. Acceptance and reform will take time."

She stopped. Tears still streamed down her face. Her expression wasn't confusion or hurt. She was enraged—something I was unsure I could fix.

I took her by the arms. "I love you." She looked away from me. I shook her gently until she looked back into my eyes. "I love you, and that has never been a lie."

"I and everyone I love are prisoners here. Never try to see me again."

She jerked away from me and bolted through the doors back out into her world. I wanted to catch her and say whatever words could make this right, but I couldn't risk drawing attention. I was devastated thinking I'd lost her. It couldn't end like this. I went to the apartment and made a plan.

CHAPTER 16

Detective Burly Edwards: Today is November 2, 1952. Present are me, Detective Burly Edwards and Officer Roy Gordon, both representing the Fayette County Police Department, Frances Owens, presently being held for questioning, Jerry Bob Owens, husband to Mrs. Owens, Lieutenant William Epps from the Georgia Highway Patrol, and Simpson Ballard, the attorney for Mrs. Owens. Frances, tell us what happened on October 31, 1952.

Mrs. Frances Owens: Me and Little Jerry and Junie was heading down Highway 92 coming back from my momma's house in Winston. She'd been sick, and I...I. (Inaudible)

Detective Burly Edwards: Roy, get her some Kleenex. Go on, Mrs. Owens.

Mrs. Frances Owens: I was trying to help out Momma, and I was late leaving cause I took Little Jerry to do some trick-or-treating. Momma had bought him this precious, little cowboy costume with the gun and hat and... (inaudible) I shoulda stayed another night. It was about 10:00 or quarter past. Junie and Little Jerry was asleep on the front seat beside me. I was trying to hurry back home cause Jerry Bob had already got off work. I was almost to Fayetteville. I'd just passed over Ginger Cake Creek when I smelled Junie's diaper, and I didn't want her to go all the way back home like that. So, I pulled off the road, right after passin' the church. (Recording paused.) I finished changing her. She and Little Jerry kept right on sleeping. I was going around the front of the car to get back behind the wheel when something came up outta the blue. It was like a fog. I just thought it was...it got thicker and thicker. It got so bad, I couldn't even see up over the hood. I sat there a minute wondering if I should go on or wait awhile 'til it cleared up. I needed to be getting home, so I cranked up the car and pulled out in the road. All of a sudden, a bright light just appeared outta nowhere. I slammed on the brakes, but I put my hand out to keep the youngins from going in the floorboard. I got scared thinking it was one of them giant tractor-trailer trucks about to run head-on into us. So, I reached over to grab up the kids... (inaudible) and when I looked over to grab Junie, she was gone (inaudible). They got her. I know they got her (inaudible). The next thing I remember was being woke up by Roy and Lieutenant Epps. (Mrs. Owens pointed to Officer Roy Gordon and Lieutenant William Epps.)

Detective Burly Edwards: Frances, had you been drinkin' that night?

Mr. Jerry Bob Owens: You miserable son of a... (inaudible).

Mr. Simpson Ballard: Sit down, Jerry Bob. Sit down. I'm warning you. If you want to stay in here with Frances, you gotta simmer down. Gosh dang it, Burly, I swear, you know full well Fran hadn't been drinkin'. For the love of Jesus, she's in the church more than Preacher Robinson.

Detective Burly Edwards: Simp, you gonna have to let me ask the questions we gotta ask. Were you drinking, Frances?

Mrs. Frances Owens: I ain't never touched a drop, and anybody that says I do is telling a black lie. Look, I know it sounds crazy. Lord knows, I love my kids, I love my Junie. I wouldn't never do nothin to her. I love... (inaudible).

Mr. Jerry Bob Owens: I tell y'all whatcha oughta be doing is getting the hell outta here and findin' my baby girl. Something's done got her, and I don't care if it's some maniac or some G. D. little green men or President Harry S.O.B. Truman. Junie's gone, and we ain't got her and (inaudible) Fran, Frannie honey, you okay? (Recording was stopped.)

Notes:
Mrs. Owens was transferred to the county hospital and released into the custody of the Pine Wood Psychiatric Facility.

Update:
As of November 21, 1952, this case is closed. Mrs. Frances Owens was found hanging in her room at Pine Wood Psychiatric Facility. Her death has been ruled as a suicide. No further charges are expected to be brought forth in this case. At this time, the missing child, June Owens, has not been recovered (6 months old, at the time of the disappearance).

—Fayette County, Georgia
Police Department Interrogation Recording
November 22, 1952

DISBELIEF

NO ONE WAS AT HOME. I SLUMPED AGAINST MY closed bedroom door, wanting to scream and cry and curse. I wanted to wake and discover this was a nightmare. How was it possible? I'd rather Bram be a liar than for my entire life to be a lie. Of everything I saw and everything he told me, I wasn't sure what was real. My thoughts were spinning, and I would've welcomed the chance to forget the facts I had been told. I'd love to call the inspector and his nurse to come with her pills or medipens, or whatever. At this moment, anyone could have convinced me of the joys for releasing the hurtful memories. I would've given back everything I'd learned to have the life I woke up with this morning.

"Ellis, may I come in?"

There was a knock at the door. I jumped, thinking I'd have time to collect my thoughts and pull myself together before seeing and talking to anyone. I didn't want to let him in, but I had no choice to answer. I stayed for a second longer leaning against the door.

"Ellis?"

I wiped the remaining tears and opened the door with my head tilted toward the floor.

"Hey, is something wrong, Junior?" Dad asked, lifting my face to his.

"It's a tough day, Daddy." I looked away. I wanted to be his baby girl again because he could make everything right. He sprayed Bogeyman-Be-Gone water inside the closet to make the monsters go away, he kissed boo-boos to get rid of pain, and he helped me bury the wild bunny we fed every evening until we found it dead. I'd break down if I looked into his eyes. This monster had no cure.

"Hey, what's this?" he asked. It was obvious I'd been crying. I'm an ugly crier. Blotchy, red face with swollen puffy eyes, even the end of my nose turns hot pink. There was no way to hide this.

"I need to be alone. I think I'm overwhelmed with the end of school, the placement test, Mrs. Young, life…I need to let my mind rest."

"That sounds like a heavy load to carry. Should I call Dr. Adler?"

Was she a part of this crazy experiment? If Bram studied for the release program, were the therapists aware? Why didn't I ask him? Was it possible Dr. Adler knew of the conspiracy? She and my Dad had been the allies I depended on. I didn't want to believe she could have been part of this ugliness.

"No. My regular appointment is tomorrow. I think it's just a little anxiety. I don't know…leaving behind my childhood or something equally profound." I forced a smile and tried to sound lighthearted for his sake, but I was kidding myself. My dad could read me with no trouble. He'd sense this was an act, and he'd know I did it for his benefit.

"Leaving behind your childhood? Ellis, no matter how old you are, no matter how you started out in this world, you will always be my baby. Do you understand? You are, and you always will be my baby. No matter what happens." He paused. "No matter what. Now, I'm making your favorite chicken casserole. How does that sound?"

"No, Dad. You don't have…"

"But I do. I want to; I need to. I want to do whatever I can to make you happy, even burn a casserole until we can make you smile again."

"Thanks, Pop." I was desperate to hug him, but I couldn't. If I did, I'd shatter into a million pieces. I remembered Bram said telling the truth would be risky for my family. I couldn't let my actions endanger him or my mom. I stepped back and took a deep breath.

"Chicken casserole sounds great," I said. He smiled, but it wasn't sincere. He looked helpless. "It's just one of those days. You don't have to worry, Dad."

"But I do. It's part of the job. Love, protect, provide for, take care of, teach, worry about…that's what loving parents do. When you become a parent, you'll do the same."

I knew that would never happen. What kind of person could bring a child into a world where we are held captive? I refused to subject another human to that fate. I tried to smile. "I hope I'm a parent just like you."

"Okay," he laughed, "enough with the flattery; I'm going to make dinner. You don't have to praise me to get your casserole." He turned away.

"Dad? If it happened again—the end of our world—I need you to remember you are…"

His expression changed, and he stepped toward me. I put my hand up to stop him from coming closer. I could tell instead of reassuring him of my love and respect, I'd worried him more than ever.

"It won't happen again, Ellis. I promise. I understand what you're trying to tell me. But know this—if life drastically changed tomorrow, I will have had the incredible luck to love and have been loved by two special women." He smiled and turned toward the kitchen.

My gut told me my mom wasn't one of those women.

CHAPTER 17

The dreams of humans are collected to determine the presence of underdeveloped senses not previously studied. Often these dreams are prophetic, suggesting they can calculate and postulate with a great degree of accuracy a probable outcome for any event. No evidence exists thus far in determining whether the human species can predict future events. Dreaming is likely the evolutionary prerequisite for developing two known senses presently not found in humans. For these reasons, the recollection and recording of these dreams must be encouraged to determine their significance in understanding the human mind.

—Professor Jdochleur Daulchmanu
Human Research Department
Nurahatum University, 2020

CONFESSIONS

THE NIGHT BROUGHT HEAVY SLEEP, BUT IT WASN'T peaceful. My normal eight hours still left me exhausted the next morning. The dreams were unending. The entire night felt more like work than if I'd actually done physical labor. I lay in bed with my eyes closed, trying to remember the dream. When I let my mind wander, my grasp slipped from what occurred. I was a believer in dream significance. They were explanations of the waking world's mysteries. Not mystical prophecy, but a heightened awareness of suppressed feelings. If I tried to understand my dreams, I could understand myself, and I needed that more than ever. The person I'd been for twenty years was gradually becoming a stranger.

I steadied myself at the edge of an enormous cliff. Rhythmic gusts of wind threatened to sweep me away. I wanted to see what lay beyond, but I was scared.

In my hand, a knife, pulsating with energy flowed into my fingers and up into my hand—creating in me a sense of empowerment.

Behind me stood every person I'd ever known. Their twisted faces stared with horror-filled agony. Their eyes pleaded for me to stop. What was I doing? The mob marched toward me in step; the sound echoed off an invisible surface. My mother led them but turned away when I reached for her. The inspector took her place now leading the angry charge.

Hands on my shoulders startled me. Ana and Mrs. Young, balanced at the cliff's edge, with knives of their own, willed me to fight. We slashed the scene before us, knives finding their mark, severing an invisible cord that bound us to Horizon. The release thrust me backward over the cliff, plummeting toward death. I closed my eyes. Is this what I fought for? Instead of ground, I plunged into still, warm water, enveloping my senses, quiet and welcoming, until my lungs pleaded for breath. Breaking the surface, I gasped for life-saving air—the sweetest I'd ever known. I was alive, and I was free. An unfamiliar voice called my name, and I was grateful not to be alone.

"Ell, breakfast."

I opened my eyes. Was I just dreaming or did the dream occur earlier in the night? It must have meant something. I grabbed my dataport and frantically typed as much as I remembered. Reality caught up with my awareness. The prior day's event flooded my mind; my heart sank. Was he crazy, or were we surrounded by aliens? Was I crazy? What did I truly see? I saw people speaking a language I didn't understand in an underground part of Horizon I'd never seen. I didn't see little green men or anyone floating in mid-air. I didn't want Bram to be a liar or be crazy, but I didn't want him to be an alien either. There was a knock at my door. I jerked.

"Ellis? Are you awake?" My mother waited for a reply.

"One moment, I'm not dressed," I called back to the closed door. I finished writing my dream and closed my port. The crumpled pants lying in a heap beside my bed and my nightshirt were the quickest outfit. Something weird was happening, and the sensation hung in the air the way some people can smell a summer rain coming. My skin tingled, and the hair on my arms felt charged with electricity. I'd felt this way before. One of those times was the day of Mrs. Young's death. I rushed to the kitchen, where Mom and Dad were waiting.

"Dad? Why are you home?" I asked.

"I took a few days off to celebrate the holiday. Your mom and I could use your help getting the picnic planned for tomorrow."

"No ham sandwiches and chips?" I asked.

"Tomorrow is graduation and career placement. An extra special day needs an extra special lunch," he said.

Mom handed me a plate of eggs and bacon with a piece of toast. "You're not eating?" I asked. I gulped juice already poured for me.

"We've been talking," she said. That wasn't an everyday occurrence, nor was it common for my dad to take so much time from work.

"What's going on?" I laid my fork beside my plate, sat back, and folded my hands in my lap.

My mother looked at my father, waiting for him to begin. He was silent.

"We have a surprise," my mother announced.

"Greta, we should postpone this…until after the picnic," said my father.

"Nonsense; now is perfect. Your father and I have secured you and Ana an apartment."

"An apartment…for what?" I asked, baffled by whatever reaction my mother had assumed this announcement might create.

"A place to live. You both will receive your placements tomorrow, and since a place has become available, you and Ana could be roommates. Moving out is part of maturing and making a life for yourself. You will have privacy and begin dating. It will be the next step in your maturing."

"You're kicking me out?" I said. I leaned forward on the edge of the chair.

"No, you don't have to move," said my dad. "It's an option. These apartments become available occasionally, and your name was on the list of singles eligible for such housing."

"And you both live here?" I asked. There was silence.

"We've considered moving into a townhome near the hospital suitable for couples. A growing family can take this house." As my mother spoke, I watched my father. This wasn't his idea.

"You're separating," I blurted out. Now the silence was complete. I looked at my mother and back to my father. She looked down. "Dad?"

"Nothing is decided," he said. My mother snapped her head in his direction. Whether what he said was a lie or possibly wishful thinking, her scowl spoke volumes.

"Mom?"

"Ellis, we have done our duty by you. Now, we will take a different path," she said.

"Duty?" I screamed. "You consider me a duty?"

"You will lower your voice. I don't deserve to be spoken to in that manner," she said.

"Ellis, she didn't mean that," said my dad.

"No, Dad, she did. She's always felt this way. I'm meeting with Dr. Adler in a few hours, but before, I'm going to Ana's." I rose to leave the kitchen and turned to face my parents. "Mother, thank you for breakfast and for doing your duty." I paraded out of the house in triumph.

My grand gesture was a failure. I had just left the house looking as if I had slept in my clothes, which was partially true, and I didn't stop to get my bike. So now, I walked instead of rode to Ana's house. My trip might take fifteen minutes instead of five, but I didn't care. I wanted to think, and I wanted to forget. From a psychological standpoint, that kind of thinking should cause crazy alarms to go off. I needed Dr. Adler more than ever. Someone in my life needed to explain my mother and make sense of what my family was experiencing. Everything was unstable, and I craved normalcy. I didn't have a fantasy with a prince on a white stallion. Happiness could be coming home from a job to a husband and family who loved one another. No judgment, no blame, and no guilt. Instead, I had aliens, apocalypse, and apathy. Bram's craziness was enough to make my head explode. I needed someone to talk to about the gigantic load of crap dumped into my life. If I told Ana everything, I could get a small amount of relief, but she had her own issues with anger, and I wasn't sure she could keep quiet. I remembered what Bram said, and I didn't want her to be in danger. Dad had his own problems. I couldn't talk to my mom because—just because. Bram was not a choice because he was a liar, lunatic, or alien. I felt alone in so many ways, and I didn't want that life. I should be delirious with happiness—graduation, career placement, and a boy.

I pulled myself from deep thought as I passed Mr. Hap's house. A child chased a butterfly in the yard with her parents watching. His house became available the way my singles apartment had. The parents laughed and took pictures of her; they looked joyful. I didn't grow up that way.

I remembered my father at every point in my life, but my mom was not as involved. She was always doing something or working on something, or merely away for reasons I never questioned. Whatever our relationship, I loved her. Not in the way I loved my father, but I loved her. I tried to remember special times we'd shared. We made cakes for my birthday parties. She helped me through the awkward years between girl and teenager. She helped me pick out clothes and style my hair. When I was twelve, I had my heart broken by Tommy Trellis. She sat with me, talking and giving me fresh tissues for tears and nose-blowing, and she told me how everyone went through heartbreak. The only time I can recall my mother making a joke was when she told me Tommy had done me a favor. At first, I was angry until I asked her why. 'Do you want to go through the rest of your life being Ellis Trellis?' Both of us laughed so much. It was one of the few times our relationship felt normal. Mom told me she had her heart broken by someone she loved, but didn't love her in return.

I froze. Could it be? Was my dad in love with someone else? Had he broken her heart? Was that why they were separating? I wanted to go home and tell her I was sorry for overreacting at what she said. I couldn't imagine my father being unfaithful. If I was honest, though, they'd never acted as if they were in love. Thinking back, I never saw my father and mother kiss or hold hands. Surely, my mom didn't mean Dad broke her heart because they were married. Perhaps she had been hurt before The End. Someone in her old life must have been her unrequited love. She'd never, even if I asked, tell me any details—not because it was forbidden to discuss old memories, but because she didn't do *heartfelt*. I couldn't imagine my mother allowing anyone close enough, giving him the emotional power to hurt her. As unkind as it sounds, I couldn't picture her romantically involved with *anyone*.

I hadn't realized it, but I had been standing dead still while processing the possibility of my father and mother separating over infidelity.

In the distance was the park where a team of workers assembled booths for tomorrow. Every year, on the first of August, we celebrate The Beginning. It was the day Horizon officially opened, and the survivors moved into their new homes. I was too little to remember, but we stayed underground while being treated for our injuries. Now, I didn't know what was true. We were told we'd been rescued and placed in a bunker while our environment was repaired. The day Horizon was opened, Mr. Hap had come from the bunker. He knew facts, and those memories hadn't been taken. A butterfly flitted by me, similar to the one the little girl had been chasing in Mr. Hap's yard. He'd described coming to Horizon like butterflies, coming out of cocoons, fresh and new, into a world we had never seen. We'd been reborn.

Why hadn't I thought of it before? I wasn't alone. I could go to Mr. Hap. That was my starting point. I needed facts, and he needed my help to get released. I snuck back to my house, grabbed my bike, and headed for the hospital.

I had no plan. What possible excuse brought me to the hospital on a day when my Dad was at home? I needed access to his office, and I had to act calm.

After parking my bike in the usual spot, I smoothed back my crazy hair, made crazier by a combination of rushing wind and sweat. I slowed my breathing and smiled as I strolled into the large lobby. Every piece of furniture was white. Sunlight from massive windows flowed through azure glass globes hanging from the ceiling. Filtered rays of blue cast onto the walls. Miss Kate sat behind the welcome desk today. I smiled and raised my hand to say hello. She was with a couple who looked desperate for help. She waved back and smiled. Inside the elevator, I pressed the number three. In seconds, the doors opened, and I collided with a nurse named Jake.

"Hey, whoa you," he said. "Whatcha doing here today? I thought the big guy was off."

"Hey Jake, how are you?" I said, avoiding his question.

"I'm good, thanks. Busier than a vacuum cleaner in a dirt factory, though. I had better run. See you around, Ellis." He stepped into the elevator, and I breathed easier. On any other day, I'd have asked him to explain what the expression meant, but today I had more important issues.

I turned and walked toward my Dad's office. Familiar faces passed me, which required only a smile instead of conversation. His door was locked. "Oh, muddy puddles," I said aloud.

"Muddy puddles, huh?"

I turned and found my dad's nurse standing behind me.

"Hello, Mrs. Lawrence," I said, without a hint of my desperation. "I'm here to pick up something I left in Dad's office. Will you unlock the door?"

"Why, sure, Honey. Why didn't your Dad give you his key?"

"Well, I...didn't realize I left my book until I nearly got to the Archives. I didn't think about needing a key." I took a chance, and said, "I'd rather not go back home, it's a little tense right now."

She understood what I was insinuating, so I suppose my Dad must have let the apartment slip to his nurse. Could Mrs. Lawrence be the other woman? I stifled laughter. She was at least twenty-five years older than he was.

"Honey, I'm sorry. Don't worry; everything will work out for the best." She unlocked the door. "I promise things will get better." She emphasized each word of her sentence. The way she spoke convinced me she knew something. She may have thought she was consoling me, but it had the opposite effect. The door stood open in front of me.

"I hope you're right. Dad hasn't been himself, lately." I walked into his office and turned back to her.

"You hang in there, darling." She put her hand on my shoulder.

"Thanks for letting me in, Mrs. Lawrence; I'll lock the door when I leave."

Instead of speaking, she gave me a smile and a squeeze before leaving. I walked in but peeked out to see if she had gone. She was rounding the corner, so I shut the door. I ran to the cabinets full of papers. I couldn't make sense of any records. There were no patient files. Dad's dataport lay on his desk; I'd give it a shot.

I grabbed it and clicked the power button. The screen requested a fingerprint or password. I had to take a chance. I typed E-L-L-I-S. The home screen blinked waiting for me to tap the enter button. I paused and considered the consequences of my actions. I pressed enter. Done. It couldn't have been easier. There was a file named patients. I clicked on it and searched the name, Parsons. Parsons, Henry Albert flashed on the screen. Henry Albert, I thought Hap was short for…happy. I clicked on the name, and his entire file opened. Running short on time, I scanned the page for a location. Room 318. The door began opening. I clicked the off button and scrambled to the door. The screen needed time to go black, so I shoved the door closed, checked it, and opened the door again.

"I'm sorry, Mrs. Lawrence, did I hurt you? The chair tripped me."

"I'm fine, dear. Are you?" she asked, looking for signs of injury. I'm such a liar. "Did you get what you needed?"

"No, I didn't, please don't tell Dad. He gave me the book for graduation. I've searched everywhere. I thought maybe I laid it here when I visited last time because I wanted to show him an interesting passage. Retracing my steps might help if that's okay."

"Sure, honey. You go right ahead. What is the name of the book? I'll search, too."

I hesitated, "It's a…very old psychology book called *Diagnostic* something, something, something—*DSM* for short.

I dug my hole of lies even deeper. Dad hadn't given me this book for graduation, and I was positive, the guide was only available to the release therapists. I hope she didn't know that. The lies were stacking up around me, but my intentions were honorable.

"Honey, I know that book. It's right there." She walked over and pulled a heavy, leather-bound volume from the shelves behind my father's desk. "It does have a long title," She laughed, teasing me.

"I can't believe it." I needed to have a reason to walk around and find Mr. Hap's room. "Wait," I called to her as she walked toward the door. "This isn't my copy. Dad must have one of his own."

She looked genuinely sad for me. I am evil. Mrs. Lawrence had always been so kind. Every Christmas and birthday, she'd always given me a very nice present. Here I was, lying to her repeatedly.

"I'll tell the others at the desk, and they can look, too. You go right on and retrace your steps. I'll send you a dataport message if we find it." We walked out of Dad's office, and Mrs. Lawrence reached behind me to pull the door until it closed.

"Thanks. You're a lifesaver. Please tell everyone not to mention it to Dad. He was so excited to give me the book. I hope to be placed in the release program tomorrow. This book will help me."

"Don't you worry, honey. I'll tell them. If it's here in this hospital, we'll find it. You go and start looking. There's nothing more frustrating than searching for something that doesn't want to be found." She gave my shoulder another squeeze and smiled at me.

I walked away, looking around as if I might have stopped at the nurse's desk and had reason to lay the nonexistent book somewhere. I hoped she wasn't watching, but I didn't take the chance on breaking the charade, so I kept on pretending to look as I rounded the corner. Once out of her line of sight, I sped up to get to room 318. I walked in quietly and shut the door behind me. A person lay in bed with their back to me.

"Mr. Hap, is that you?" I tiptoed so my shoes wouldn't make noise. Machines surrounded the person I hoped was him. I considered stopping to turn back, but I couldn't. I drew closer to the bed.

"Mr. Hap?" I crept to the far side of the bed. It was him. "Mr. Hap, it's me, Ellis." He lay so still with his eyes open. "Mr. Hap...are you okay?" His stare was blank. I leaned closer to his face, hoping his lack of response was because he couldn't see me clearly. "Mr. Hap, please talk to me. I'm Ellis, your neighbor." He said nothing. I knelt beside his bed, "I'm so sorry."

He said nothing. I slumped to the floor devoid of any hope and sat with my back against his bed looking out at nothing, just as he did. He didn't deserve this.

"I'm the reason you're here, and I'm sorry. I really wish you could talk to me; I need your help. Horizon isn't what we thought."

I continued to sit but glanced over my shoulder at him. He was alive, plenty of monitors proved that fact, but he wasn't aware I was in the room. For that matter, he wasn't aware *he* was in the room. I continued to sit against his bed, looking toward the same window. I grieved his absence. Although he hadn't spoken, just being near him, made me feel less alone. Possibly, he had been more of a companion than I realized.

"Mr. Hap," I whispered without looking at him, "this might not have happened if I had talked with you more. They stole your memories of Lilly Rose and replaced them with stories hateful and untrue. They tried the same with Ana and me. You loved her, Mr. Hap. You should know that. You told me how beautiful she was when you first met. I wished I had known her. Lilly Rose loved to grow flowers in her garden. They robbed you of forty wonderful years, and I don't know how to stop them."

"Forty-five years," a voice ripped through the silence. The sad, monotone words had a frightening sound. I scrambled to stand. I needed to see if he had spoken or if I had imagined his words. His face had not changed expression.

"She loved roses," he said. His tone was weaker than before.

"Yes," I said too loud. "Mr. Hap, do you know me?" There was no response. My mind raced. What was I doing wrong? "Why did they want the memories of your wife?"

"Control the mind, control the person," he responded.

"Who are they, Mr. Hap?"

"I wanted to surprise her, so I planted the butterfly bush. She was at her bridge club. I wanted to have it planted before she got home."

"What happened?" I asked in a hushed voice. "Tell me."

"She was due home any minute."

"Mr. Hap, please tell me," his monitor beeped faster. He blinked for the first time and then closed his eyes so tightly tears seeped. His contorted face grimaced as if he was in pain. The monitor was now flashing lights, and the beeping intensified. "What happened, Mr. Hap?" I urged.

"Her car was almost to the driveway. She saw me in the yard and waved. Then, there was a flash of blinding light." An alarm started sounding from his machine. He thrashed at something invisible before him. I tried to stop him. I needed to quiet him.

"Please, Mr. Hap," I said.

The door opened. I fell to the floor and slid underneath the bed in a streak.

"Mr. Parsons, can you hear me?" said a female. "Give me the medipen," she said to someone with dark shoes and pants. "Try to relax, Mr. Parsons." Abruptly, he stopped moving in the bed, and the alarm stopped sounding. The beep of the machine became slower and steadier in rhythm. "That's better; you rest now."

The person dressed in the dark colors now spoke, "The chart says Final Release should be called in if his behavior patterns don't change."

"Warn Ellis," he said, barely understandable. I froze.

"What did you say, Mr. Parsons?" the nurse asked.

"The butterflies will die."

CHAPTER 18

Final Release Protocol

Final Release is an ethical and humane solution for humans who cannot maintain societal, physical, or emotional expectations within the Habitat research program.

—Expectation One:
Humans must live peacefully and lawfully within the Habitat.

—Expectation Two:
Humans must possess physical quality of life.

—Expectation Three:
Humans must have or be capable of achieving emotional stability.

—Expectation Four:
　　Humans must be productive workers within the
　　Habitat.

The first level of assessment is performed by the personal release therapist. If a human fails to meet one or more expectations, the release therapist will conference with the patient's medical physician. The medical physician will perform tests to conclude if the failure can be corrected. If the medical physician and the release physician agree a patient is incapable of normal functioning, a report will be submitted to the Final Release Committee. The committee shall review the information and determine whether the human shall be eligible for Final Release or further treatment. Humans ineligible for further treatment will move to the Final Release ward. The Final Release date will be at the discretion of the committee not to exceed one week from patient admittance.

—Garash Nirgal
Director of Human Affairs
January 2037

FINAL RELEASE

I DIDN'T STOP UNTIL I REACHED THE OUTSIDE OF the hospital. My mind raced. I didn't know what Final Release was, but it sounded…final. I'm sure it didn't mean his release to go home. I had to act before time ran out. I wanted to break down, but I had to stay focused.

Our whole lives had become one release after another. We released our planet and our families, we released our memories and opinions, and we released our freedom. Now, we were expected to release our lives if we didn't conform. This wasn't a research observatory. This *was* prison. Aliens locked us inside this town. If we ignored the rules, we paid with our lives. Citizens who remembered the freedoms of pre-war Earth must suffer, be reprogrammed, or be released in the ultimate, final way. I understood what Dad meant when he said I was lucky to have no memories of the past world. Had he given up those memories, or was he suffering in silence? I needed time, and I needed a place to go.

I had to be alone, but Bram said we were watched constantly. Ana's house was the safest place I knew. I didn't want to involve her before, but this was too big to handle alone. As I rode through town, I searched for signs of hidden cameras. Perhaps they were watching me now, waiting for an excuse to take *me* to the Final Release ward. Horizon's utopian façade masked a horrible reality.

Ana's house was near. I could see her and Mrs. Hamilton kneeling in the flowerbed. When she looked up and saw me, I thought of Mr. Hap. He watched his wife driving toward him as he planted the butterfly bush. Could that have been when the explosions occurred? A chill spread over me.

Lost in my thoughts, I didn't see the official's car until the horn blared and the tires screeched. I wobbled on my bike but didn't lose control. The driver was Thomas Ryder, the inspector, and I wondered how long he'd been following me. He smiled. Goose flesh rose on my skin. I crossed to the sidewalk that ran along the front of Ana's house. By now, she and her mother had jogged toward me.

"Are you okay?" Ana asked, having reached me first.

"Elleees," her mother added. She grabbed me and pulled me to her. She wrapped her arms around me in a tight embrace, more genuine affection than I'd experienced with my mother. "Are you okay, cariño?" She pulled away, looking for possible injuries, and pulled me in for another tight hug. "What are you doing, not watching?"

"I'm fine," I said, not wanting to pull away from her, enjoying the tenderness.

Beyond us, Inspector Ryder parked in their driveway. He eased out of the car with a smugness, suggesting he enjoyed his authority more than he should. *Is he an alien?*

Mrs. Hamilton pulled away and turned over her shoulder to look in the direction I faced. She broke from me and walked toward Inspector Ryder.

Ana leaned forward and whispered, "I've got something very important to tell you."

"Hello, Inspector Ryder," said Mrs. Hamilton. He walked in our direction.

"You should be more careful, Ellis," he called over to me, leaning around Mrs. Hamilton. "You could have been killed."

For a moment, I wondered if he suspected I knew everything. I purposely didn't respond.

"Were you coming to see us, Inspector?" said Ana's mother.

"Yes, I'm checking on everyone's progress since Mrs. Young's heart attack." Ana and I walked to where he and her mother stood.

"How are you, Ana?" he said.

Everyone looked at her. She stepped forward. She had not talked with him since learning the truth about Mrs. Young. If he gave her more drugs like those that we had in the Fountain, could she resist confessing what she now knew? Had I put her in danger by telling her what really happened? If the inspector discovered our secrets, Ana and I could be hospitalized like Mr. Hap.

"Thanks for checking on me, Inspector," said Ana. "I'm fine. The Celebration is tomorrow, and I'm receiving my work placement."

He didn't acknowledge graduation with congratulations or a

smile. This was not normal behavior. He never took his eyes from hers and never blinked. I think he was looking for those signs people give when lying. "Have you had any issues with Mrs. Young's moving forward?"

"Issues?" she asked, wrinkling her nose. "You mean being depressed?"

"Any emotions or memories," he answered, now looking at me as if I might try to influence her answer.

"Yes," said Ana. Inside my head, I screamed at her. "I'm not sure how this will sound, but I wish she died somewhere else. Before, Ellis and I ate there every week. Now, I don't want to be reminded of her death every time we go there. Not thoughts of sadness, but as if I wished she hadn't involved us in her passing." She looked at her mom. "Is that too horrible to admit?"

"No, mija," replied her mom. "Don't you worry. Right, Inspector?"

"Talk to your therapist," he said to Ana. "Do you have other concerns?"

"No," she answered.

"Call me if anything changes. And you, Ellis," he said, now stepping closer to me than I felt comfortable with. "Watch out; you risk your life when you're careless."

I could have thrown up right then. He was vile, and he suspected me, so I said nothing. I kept calm because had I spoken, I would have confirmed his suspicions. So, I forced a smile and thought he was the one who'd better watch out. He might not be the leader, but he was the closest I had, and I hated him.

When he drove away, I could tell Ana's spirit lifted. From where I stood, she had half of the information I knew, and she thirsted for the truth. I had it within my power to hold everything else from her. She'd be safer if I did. As her friend, I couldn't let her live in the dark, not knowing our lives were lies. I was willing to risk our happiness, our sanity, and even our lives to get the truth.

We walked back toward their yard, Mrs. Hamilton, with her arm around Ana and me behind, feeling a bit jealous. Ana felt safe and loved. The actual truth was, we weren't safe—no matter how many arms held us, and no matter how often we were assured of being loved.

"Ana," I said, "They are setting up the fireworks at the park. You want to ride over and watch?"

"That sounds fun," she said. "Are we finished, Mamá?"

"Yes, you don't want to be too tired to enjoy tomorrow," her mom said. Ana grabbed her mother and gave her a quick squeeze.

She got her bike, and we headed toward the park. She immediately began talking, not allowing room for me even to respond. She covered every subject except for our crisis. She and her mother had made a pie for the contest, and they prepared a special picnic. Ana told me what she was wearing and discussed the prospects of our assignments. She didn't mention Mrs. Young or any mystery that had once consumed us.

"You will get the release therapist assignment, Ellis. You're perfect for the job. I hope I'll be placed with the historian department. Please don't let me get something like a clerk or waitress. I have to be involved with the Archives; it's what I've always wanted to do. I wonder what assignment John will get."

The more she talked, the faster she talked. This wasn't the real Ana. She spoke in the same way with Inspector Ryder. Maybe I was paranoid, but I sensed she didn't want me to say anything until we were at the park. In a few minutes, job assignments, picnics, and possible boyfriends wouldn't be a priority.

"Where do you want to go? There?" She pointed to workers setting up fireworks by the far end of the lake. Her hand shook.

"Why don't we go to the knoll?" I suggested. She didn't answer. I lead the way, not speaking anymore.

When we arrived, she looked around us. "Okay, let's start." Her smile vanished. "You go first," she said.

"Everything has changed," I said.

From there, I began my story with Mom and Dad separating and arranging an apartment for us. Next, I moved on to Bram and our meeting at the Archives. I described his home and the underground. She never interrupted me, and her expression hardly changed. I gave her the details of the war and how the Habitat came to exist. I described my visit with Mr. Hap at the hospital. When I finished, she didn't speak for a long time. It was as if she needed the time to calculate everything. This morning, I felt overwhelmed and couldn't organize my thoughts. Today, we both learned Horizon was a lie. Now, I had someone to share this burden with, and I welcomed the relief.

"Okay, what do you want to do?" she asked.

I loved her. She trusted me and never questioned the truthfulness of the information I told her. "I don't want to live a lie," I said.

"Then, we need an alien-butt-kicking plan."

"Are you sure? Once we get involved, I doubt we can turn back," I said.

"Living like lions, sister."

Ana and I parted ways at her street. Our plans were complete, and I biked to my appointment while she rode home to prepare for the following day. Ana accepted everything I told her. She reacted with a bizarre calm as if the news wasn't a surprise.

I rode to the Orchard building for my scheduled release session.

I wanted to hate this place, but I'd been conditioned for years to think of it as a source of healing. I entered the building and noticed, for the first time, a carving into a stone situated over the entrance. It was two suns. If it had meaning, which I'm sure it did, I doubted I'd learn it. I had a habit of trying to find hidden meaning in everything. I deciphered words, thoughts, and ideas into that which held a deeper meaning. So for me, this carving meant I was going into the sun. The sun gave light, so everything was visible. Perhaps here, nothing could be hidden in darkness, and everything was visible. I had to make sure this wasn't the case with my release session. I couldn't allow myself to be transparent.

I knocked, and Dr. Adler called for me to enter. I walked into the same office I'd known for over ten years. Nothing had changed. I supposed if she was on their team, she had to maintain a constant and steady environment. If, however, she was on our side, she may have her own doubts and be waiting for someone to become her ally.

"Hello, Dr. Adler," I said.

"Hello, Ellis. How are you?" she asked.

"I'm well. Just waiting for tomorrow," I said.

"Are you nervous?"

"No, there are more important issues I want to discuss."

"Oh, certainly."

"My mom and dad are separating."

"Are you sure?" she asked, putting her port on the side table.

"Yes. They announced it this morning. They said they had arranged an apartment for me to share with Ana. I believe my dad is getting an apartment near the hospital."

"And your mother?"

"I don't know, but I believe she insisted on the separation. I've suspected for a while they weren't happy together. I asked him not too long ago if divorce was a possibility."

"How does separating cause you to feel?" she asked.

I sat for a while, thinking through the seriousness of the question. Parents were supposed to be a source of security that children needed in this post-apocalyptic world. We were supposed to find safety within the family unit. While devastating, my parents' impending divorce was now at the bottom of my worry list. It was just another piece of the mounting insanity piling up in my life.

"Ellis? Can I get you a glass of water?" Dr. Adler's voice drew me back into the present. She was now beside me, on the sofa, holding my hand.

"I'm sorry. I…"

"It will be fine. You're shaken by this news. I understand. You love your father. I recognize what this must mean to you. Let me give you some medicine." She stood and walked to her desk.

She believed I was cracking up because my parents were separating, when in actuality it ranked pretty low on the crap-o-meter. There were other issues far more pressing than my parents' marital status.

Once again, I had appeared disconnected from my surroundings. Dr. Adler was back at my side.

"Ellis, I'm calling your father to come and take you home. I don't want you going back alone. I believe you are suffering from too much stress. This family situation, coupled with the end of school, placement tests, and the incident at the Fountain—has caused what I believe to be an emotional overload." She held her hand out. In her palm laid a small blue tablet. It didn't look similar to the medicine given at the Fountain. But how could I be sure? She held a glass of water. "It will help relax your mind."

"I want a break from stress," I said, "but tomorrow is the day I've looked forward to my whole life. I want to savor it—good and bad. Maybe it's normal to suffer through some parts of life, but that makes the good times even more wonderful. You're right. The last two weeks have been the most difficult, wonderful, hurtful, confusing times I can remember. It's overwhelming to think about, nevertheless, live it."

She laid the tablet and water to the side on the small wooden sofa table.

We talked nonstop for the rest of the hour.

"The last time we spoke, Ellis, you had more positive than negative in your life. Why has so much has changed?"

"Because I've changed," I said standing. She stood with me. I walked to the door. "I hope I'll see you tomorrow at The Celebration."

"Will I get to meet your young man?" she smiled.

"No. That's also become a negative in my life. He wasn't the person I thought he was," I said.

"I'm sorry. You never told me his name."

"It doesn't matter anymore. Although, if anything in my life felt perfect, it was him. I can't explain it because it doesn't make any sense, but I think I love...loved him. Anyway, it's over, and it's for the best. We weren't suited for one another." I opened the door and walked into the hallway but stopped and turned back to her. "You would've liked him; his name was Bram." I walked away, thinking that would probably be the last time I ever spoke his name.

CHAPTER 19

Today marks the one-year anniversary of our re-birth—a day when citizens of Nurahatum triumphed over nature. We met our impending extinction face to face and prevailed in a way no other civilization has since the beginning of recorded histories. Our de-scendants will look back on this event and celebrate us. History will not forget our achievements, sacrifices, and ingenuity. We are the saviors of our people. We are saviors of a future yet to be written.

We must memorialize those who gave their lives so we might have ours. Our future is full of promise. We have achieved so much, yet let us not stop striving to excel. We will create challenges anew for our people. The quest for true utopia must never stop. This planet, rescued from reckless caretakers, is now made per-fect and has created a home for us all. With mercy, we took pity on a race of inferior creatures and fashioned for them a new chance of survival. We will nurture them. We will be gods for them, and they will enjoy a peaceful existence. The blessings we bestowed gave them a chance to live as superior races do—without fear, war, division, and other dangers.

We are mindful of our responsibility as their saviors. Without us, humankind would be extinct. Their inability to maintain civilized relations has provided us the opportunity to colonize and survive. In that way, they unwittingly have been our saviors.

As we celebrate today, let us remember for as long as we remain of one mind, we shall always be triumphant in our goals. We will continue our way of life and endeavor to increase felicity and success. Praises for The Beginning.

—Emperor Dalgrim Tilmun
New Earth
January 1, 2033

CELEBRATION

I WAS STARVING FROM THE MOMENT I WOKE. WHEN I came in the night before from release therapy, the house was quiet except for the sound of running water coming from my parents' bedroom. There was a note on the kitchen counter, in my father's handwriting, saying dinner was in the fridge. I lumbered to the bedroom without even checking what had been cooked. All I thought about was sleep and meeting Ana at the Archives during the fireworks. We decided the best way to get concrete proof was in the records department of the restricted section. Everyone comes to see the fireworks display, so downtown would be deserted. Ana received security codes for the main entrance two days ago because Mrs. Croft was ill. Those codes and the stolen security badge would allow us total access to all areas of the Archives. With proof, we might convince the rest of Horizon we were a science project for an alien race. We would demand our freedom, and if necessary, we would fight.

Today, the town was preoccupied with happiness and laughter. Whoever watched us would see a carefree society. I got out of bed, dreading the meeting with my mother. I heard no sound from the rest of the house, which was unusual. By this time on Celebration Day, our lawn chairs, food, and other amusements were packed to take to the park. My father liked a particular spot within the area he thought provided the best views of the entertainment throughout the day. From the window, I saw excited families packing their carts.

No one was home. I was attending The Celebration with or without my family. I couldn't explain why, but placement still mattered to me. I'd never have a job in Horizon because Horizon would soon cease to exist. Still, I needed to know my years of hard work had meant something. Inside the fridge, a plate meant for me from the night before held a sandwich and chips. We didn't do sandwiches for dinner; this meal had been thrown together.

After eating, I placed my plate in the sink. House rules dictated everyone washed their dirty dishes. In rebellion, I spun around and walked toward my room. If Mom didn't like it, she could wash it herself. I heard the cart drive into the garage. I took a deep breath and walked back to find out who had come home. It was Dad.

"Hey," he said with a smile. "Happy Beginning." He pulled bags from the storage bin.

"Happy Beginning," I mumbled. "Need help?"

"Yes, please. These," he said, handing me two bags.

"What is this?"

"This is your Celebration picnic. I thought today needed something extra special, but I didn't get to cook as I had hoped yesterday."

"I shouldn't have run out on you."

"It's okay." He walked past me into the kitchen. "Your mother thought providing you an apartment might soften the blow of our separation. I'm the one who should apologize because you thought you had no choice but to leave us." He placed his bags on the counter. "Now, let me ask you a question. Did you find your book at the hospital?"

I stopped unpacking the bags. I turned, unsure of how upset he was. He looked grim.

"Dad, how did you hear so soon?"

"One of the emergency room physicians called and said Mrs. Lawrence had the hospital on a massive, widespread search for your book. She wanted to give me her copy. Will you tell me why you lied?"

I had to make quick decisions with my story.

"You won't admit it, but I'm the reason Mr. Hap is there, and I had to see him. If I hadn't said something to you, he might still live in his home and be tending his flower garden."

Dad stopped everything. "Ellis, do you honestly believe you're the cause for Mr. Parsons being in the hospital? He is there because he is ill. You saved him. He could have progressed to the same condition as Mrs. Young, and I'm certain you wouldn't have chosen that tragic ending for him."

"You should see him, Dad. I didn't save him. I doomed him to a breathing non-existence. He's not free to live his life. He is medicated into compliance."

"Ellis, you're wrong. Mr. Parsons has progressed in his illness. Keeping him medicated is keeping him safe until we can decide how best to treat him. Please understand, I could never harm Mr. Parsons, nor allow anyone to harm him. I'm not angry because I understand your motives were unselfish, but we both could have gotten into trouble for you being there without permission. I wished you had discussed your intention with me. Is this why you have been acting so sad lately?"

"Yes, partly, but you'd never have allowed me permission to see him. What is Final Release?"

"Where did you hear that?" he asked.

"The term was written on his chart."

"Ellis, charts are private."

"What does it mean?" I repeated.

"It means he may be beyond help and will be transferred to the ward for people who cannot get better. However, before you get upset, I promise I will not let that happen. I'm doing everything I can to help him recover. Please do not risk our getting into trouble by visiting him again. I will try to determine a time for you to have a supervised visit. Now, let's not talk about Mr. Hap any further. It is done, so there's no point in discussing it. Let's focus on something positive. Tell me about your meeting with Dr. Adler."

"The same as always. We talked about you and Mom, mostly. Where is she?"

"Your mother is moving her belongings to an apartment and slept there last night."

"Great. I'm not surprised. She didn't waste any time. Dad, it's not my business, but is there a third person involved in this break-up?"

He stopped mid-air putting a jar of preserved peaches into the picnic bag. "Ellis, you are wearing me out. Where are you getting these ideas? I'm not comfortable discussing your mother and me when she is not present. When everything is less hectic, the three of us will get together and try to answer as many of your questions as we can. I'm not admitting to nor should you assume anything because I don't give you a direct answer. We should discuss the separation when we are together. I hope you show me the same consideration when you and your mother are together. Please do not exclude me from those conversations."

"Okay," I said, "but I believe I deserve to know what caused the break-up."

"Point taken. What should we pack for the park?"

"Dad." He stopped and looked at me. "She's not coming?"

"I don't know, but I hope she will."

On my day, she is decorating her new apartment, and Dad was left responsible. I was angry, and I hoped she didn't come because I didn't want today to turn into a catastrophe. I decided to talk with him later about us continuing to live here instead of me taking an apartment with Ana. He shouldn't live alone, and I believed he'd agree with me.

"So," he was saying, "gourmet sandwiches—grilled eggplant and goat cheese or chicken salad?"

"Surprise me," I said, "I need to shower now so we won't be rushed for the announcements."

"Go, I'll get everything together." I turned to leave. "Ellis, have I ever let you down?"

"No."

"Then stop worrying and enjoy this day. I promise there will be big changes in the future. I am determined you will be happy. Let me worry about your mother and the living arrangements. All you should do is focus on today. Okay?" I nodded and walked away, feeling no better about what the future would hold.

I took my time getting ready because I wanted to look my best. When I finished showering, I did my hair as carefully as I ever had. I looked in the closet to get the outfit my mom found. For a moment, I missed her. After slipping on the dress, I noticed the tiny embroidered purple violets. It made me think of Mr. Hap's wife. It may be petty, given everything I had learned over the last two weeks, but I was still a normal girl with normal feelings, and I missed Bram. I wanted him to be the one I spent my life with, but that was impossible now. My port chimed.

"Hello?" It was Ana.

"Are you still at home?" she asked.

"Yes, why?"

"You won't believe who I spoke to earlier."

"Who?"

"Bram. He's here and wants to talk as soon as possible. He acted as if it was an emergency. I didn't let him know I knew what he was. You know, the "A" word. That sounds incredibly weird coming from my mouth."

"Ana, our lives complicated enough. I don't have time for him."

"Ellis, if you think I believe you're over him, you're stupid. Can I say it any plainer? I'm not suggesting you two should get together and start naming your weird-looking hybrid-children, but you need to be honest with yourself."

There was a knock at the door.

"I've got to go. I'll meet you at our regular spot. See you soon." I tapped out of the port and opened the door.

"Wow, who is this adult? Have you seen my little girl, Ellis?" my dad asked. I laughed. He held out his hand to me as he had hundreds of times before in my life. "Ready?" I nodded. He squeezed my hand and kissed my forehead. "Excellent, let's find out what Ellis Bauer's future holds."

The Beginning Celebration was crowded, and most families were already at the park. My dad and I arrived fully prepared with lounge chairs and coolers of drinks and food. The park was packed with many types of amusements, including games for little kids to win candies and older kids to win Take credits. One of my neighbors, an art teacher at the Hobby Center, was face-painting beside several tables of vendors selling their handmade crafts. The main stage hosted big events—the high school seniors and kindergarten students would graduate, and the Placement Program would announce work assignments. Each year cooking, art, crafting, and flower contests created lots of excitement. At the end of the evening, before the fireworks, the Council Chairman always delivered a speech.

We found our spot by recognizing Mrs. Hamilton's large hat on their picnic blanket. Dad put up a small canopy tent for shade while I scanned the crowd looking for Ana. A small part of me hoped Mom might come to see my placement. This year would be very different for our family. Before, Dad and I always entered the three-legged race. We never won, but still had fun. Since I was dressed up for the placement, there would be no races for us this year. I paused; there would be no races ever again for us here. Everything would change soon. For a moment, I began questioning my decision to reveal the truth. I looked around; everyone was happy. I would be responsible for ending the joy I saw before me now. If we were going through with our plans, I had to stay strong.

"Dad, I want to find Ana. I'm sure she and her mom are at the pie contest now. I'll be back soon." As I walked away, my Dad's miniport chimed. It had to be Mom, so I was glad to be leaving. I made my way across a slight knoll to the main stage area. In the distance, I saw Ana speaking with a man I didn't know.

"Ellis."

I turned. Bram was behind me.

"Why are you here?" I asked.

"Please, I have to talk to you. Something has happened. I can't lose you this way. I believe you still care for me," he said.

"The person I cared for doesn't exist because you created him."

"Don't say that, Ellis. Please come with me so we can talk."

"If you'd been honest with me from the beginning, maybe we could've worked through some of the issues, but be realistic. You are what you are. I am what I am. I can't live like a prisoner, Bram." The last part I said in a hushed tone, but still, he shushed me.

"Ellis, you need to keep your voice low. I need to tell you something.

"Ellis, who is your friend?" Without turning, I knew Dad was behind me. I froze, my eyes glued on Bram, who was frozen, as well. Dad walked around me to face him. The two men in my life stared at one another with blank expressions.

"Dad, this is…" He'd soon learn the realities of our town, so I refused to lie more than I had. "Bram Potter. Bram this is my father, Alex Bauer." The moment was tense because neither moved nor spoke.

After an uncomfortable hesitation, Bram finally spoke. "Hello, Mr. Bauer. I am pleased to meet you." Bram extended his hand.

My father did not attempt to shake it. I had never seen my dad act this intimidating. "Hello," he said. "Ellis, your mother is at our spot, and she needs to talk to you privately. I will keep Bram's company while you speak with her."

I felt uncomfortable leaving the two together; clearly, Dad was upset about something.

"Happy Beginning, Bram." I walked away without waiting for a response. Surely, my bland goodbye to Bram sent a message to my father he need not worry this boy was trying to steal his little girl.

My mother stood at our spot, looking agitated.

"Hello, Ellis," she said. "You look so grown in your dress."

"Thank you. Are you staying for the picnic?" I asked.

"Yes, if you don't mind," she responded.

"You've moved out, haven't you?"

"Yes, although I haven't gotten all of my belongings, yet. One day you will understand. Several reasons make our staying together impractical," she said, reaching across to pull a string off my dress. "In our world, Ellis, being strong and independent is difficult. I want you to rely on your own strength and talent. You have become such an intelligent, sensitive young adult. However, you must be prepared for what the future may hold. A day may come when Horizon is different, and I want you to be ready to survive whatever lays ahead. You must realize what I'm doing is best for many people. It may be difficult to understand, but never forget, I *am* on your side."

She leaned toward me and placed her hand on my shoulder. She gently kissed my forehead—something she'd done only a few times during my life. I didn't know this side of my mother. Her words struck me as sincere, but there were volumes she allowed to go un-said. In the farthest part of my mind, for an instant, I wondered, could she know the truth of Horizon? Is that why I needed to pre-pare? The thought vanished—I had now officially become paranoid.

"You missed the contest, Ellis. Hello, Mrs. Bauer," said Ana. Her mother stood behind her, holding half of her famous caramel-apple empanada pie.

"Hello, Ana. María, how was the contest?" asked my mother.

"Always the same. Josie McCoy won again. Listen, honey, what can you do? This time, she had something called egg custard pie. Five years in the row, she has won. Oh well, maybe next year."

My dad appeared. "Ho-la Ma-ría, ¿Có-mo est-ás?" Ana and I laughed. My dad had such a low, serious voice. He spoke in such choppy, over-accented syllables—his Spanish sounded comical.

"Muy bien, gracias. Look at you. Your accent is getting better,

Alex. Oh, I made those fajitas you enjoy so much," she said, half speaking and half singing her words.

As Mrs. Hamilton searched through her picnic basket, I noted my mom's reaction. Could Ana's mother have been the reason for Mom and Dad separating? No, that was absurd; I was letting my imagination go on a rampage.

The announcements for placements began at two o'clock, so we had another hour. Ana and I sat on our blankets under the tent, and we feasted on our combined picnics. It was nice and somewhat relaxed. I kept trying to judge my dad's behavior for a sign of how he felt meeting Bram. I couldn't decide if he withheld discussing Bram because of Mom or because of Mrs. Hamilton and Ana, but I was surprised meeting a boy I was talking to didn't come up in conversation. 'So tell me, who is Bram?' or 'I don't know this boy's parents.'—nothing—my dad said nothing. Instead, everyone was on their best behavior, and no one could have suspected anything was wrong. When we finished the last of Mrs. Hamilton's delicious desserts, I looked around at the entire scene. The people of Horizon were happy and appreciative they were alive, and they were content. What I wanted, no…what I was doing would destroy everything.

An announcement rang out for placement students to come forward. The results were being presented in fifteen minutes. Without thinking, I turned to my mother. "Wish me luck?" For a second, I thought, why did I reach out to her for emotional support? She took my hand, squeezed it, and smiled.

Ana and I walked toward the main stage to line up with the rest of our class.

"Did you see him yet?" she asked.

"Yes," I said, looking back to judge whether we were far enough from our family to continue the conversation. "He had something to tell me. My dad walked up on us, and I choked."

"Holy cow. What did you say?"

"I introduced them as if I had run into a friend and nothing more. Except, Dad acted weird. He acted as if he knew Bram and I weren't casual friends."

"You imagined that part," she suggested, "he couldn't know him."

We reached the stage and climbed the steps where our instructor, Professor Zhào, was waiting.

"Hello, girls. You look lovely, indeed. Take your places in line; we will begin shortly. I am so pleased for you." Professor Zhào, who was about a hundred and fifty years old, must have taught school for seventy of those years before The End. Ana told me I had no concept of age, and she was most likely sixty-five.

"Are you meeting him later?" Ana asked.

"Bram? No. I can't. When I look at him, I want to melt. I want to forget what he is and where we are—a part of me wants to live the lie. But I can't and I won't. That makes sense, right?"

"I understand you're caught between following your heart and following your head. Only you can decide which will win out," she said.

"Hey, that's smart advice. You're not trying to get my therapist job, are you?"

"Me?" she asked. "Umm, no. What misery, listening to people yak about their problems all day. Ugh, kill me if I get that assignment." She laughed. "So, what if Bram tries to see you again?"

"I have a speech already written in my mind, but it's complicated," I said.

"You're being very secretive today," Ana said. "So that means it's my turn tomorrow. Just remember that, okay?"

I laughed. Instantly, I felt the need to thank her for being my friend. I couldn't imagine not having her in my life. "Ana, I want to tell you…"

"Welcome." The school superintendent, Dr. Williams, was at the microphone. She had to bend forward to speak because of her height. Before The End, she had been a professional basketball player who quit to pursue what she called her true joy—education. Her duty was announcing the placements. Twenty students were in our class, but several looked to be absent, and I couldn't imagine why. No one misses their placement day.

"Let us begin with a moment of silent reflection and gratitude."

Everyone became still. Some lowered their heads in prayer. Some people just stood, but everyone respectfully became quiet. This was the observed ritual of our community gatherings. But this was the first time I had a front-row seat looking out over the entire town. Every one of these people, those I knew and those I didn't know, would have their lives ripped apart by what Ana and I would do. I felt overwhelmed. The responsibility became more real, seeing how many lives would be affected.

"Thank you. I have the privilege of announcing the Career Placement results for the class of 2052. Let me first thank Professor Zhào for her continued excellence in helping our Horizon youth find and utilize their talents that benefit our community." Everyone applauded, and the professor bowed her head to the audience in gratitude. "When I call your name, please come forward to accept your placement." Professor Zhào, who now held a stack of papers, joined Dr. Williams.

"John Frederick Anderson, communications." John stepped forward and gave a quick wink to Ana. He took the certificate, shook hands with both adults, and gave a big wave to the audience before exiting the stage. I looked at Ana; she liked him. Now, she knew he liked her. She lowered her head, but not before I saw her enormous grin.

"Isabella Blythe Bailey, food services." My nickname for Bella was BeBe, and she was a fantastic cook who brought our class treats all the time. She looked relieved and let out a high-pitched squeal of delight. I could hardly breathe; I was next. Please let it be a therapist. I took a step forward.

"Ellis Elizabeth Bauer, patient services." I stumbled forward and stopped. What did she say? I looked over to where Ana stood. She motioned for me to walk forward. It must have been a mistake. Patient services was a help desk to answer questions and make appointments.

"Ellis, that's you." She pointed forward, where I walked in a fog to receive a meaningless piece of paper.

"Congratulations, Ellis," said the superintendent. She reached to shake my hand, and instead, I walked to Professor Zhào.

"Congratulations, dear," said the Professor as she placed her hand on my back and maneuvered me toward the stage exit. I descended the steps, not taking my eyes from the paper in my hand.

"Wynn Karsyn Grey, patient services," said Dr. Williams.

This is crap. So my tests proved I would be effective in helping people find the hospital bathroom? I don't know how long I stood at the bottom of the steps, but Wynn tapped me on the shoulder to get by.

"Hey Ellis," Wynn said. "I got patient services, too. We are working together. Isn't it awesome?"

I was mute.

"Hi, Wynn." I looked at my dad standing in front of us. "Congratulations to you," he continued to speak to Wynn. "Ellis, come, let's go to our spot."

"Ana Gracia Hamilton, Archives." At least, she received the position she wanted.

"Dad?" I said, letting myself be led by his embrace around my shoulders, "Why?"

"We'll figure it out together, I promise."

"My calling is to help people, Dad," I said.

"It is, Ell. I believe you are meant to help people. There are many ways to help, and you will. Be strong." We walked back to where my mother stood. She looked as if she were truly sorry for me.

"I'm sorry, you didn't get the position you wanted," my mother said. "You would make a magnificent therapist."

"Thanks. I think I'll walk around and see the booths." I had to get my thoughts together. "I'll be back soon. I just need to be alone."

I walked aimlessly through the crowd winding up in the spot I'd come to three times during the last week. The first time I visited the knoll overlooking the lake with my dad, I felt calm, but I didn't realize how often I would seek this place for its solace and privacy. I sat on the ground, not caring if I stained my dress. I had two more hours to act as if everything was perfect in Horizon. I intended to commit a crime which might cause my family and me serious trouble, so I needed to stay away from Bram and convince myself I didn't care what placement I'd received. I was acting stupid. The placement was no longer of any consequence. The way we lived our lives wouldn't exist much longer.

I stood and dusted grass off my dress. I wanted to return and have time with my parents. Ana and I would be leaving for the Archives soon. This might be the last time we were together as a family. It might also be the last time to see the town together and happy.

"Ellis."

I jumped. "I've been trying to find you everywhere. I thought I was too late."

"Forget it, Bram. I can't do this." He tried to take my hand, but I brushed away from him and began walking back to join the others.

"I love you, and you love me," he pleaded.

I stopped without turning to face him. "You're wrong—that was a different Ellis, and I'm not her anymore."

When I arrived back to our spot, Dad was alone.

"Hey, Ell. You okay?" he asked.

"Better than okay. I'm sorry I overreacted with my placement. In the grand scheme of life, my career isn't my primary focus now…"

"I don't want you to downplay your feelings. You have every right to be disappointed. Many times life presents hurdles. We will find a solution together. Someone once told me, 'We are not defined by our challenges, but by how we attempt to overcome them.'"

"That's very inspirational, but I wonder if the speaker ever really lived through a series of crappy events."

"I think so; it was my father," he said.

"Dad…Dad, I'm sorry. I didn't…"

"Everyone has crosses to bear. It's important to focus on the real blessings. We might not see someone's burdens, but that doesn't mean they don't exist. So many times, we are saddled with disappointment. Ask yourself, could it be worse? If the answer is 'no,' then you *are* at a very desperate place. But if the answer is 'yes,' then be thankful."

"That's the first time you've ever mentioned your family," I said.

"And that has been a mistake. I think it's time for the rules to change. We can learn a great deal from the world before. Do you see, Ellis? You have helped me understand the importance of memories.

Whether you are a therapist, or something entirely different, you *are* meant to help people."

"Thanks, Pop." I hugged him as tightly as I could. "Where is Mom?"

"She went back to the house to pick up personal items. She thought it might be easier on us if we weren't home while she packed."

"So, no change there?" I asked.

He shook his head. "Everything will be fine, perhaps even better. Time will bring new and interesting changes for us. As long as we stick together, nothing else matters, right?"

"Right," I said, hopeful we might have a future. "Dad, have you seen Ana? I was supposed to meet her here so we could check out some vendors before the fireworks."

"Yes, before I walked your mother back to her cart, Ana came here. The reason I noticed is she grabbed a chicken leg and her backpack. I thought that was funny."

"How long ago?" I asked.

"Thirty minutes, I suppose. Why?" he asked.

"No reason, I thought she might be ready to check out everything by now. I'm sure she will be here soon."

"Well, I'm going to the bathroom. If you aren't here when I get back, I will know you have gone with Ana. Don't be late for the fireworks." He walked away, and I scanned the crowd for my pal. In less than ninety minutes, fireworks would light the sky. Ana and I needed to get to the Archives.

Mrs. Hamilton's gigantic hat caught my eye.

"Mrs. Hamilton," I called. "Wait, have you seen Ana?"

"I'm looking for her, too. I wanted to check if she was okay."

"Is something wrong, Mrs. Hamilton?"

She put her hand on my arm and paused before speaking. "No, cariño. Ana has been a little quiet lately."

"Don't worry. When I find her, we'll come back for the fireworks. We both have been focused on our placements. I'm sure she worried she might not be chosen for the Archives assignment."

"You are right, Ellis. I hope you both remember how someone else labels you, does not matter." She cupped my face and smiled. "Have fun," she said.

I worried Ana had already left without me. She should have waited. I needed to make my way to her house, where I left my bike. We decided it might be easier than going back to my house to get it. I set off taking the long way around the park, hoping no one saw me. I was sure Ana had gone home for her bike and was upset because I was late. If she had to wait long for me at the Archives, someone might have seen her, so I jogged once I was out of sight from the park. I came to her house and saw her bike was gone. She had left already, so I jumped on my bike and pedaled fast. Why did I have on this dress? We had an hour and fifteen minutes until the fireworks. We could still make this happen.

I crossed through town, now deserted, and turned toward the building. We didn't expect to be separated when we came, so I didn't know which door she had planned on using. I rode casually by the front of the building and saw no sign of her. After checking every entrance, I got nervous. I ditched my bike and walked to each one. I knocked hoping that if she was inside, she might hear me. There was no answer. I had no choice but to ride back to the park and hope our paths crossed. After making one more spin around the Archives, I rode back through town and around to the park. I was nearly to our spot before I realized I'd need an explanation of why I now had my bike. No one was there. In fact, our spot was missing. Our chairs and blankets, along with our food, was gone. Even Mrs. Hamilton's picnic things were missing. No one ever missed the fireworks. Why did they leave? The sun was glowing with reds and oranges. I needed to find out why everyone left. As I rode past the lower end of the lake, I noticed how the sun reflected on the water. If this was a habitat, at least they wanted it to be beautiful for us.

I pedaled home not knowing the end of this day would bring the beginning of something far worse than I ever imagined.

CHAPTER 20

"I'm scared...I want Momma and Daddy. They scare me. The doctor talks funny. A woman tells me to breathe. She is rubbing my head. I'm gonna be brand new. She says when I wake up, I can have some of my brother's Halloween candy. I don't know where I am. Where's Momma and Little Jerry? Everything is white. I'm freezing."

(The patient starts to whine and cry.)

"She gives me a drink. It tastes good. I'm so sleepy. Something is wrong with my mouth."

(The patient struggles as if her mouth is forced shut; after two minutes, the patient relaxes.)

"I want to go home. She tells me to shut my eyes, and when I wake up, Momma will be here. They make me smell something. They tell me don't be scared. I close my eyes and I ain't scared no more."

—Ana Gracia Hamilton
Sleep Therapy Session Transcript
July 17, 2052

ANA

ICOASTED INTO MY DRIVEWAY CROWDED WITH OF-ficial cars. I jumped from my bike while it still rolled forward, not quite losing my balance.

"What is this?" I said, brushing my hair out of my eyes. My father, along with officials and Inspector Ryder, walked toward me.

"What is it?" I repeated, this time to the officials.

"Ellis," began my father, "Ana..." he stopped and braced my arms with his hands.

"What?" I asked.

"She's missing," my dad said.

Silence. "What do you mean she's missing? She must still be at the park. Check there or at the Archives. Maybe she forgot something and had to—" I stopped, catching sight of Ana's bike in the back of an official's car. It looked odd. I broke away from my father and took several steps toward the twisted pile of metal. "Why do they have her bike? What happened to her bike?" I said, turning to redirect my question to an official. "What have you done? Why does it look like that?

"Let's go inside, Ellis," said the inspector. My father took my hand in his, and I followed as if in a dream, still looking at her bike as I was led away. No one ever disappeared in Horizon. This didn't happen; it wasn't possible.

"She can't be missing."

"When did you last see Ana?" asked Inspector Ryder.

"At The Celebration, we had lunch and then received our placements. Come on, she is somewhere, lost in the crowd. We are meeting there to watch the fireworks together. She is probably wondering where I am."

"Did you ask her to come here?"

"Here, to my house? No, why would I do that? It makes no sense. We've been at the park today," I said.

"You are lying," my mother spit out. "She said you told her to come and borrow the new brown dress I gave you for your birthday."

I stared mouth open, taken by surprise at my mother's angry tone. "That's ridiculous," I said. "That's crazy. It's ugly and not even her size. You must be the liar!"

My mother flinched, appearing seized with hatred.

Inspector Ryder asked, "Where have you been?"

"I've been—"

"Does Ana have a boyfriend?" asked another officer.

"What? No. What is this? Where did you find her bike?" I sensed a wave of heat spread across my face. "There is no boyfriend. This is…"

"Have you and Ana been arguing?" asked Inspector Ryder.

"What? This is ridiculous. I have to go to Mrs. Hamilton."

"Officials had to take Ana's mother to the hospital," Dad said. "This incident has affected her tremendously. She is being given something to ease her condition."

The sound of a crash, coming from my bedroom, broke into our conversation. I raced to see officials holding pieces of a glass frame that held my favorite picture of Dad and me.

"What are you doing?" I screamed at them.

"We are gathering clues," said the official.

"Clues to what?" I shouted. I snatched the picture from the hands of the idiot official, obviously, the one who destroyed it.

"You think I know something, but you're wasting time. This is insane. What if she fell off her bike and hit her head? She could be hurt and wandering around somewhere in town. This is useless—she isn't here. You're being stupid!"

"Be quiet this instant," bellowed my mother. "How dare you raise your voice to an official? You will apologize at once for your disrespect and anger."

I spun around, dumbfounded she would side with the imbeciles who wrecked my room and believed me capable of hurting Ana. I walked toward this stranger who raised me, and she returned a venomous gaze.

I broke the deafening silence. "You are correct, Mother. I spoke in anger, something I know well because it's the only way you've ever talked to me. Why are you such a hateful witch?"

She lunged forward. "You ungrateful orphan," she screeched. The blow to my face from her hand knocked the wind out of me. The emotional sting was far greater than the physical pain.

"Get out of this house, I don't want to look at you," said my mother.

"I'm leaving," I said to my father. "I'm finding Ana, and if you love me, you won't try to stop me." He took a step toward forward with his hands outreached, but my mother stopped him with a pull on his shoulder and a look he comprehended.

"Let her go," she said to him. I shoved my way past the crowd gathered in the room because I refused to let any of them see me cry. I barreled through the door and swung it closed as hard as I could. That gesture would show I intended to shut her out of my life forever. I turned back to savor the moment, but the door slammed so hard it snapped back open. The flesh on my arms tingled with raised bumps. Stupid door—it meant nothing. I could live with having only one parent, and that is exactly what I intended to do.

CHAPTER 21

Dr. C. Adler: Four, three, two, one. (Pause) Describe your mother.

Ellis Bauer: She's incapable of love. (Pause)

Dr. C. Adler: Your mother loves you. Tell me your feelings
about her.

Ellis Bauer: Most of the time, I don't believe she loves me. It's almost as if she only pretends to care. (Pause)

Dr. C. Adler: Your mother performs many loving acts for you. She adopted you as an orphaned baby of The End. She raised you as her daughter.

Ellis Bauer: She provides me with the necessities,

but that doesn't mean she loves me. You care for my happiness, and you listen. I think that makes you more of a mother. I trust you, and that is the closest thing I have had to a mother-daughter relationship.

—Ellis Bauer, patient
Attempted Memory Reconstruction Transcript
May 2050

SANCTUARY

I PEDALED WITH A FURY, EITHER RUNNING FROM something or to something, I had no idea, but I knew I needed a safe place. The anger at my father, because he didn't defend me to my mother, welled up. He had never taken her side before today. Although I told him not to follow me, I needed a person to listen and help.

I turned toward the Orchard building. The only person left in my life I could depend on was Dr. Adler. She could help me now. I didn't see her at The Celebration, so I hoped she might be in her office. She always had the answers, so I planned to tell her everything. My mistake was keeping Mrs. Young and Bram a secret from her. How did I expect her to help me with these last two weeks if I didn't confide in her? I was stupid to have hidden the truth; she cared for me more than my own mother. If Bram was telling me the truth, I might be putting her life in danger. If aliens don't exist, she could have me committed. I hoped she believed me because I didn't know if I'd survive another heartbreak today. And I definitely could not lose another person I loved.

I slammed into the bike rack, almost flying over the handlebars, and sprinted up the front steps. No one was in the lobby, and I was glad because surely I looked crazed. If the doctor wasn't here, I wouldn't know where to find her. I didn't bother to knock at her door but threw it open instead. I startled her as she was tapping on her miniport.

"Please," I began, "I need your help." By this time, I choked with breathlessness.

She rushed toward me and held out her hand. I ignored it and wrapped my arms around her instead.

"Sit, Ellis," she said after a moment. She led me to the patient's sofa, but instead of returning to her chair, she walked to the door I had entered and locked it. She made her way back and sat with me on the sofa. "Tell me everything."

"I don't know where to begin. There is so much I should've told you," I said. She reached over to move a piece of hair hanging in my eyes.

"Calm yourself; you are safe here. Let me get you a cup of tea."

"No." My breathing was slowing to a more normal pace. Sitting beside her, I smelled the fragrance of lavender mixed with gardenia, and I did feel calmer. "Ana is missing. Officials were at my house. They are convinced I know where she is, but I don't. She may be in danger, and I must find her. Please help me."

"Why do you believe she's in danger?" she asked calmly. Too calmly. Was she putting on her therapist's hat for me? Why wasn't she alarmed Ana was missing? I told myself to shut up. I was losing a grip on what little sanity I had left.

"They couldn't find her, but they found her bike behind the lake in the woods. The metal was twisted. She should have met up with me at The Beginning Celebration, but she didn't."

"The officials should have no reason to suspect you could harm your best friend."

"I don't think they believe I did," I said. "Ana may have done something forbidden, and they believe I know it."

"Ellis, you are upset, and I'm having trouble understanding what has happened. Tell me everything."

My story began. She was the person I believed could help me, so I held nothing back. It all came out in a great flood. First, I talked about Mr. Hap and his forgotten memories, then Mrs. Young and how the officials had convinced everyone to forget the suicide. I told how I had met Bram when Ana and I were attempting to enter the restricted zone at the Archives. I told her his story about aliens and the Habitat. I confessed to her our plan to go back during The Celebration for evidence. Finally, I told her I suspected Ana found something and hid it in my house. When I finished, I had purged every secret I carried. They were now out in the open, even if only to one person.

I took a deep breath as if I had just run a marathon. I looked at Dr. Adler, expecting her to be staring at me as if I had gone insane; her gaze had not changed. She didn't have the slightest look of surprise.

"Why aren't you shocked? I promise it's the truth," I said, looking for signs she understood the magnitude of what was happening. "I'm not making this up," I added.

"Ellis, you have to get yourself together, they may come for you."

The sound of The Celebration fireworks caused me to jump. "Who…who is coming for me?"

There was a violent knocking at her inside door. I jumped. "Shh," she whispered.

"Mom, let me in," yelled the voice. The knocking became frantic now. "Mom!" It was Bram's voice, but that was impossible. *Why would he be…*

Dr. Adler unbolted the door. Bram rushed in and grabbed her by both arms. "Something is wrong at Ell..." He turned and saw me. He released her and came to me. "Ellis, are you okay? I was so worried." He took me in his arms, but I pushed him away.

"What...Mom...your mom?" I couldn't grasp what I heard. I fought his embrace and yelled out, "What is this?"

Dr. Adler came behind him and spun him around to her. "Listen, we have little time."

I lost my composure. Hot tears flowed; I slumped back into the sofa. I didn't think I could survive this. Panic and shock tried to take over my body. I shook uncontrollably.

"They will be here soon, Bram. You must leave and take Ellis with you. Her life is in danger. Do you understand what I'm saying?"

Banging on the office door caused us to freeze, and my dad's voice shouted, "Claire! Hurry, let me in!"

Dr. Adler ran to the door and threw it open.

"Ellis," yelled Dad as he rushed in. "We have to leave now." Without another word, he grabbed me by one arm and pulled me.

"Dad, what is hap..."

"Alex, wait," said Dr. Adler, who had re-locked the office door. "We have to follow the plan. We can't back out now. What if we..."

"There's no time, Claire. Give me your keys..."

"Open the door!" My father put his hand over my mouth. He then motioned for me to be quiet.

We crept toward the other door in Dr. Adler's office. The person continued pounding, and then the door exploded inward. Inspector Ryder burst into the room. He raised a weapon and pointed it at us. My dad jumped to shield me. "Stop! I'll take that, Dr. Bauer," said the inspector, reaching for the brown satchel my dad had in his hands. The inspector grabbed the bag. Sound exploded and light streaked through the room. The inspector fell backward into a bookcase. More sound tore through the room as his own weapon discharged just before he hit the floor. I was shoved forward and fell into a side table. The ringing in my ears was as loud as the sound itself. I could hear nothing else. Inspector Ryder lay twisted and still just inches from me. Something pooled beneath him. He had dropped the bag that I now reached for in my stupor. A shriek shattered my deafness and jarred my senses. I turned. Dr. Adler was kneeling over my father.

She was pulling at him and crying. "Alex...no, no, don't go. Please, no!"

"Dad!" I screamed. "Daddy!" I scrambled on my hands and knees from the body of the official to where my father lay. He, too, lay in a pool of blue liquid soaking the white shirt I gave him for Father's Day.

"Ellis," he struggled to say, "Trust Claire." He lifted his hand to my face. Dr. Adler held his other hand. "I love you so much...you have meant everything in the world to me. I'm sor...sorry I've put you in danger. Don't be angry with your mother. She was trying to save you. Go now. Take the bag, you'll understand."

"No, Daddy." I kissed his forehead. "I love you, and I need you. Please, Daddy, don't leave me. No! Don't..." One of my tears fell onto his face and trickled down. I leaned closer. He smiled and closed his eyes. His last breath brushed against my cheek and then—silence and nothing.

A thousand things splintered within me.

"Come away, Ellis," someone spoke.

Those were the last words I would comprehend during the madness fracturing my life. Darkness began to drown my mind, and I was so grateful to slip away.

"You must go, Bram. Use the back way. Take my car and identification. Listen to me," my mother was screaming with tears streaming down her face, and I understood. I understood so many things.

Ellis and I were running for our lives. We had to escape the Habitat. Mom shoved the keys, identification badge, and a paper into my hands. She raced to her desk and came back with a medipen she jabbed into Ellis's arm.

"The medicine will sedate her in fifteen minutes and will last about four hours. Leave now and once outside the Habitat, read this paper. It will tell you where to go, but don't contact me because it will be unsafe. I'll meet you when I can get away. Do you understand?" I didn't answer immediately. "Do you understand? There is no time to explain. Use this for money; it can't be traced." She handed me a money card and began pushing me to Ellis. "The officials will be here in minutes, and I need...I have to plan a convincing story."

I had never seen my mother cry this much. She shoved supplies into the satchel Dr. Bauer had brought and looped the bag around my shoulder. We both pulled Ellis to her feet, and she didn't resist. I felt her body relax against my pull, and I knew the medicine had begun to work.

"I love you, son," she said. "Now go, hurry. Be careful. I believe in you," she said. As she pushed Ellis and me toward the back hall, Mom ruffled my hair.

I tried to keep calm and alert. Around any corner, someone might have been waiting to catch us. My actions weren't just affecting me. Now, many lives were depending on me making the right decisions. Ellis had begun to move more sluggishly, and though I was thankful the drug was keeping her calm, I wish she'd move faster.

An elevator took us to the underground garage, and from there, we had several checkpoints to cross. Thankfully, it was after hours for the workers, and the majority had gone home. The garage was empty. We hurried to my mother's car, looking around to see if anyone was watching and Ellis slumped to the ground. I held her tighter around the waist and began half dragging, half carrying her to the car. I'd never make it through the checkpoints with an unidentified person in the car—especially one who was unconscious.

When I opened the trunk to store Dr. Bauer's bag, I knew what had to be done. I picked up Ellis and placed her in the trunk. Her expression didn't change. Luck was with me, or I couldn't have put her there. Her eyes closed, and I leaned in to shake her, but she didn't wake. "I'm sorry, Ellis, but I have to do this." I knew she couldn't hear me, but it didn't matter. I looked at my watch and memorized the time, so I could judge when she may regain consciousness. With every bit of emotional strength I had left, I forced myself to close the trunk. Once in the car, I checked myself in the rearview mirror. I was sweating. My right sleeve had the blue stain of our blood. I stopped the car, rolled up my sleeve, so the stain was hidden, smoothed my hair, and wiped away the sweat. If I kept my cool, I could make it past the next checkpoint.

I drove toward the garage exit, where the guard station was. I lowered the window and held out my identification badge to swipe. The guard from within the station looked at me and spoke. I answered, and he turned to another monitor. As the gate opened, I breathed a sigh.

"Wait," he said. I panicked as I hit the brake. "You can't leave," he said in our language. I thought about barreling through the checkpoint and remembered I still had to board the transport to leave the Habitat. "Your badge," he said. "You can't get back in without it." He laughed. "Have a good evening."

CHAPTER 22

I always wanted a child. From the time I was young, I thought being married and having a child was a perfect life. I wanted to have the same incredible family I had as a young boy. My mother and father had a wonderful marriage, and I wanted the same for myself. When I accepted the appointment to study the Habitat from within, I couldn't say no. Part of my assignment, aside from my research, was to assimilate myself into society. I was not the only Atum to play a role, but I was the only one to receive a human child to raise in the Habitat. When I held her for the first time, I thought she was the most exquisite creature I had ever seen. I named her for my mother, Ellissyanaistra. She is my Ellis, and I will devote my entire life to her happiness.

—Dr. Alex Bauer
Private Journal
February 16, 2035

OUTSIDE

I LOST TRACK OF TIME AND WOKE ONLY LONG enough to drink when Bram told me I must. I remembered a night and a sunrise. Mostly, I remembered wanting to sleep and escape the pain.

Bram eased onto a dirt road with turns and twists around a thick forest. I couldn't muster the strength to worry about my safety. I would go wherever he took me, and I had no concern for what I left behind, including my mother. She made her true feelings known when the officials were ransacking my room. Seeing my father lay on the floor of Dr. Adler's office drained what motivation I had to survive. I recalled the blue liquid gushing from his wound. How could that be? How couldn't I have known? I agonized over Ana's fate. If someone murdered her for trying to pass me information, I would drown in guilt. I had never known this amount of sorrow, and I doubted my ability to survive the crippling torment.

"This is it," said Bram, turning to me with a tender smile. His hand reached for mine, but I pulled away first. I looked through the window of this unusual car, saw a strange landscape, and could find no joy in its newness. A month ago, I dreamed of what the world looked like beyond the wall. I should have been grateful for the freedom to experience it now. This world was reality, and I had lived in a scripted and directed stage play. I stared without speaking. I didn't want to live any life, inside or outside the Habitat. Misery consumed me. I thought of Mrs. Young and the anguish propelling her toward suicide. Before, I never understood. That's what my dad had tried helping me comprehend. Memories can be wonderful, but they can be excruciating. I wanted to sleep and forget.

I hadn't realized Bram was missing until he appeared at my car door. He opened it and held out a hand I refused. I didn't know how long he would continue to make an effort, nor did I care. I stood up with the bag my father brought to Dr. Adler's office, and I followed Bram toward a house built with dark, wood logs. This design reminded me of those I read about in a Laura Ingalls Wilder book, but I believe her home wasn't this large. We stepped onto a sizeable porch lined with wooden chairs that rocked. I had only seen those in the newborn ward of the Horizon Hospital. Bram watched me from the corner of his eye. I don't know what he thought I might do, but he continued to stare.

As the door opened, he stepped back, offering for me to go ahead of him, which I did without speaking.

"I'll make tea," he said. "Can I take your bag?"

"No," I replied, stepping back from him.

He carried bags of supplies to the large kitchen overlooking a lavish room with views of the lake. It was unlike any design I had seen before in Horizon, and it might have been impressive in another life. I walked to the window and watched the darkening sky. Lights resembling fire torches lined a wooden balcony. The same stars beginning to glimmer hung over Horizon, and no doubt shone just as lovely. Here, the rising full moon cast a magical glow on a light mist hugging the lake. The view should have inspired me to comment. Instead, despair and cold, dark wretchedness rendered me unmotivated. I was empty. There felt like a hole where my heart should be. I had nothing to give and wanted nothing in return.

I sat in a chair, consumed by my own thoughts. I didn't hear Bram behind me at first. I flinched, and he apologized. None of this was his fault, but I needed someone to blame. I remembered Ana at the Fountain telling me she needed someone to be angry with—now, I understood. I had come to understand so much in the last few days. Why people would consider death over a life of pain, why people needed to target their anger, and why my family had been a complete mystery to me. I understood why aliens didn't want humans to walk around, feeling these horrible emotions. Earth wouldn't be a very nice place to live if everyone felt the way I did at this moment.

"Here, try this." He handed me a cup with a peace sign logo on the side.

I lifted it to my mouth and stopped. "Is it drugged?" I asked bitterly.

"Sorry, all out of drugs." He smiled hesitantly, hoping to see a whisper of kindness left in me. My expression must have offered encouragement; he smiled. I didn't want him to find softness in my demeanor. I wanted him to hurt as much as I did. He walked away without speaking, and oddly, I felt easier because no matter what happened in the last days, this man cared for me. He was trying to help me in any way I'd allow, and I had unintentionally shown him a speck of tenderness with the tiniest reaction.

The tea was warm and soothing. I sipped it in total silence. Aromas and sounds drifted from the kitchen. He was cooking for me. My stomach lurched anticipating food. It must have been a while since I last ate. I stood and walked toward the sound. He didn't hear my approach, and I found him engrossed in chopping and stirring.

"Thank you."

"For what?" He looked up, surprised.

Overcome with emotion, I couldn't answer, so I turned away.

"I'm happy I can be here for you," he replied and returned to his cooking. As soon as he finished speaking, I knew he would try to console me. He didn't. A twinge of disappointment rolled over me. He'd never stopped trying to comfort me even when I pushed him away. Now, he turned away, and when he did, I felt drawn to him. I wasn't trying to play cat and mouse games. I was so confused but knew I didn't want him to stop caring. I walked to his side and stood by him unmoving.

"I need time," I whispered.

"And you'll have it—as much as you need." He stopped stirring and fixed his gaze on me.

Dinner was delicious. We ate sautéed vegetables I had never seen, along with a grain similar to rice, and fish he had caught in the lake a month before. We sat together, not speaking.

After we finished, Bram led me to the place I would sleep. He offered to start a bath for me, and I accepted. Inside the wood-planked bedroom was another small room. He opened the door to reveal an ample closet. Clothes hung in rows along the walls, and dressers beneath contained glass drawers full of folded items. I had never seen so many clothes for one person. They were unlike the kind we had at home. The colors were vibrant, and the fabrics varied. Nothing looked worn or old. I'd never had anything new. He opened a drawer and pointed out different underclothes and nightclothes. These were his mother's things. I broke away from my own grief long enough to realize I didn't know if Dr. Adler was okay. "Your mother," I began.

"She won't mind you wearing any of this."

"No, I mean, how is she?"

"She is miserable and worried," he replied. "While you get your clothes, I'll start your bath."

I hadn't expected that answer. I remembered Dad saying too many times people ask how someone is and they don't want an honest answer. They want *fine, good, okay,* but not the truth or a response too complex. I didn't want to be that person anymore.

Dr. Adler and I were not the same sizes, but I would find something. It shouldn't have been easy going through someone's personal things, but I imagined her willingness to help me. I chose a pair of underwear, pants, and a matching top. I assumed this clothing was used for sleeping. I had never felt anything so soft.

I walked to the bathroom where Bram waited by the entrance. He motioned for me to come inside the unusual room. We didn't have bathrooms this large or unique in Horizon.

"This bottle is for hair, this one is bath gel, and these are bath oils. Is it the right temperature for you?" he asked.

I stood staring without speaking long enough for him to repeat his question. I remembered the night my father took care of me in the bathroom after Mrs. Young killed herself. He washed my face as if I were still a baby. Tears fell.

"Hey, hey, no. It's okay." He stepped forward to console me and then stopped. I had not let him touch me since that last day in Horizon. He didn't want to be rejected again, and I understood the conflict he felt.

"You could change and go straight to bed. It's whatever you want, Ellis."

I discarded the memory of my father caring for me and flashed to the memory of the first time Bram said my name. The rush of feelings for him at the Archives flooded my brain. I leaned over the tub and scooped my hand through the water. I stepped closer, "Thank you. The water is fine." I wanted to reach for him, but I couldn't.

"If you need anything, call. I will be in the kitchen cleaning dishes. Put your old clothes here, and we can wash them tomorrow. I laid a toothbrush near the sink for you beside the towels, washcloths, and sponges. Wave your hand over the type of water you want to dispense." He showed me. A mixture of sadness and anger filled my mind. The citizens of Horizon were ignorant of the real world. Our keepers withheld so many remarkable inventions and so much beauty from us. He walked to the door with no other words and closed it behind him.

I undressed and eased into the bath. I allowed my hand to hover above the oversized spout. I was grateful for the sound of running water masking the sound of my sobbing.

I considered how my world, no, my universe, had changed. The future was a blank sheet for me, and I didn't know what path lay ahead—or if a path existed at all. After I finished bathing and dressing, I saw a robe hanging at the door and put it on as well.

When I came from the bathroom, the bedcovers were pulled back. These sweet, thoughtful gestures continued, and I felt my anger toward Bram melting away with each new morsel of kindness he offered. On the nightstand lay a steaming cup of tea and a small dish containing a cookie. A cream and yellow striped bedside chair held my father's bag. I took it and crawled into the large bed, hugging it to my chest. I'd never sleep in my bed, nor see my home again. I looked inside the bag and noticed the randomness of the items it contained. Inside was a first aid kit, books, folders, and a mini data drive. There was my Jane Austen book Dad had given me along with the necklace I often wore. I picked up one of the books, and out fell the photo of my dad and me. The photo survived the government official dropping and breaking its frame the day of The Beginning Celebration. A shard of broken glass no doubt made the long scratch which ran down the middle of our image—a visual reminder of being separated from my father. I collapsed into tears.

"Ellis?" Bram called from the outside the bedroom door. "Can I help?"

I needed him. I jumped from the bed and rushed to the door. There he stood. Concern covered his face. I paused and threw myself into his arms. "Stay with me," I said, my face buried into his chest.

He led me to the bed, lifted the covers, and waiting for me to slide in. He pulled the covers up and then took the bag my father gave me and put each item into it except for the picture of my father and me. Bram looked at it, smiled, and stood it against the base of the bedside lamp. He looked at me. Without words, he leaned over to kiss my forehead, then pulled the chair closer to the bed, and sat.

"Don't leave me."

"I will stay with you as long as you want me."

"You can't sleep sitting up the entire night," I said.

"Don't worry about me, Ellis. I promise to be here when you wake."

And he was.

CHAPTER 23

The last thing I remember was a struggle between Dr. Bauer and myself. He'd been shot by the inspector and had returned a shot. After Inspector Ryder fell, Dr. Bauer turned toward me. His wound looked serious. I believed he might shoot me as well, so I rushed by him toward the door. He grabbed me and shoved me backward, which must have caused me to fall, hitting my head. I have no idea how long I was unconscious. When the officials awakened me, I was told Dr. Bauer was dead, and Ellis had vanished.

—Dr. Claire Adler
Official Interview Report
August 2, 2052

PROOF

I DIDN'T WANT TO WAKE BRAM, WHO FAITHFULLY slept in a chair the entire night just so I might feel safe. Whatever happened or would yet happen between us, he was the one person in the world I had to depend on.

Quietly, I eased from the bed and picked up the satchel laying against the side table. I opened the door to the bedroom, hopeful it wouldn't make noise. I walked into the kitchen and poured a glass of juice. Carrying Dad's satchel, I stood at the gigantic windows and looked out. The sun rose on a lake so smooth it appeared one could walk on top of it. I unlatched the door and stepped onto the balcony. The torchlights from last night weren't actual torches. They were solar lights. I sat in a wooden chair beside a small table. A slight morning chill hung in the air; I pulled my robe tighter. Bram saw me in my nightclothes and slept in my bedroom. Those intimacies weren't allowed in Horizon. Our rules frowned upon unmarried couples having overnight guests. I now understood how manipulated our lives had been in the Habitat. For the rest of my life, I'll wonder what parts were real and what was orchestrated.

Gloom engulfed my senses. Gravity forced its invisible weight heavy upon me; I struggled to breathe. The bag shifted in my lap; I had to focus. I needed to plan my next move. I reached into the smooth leather satchel and pulled out the first of its contents. There were many folders filled with papers I'd never seen. They were bound by a rubber band with an attached note from Ana. It read, "Revolution has begun. Would you rather live one day as a lion or a hundred years as a lamb?" I unbound the folders and opened the one on top fearing what I might read. This information caused Ana's disappearance—I knew it, deep within my soul. Now, I had to accept responsibility for Mr. Hap, Ana, my father, Dr. Adler, and now Bram. This catastrophe began with me trying to find the truth. Me. I did this. I caused everything, but I was alive and safe. Where was everyone I'd involved in my quest for the truth? Dead? Tortured? Reprogrammed? Without warning, large tears fell. I felt black, vicious anger at everything and everyone, but mostly with myself. I didn't want Bram to hear me crying. With the folder over my face, I tried to stifle the sound. I wanted the anger, the grief, and the guilt out. I sat there rocking back and forth, for what seemed like a lifetime. With every inhale and exhale, I tried to release every hateful emotion knotted inside. At last, I opened my eyes and realized gravity had released her hold on me. The weight I felt was gone. I looked up into the rising sun. "Enough," I whispered aloud, "enough now."

I looked at the mass of papers, folders, and books in my lap. Dataports were the keepers of our information. These hand-written documents were absolute truth hidden from our keepers in the Habitat. I looked at the book lying beneath tear-stained folders. Alex Bauer was written on the cover in black ink. This was my father's journal. He had meant for me to have this information. I held the key to the truth, and the power to do with it what I chose. This predicament reminded me of the sword fixed within a stone from an ancient story read to me as a child. Like King Arthur's sword, this information was power, waiting to be seized and wielded by me. I imagined my mother's voice coming off the gentle breeze rippling the water of the lake before me. A warrior only takes up his sword when he is ready to fight. I could throw everything into the lake now and live my life as invisibly as possible, or I could read this information and take up the fight. I had to choose between being the lion or the lamb, so I opened my father's journal and read.

CHAPTER 24

She was perfect, and I loved her from the first moment she spoke. After she told me her feelings, I knew we must try to make a life together. Our love was a crime hated and punishable by death. Together, we lived in absolute secrecy. She never spoke about us, not even to her only relative. Had she told another human, she would have been institutionalized. Had I told another Atum, we would have been killed. By necessity, I returned to Nurahatum to complete final preparations for my assignment on Earth. When I left for the return to Earth, I said goodbye to my home planet for the last time, and I did not care. My life was now with my darling Sofla—Sofla Ana Castillo.

After arriving back to Earth in June, we traveled to the coast and there on a deserted beach at sunset held our own marriage ceremony. We danced in a misty, light rain and tossed pebbles into the water just as my parents and grandparents before me. We devoted our lives to each other, and for the next amazing year lived together while she helped me with my work. Until Sofía entered my life, I had never known the joy of true happiness. When she told me we were expecting a child, a whirlwind of conflicting emotions besieged me. I was overjoyed and miserable. If discovered, a Human-Atum baby would be killed. Our society struggled with that controversial issue in the past, and it remained a sensitive topic.

We did not know what lay ahead for us. I didn't know what to expect for a mixed-species child. As the pregnancy progressed, Sofía's health declined. Brave and determined, nothing could prevent her from bringing our baby into the world. Our adorable little girl was born seven and a half months later. The birth weakened Sofía, and I had no way of saving her.

We lay in bed, the three of us, with you sleeping peacefully. I read softly to your mother from her favorite Jane Austen novel as she gently stroked your hair. She smiled and said our romance had been greater than anything ever written.

On a bleak, rainy day, your mother became quiet. In the stillness of a random moment, she turned to me with an air of serene acceptance. Her last words were, "Protect our darling Ellis; she will change this world."

—Dr. Alex Bauer
Private Journal
July 31, 2052

THE ROAD

ELLIS CLOSED HER FATHER'S JOURNAL AND LOOKED out upon the wilderness. The rising sun chased away the shadows on the yellow woods beyond the water.

"I am the lion," she whispered.

THE END

EPILOGUE

B_am,

I am w_iti_g this to tell yo_ impo_ta_t facts. I ca__ot _isk seei_g yo_ __til the chaos has q_ieted.

Alex Ba_e_ a_d I we_e i_ love. We we_e o_ each othe_'s compatible mates list. We chose to co_ple befo_e he was assig_ed to leave fo_ his missio_ o_ Ea_th. While the_e, he fell i_ love with someo_e else. He e_ded o__ _elatio_ship, a_d I was c__shed. Yo__ fathe_, of co__se, was o_ my list, b_t I chose Alex ove_ him. Afte_ Alex left fo_ the last time, yo__ fathe_, agai_, asked me to ma__y him. We we_e happy, a_d whe_ we had yo_, o__ lives we_e complete. I _eve_ _eg_et-ted ma__yi_g yo__ fathe_.

Whe_ the Habitat p_oject was i_itiated o_ Ea_th, we fo__d o__selves livi_g a_d wo_ki_g i_side Ho_izo_. Alex was si_gle, a_d I was _ot f_ee. Afte_ yo__ fathe_ died, I was f_ee, b_t Alex had ma__ied.

Five yea_s ago, we _ealized we still had feeli_gs fo_ each othe_. I'm ashamed to admit this, b_t yo_ dese_ve the t__th; we bega_ a_ affai_. He was mise_able with his wife, a_d she was with him. Please do _ot be a_g_y with me. Sometimes, life is __fai_, a_d we m_st make choices that a_e ofte_ diffic_lt. This was my choice. Alex a_d I we_e ve_y happy togethe_. Yo_ ca_'t de_y the hea_t. I thi_k yo_ a_e i_ a positio_ to __de_sta_d how we felt.

_ow, I m_st tell yo_ c_itical i_fo_matio_ fo_ yo__ safety. The last thi_g yo__ fathe_ told me befo_e he died will be diffic_lt fo_ yo_ to believe. The_e was _o wa_ o_ Ea_th. The At_m c_eated this lie to j_stify claimi_g the pla_et fo_ themselves. H_ma_s we_e ei-the_ ha_vested o_ exte_mi_ated. They did _ot ca_se The E_d. We did.

___! I love yo_.

—Dr. Claire Adler
Deleted Dataport File Fragment
August 2052

HABITAT
READING GROUP DISCUSSION GUIDE

1. What other books did *Habitat* remind you of?

2. At the beginning of the book is a quote about sweet ignorance. What does it mean to you?

3. What feelings did *Habitat* evoke for you?

4. What songs does this book make you think of?

5. Discuss examples of foreshadowing within the book. Did those passages lead you to imagine eventual outcomes for the storyline?

6. Why do you think Ellis's mother acts as she does?

7. Give examples of symbolism found in the book and discuss what you believe each means.

8. Discuss your ideas about the mysteries surrounding Ana.

9. Who is your favorite character? Your least favorite? Why?

10. Discuss Glairn as a character. Why do you believe she relentlessly pursues Bram, who seems uninterested in a relationship?

11. Does Horizon represent a utopian or dystopian society?

12. Discuss the cryptic letter written by Dr. Adler to Bram.

13. Share a favorite quote from *Habitat*. Discuss your choice.

14. Control and choice are central themes in *Habitat*. How well could you have tolerated living in Horizon?

15. Imagine humans knew they lived in the Habitat. How might life differ for the Horizon 5000 and their descendants?

16. Discuss the poem from Chapter 15. Why do you think the author chose to include it?

17. Colors play a role in *Habitat*. Discuss examples of colors mentioned throughout the book. What does each symbolize?

18. Make a list of characters you believe are Atum and discuss your choices.

19. In the Atum culture, mates are chosen for each person. Give support as to why this practice would be positive or negative.

20. Several dreams are in *Habitat*. Discuss why you think the author included them and what their meanings might be.

21. In Horizon, people earn credit for work and volunteering. Discuss Horizon's Give and Take system.

22. What do you see in the future for the characters? For the Habitat?

23. Ana's mother is last seen in chapter 19. How much do you think she knows about the Habitat and the secrets about Ana and Ellis?

24. Deception is a theme throughout Habitat. Think about the different situations when characters resort to lying. What are their motivations? Do you agree with their reasoning?

25. In the Atum culture, people can choose to change their physical appearance by taking pills. What changes would you make? What does this say about positive and negative self-image?

26. Chapter 18 details Final Release. Discuss your opinion. Do you believe this will be Mr. Hap's fate? Debate the ethics of Release. How does the security department use Arranged Release in Chapter 11?

27. Why does Ellis care about her placement after she learns the truth about Horizon?

28. Do you agree with the Adolescent Human Study found in Chapter 9? How do you believe adolescents might be different, growing up in Horizon?

29. Chapter 13 explains that Earth's leaders knew of the Atum's existence. Quite simply, what do you believe? Is it possible that intelligent life exists elsewhere? Why or why not?

30. Discuss the revelations from the Chapter 24 journal entry. What will this mean for Ellis?

31. How might have the story have ended if Ellis and Bram hadn't met?

ACKNOWLEDGMENTS

In my case, it takes a village to write a book.
I give loving thanks to the following people.

Thanks to my daughter, Liz, for so many reasons. I found your letter written inside my Christmas present. I love you.

Christmas 2015

Ma,

I hope this journal inspires you to dive into your own imagination and write something extraordinary. You taught me to love words and how to get lost in the pages of a good book. I can't think of a better gift you've given me than to cherish a classic, Jane Austen novel.

I'm not sure if you'll use this journal or just sit it on your desk, but I know somewhere in your mind is a masterpiece waiting to be written.

I hope you find it.

I love you,

Liz

With loving appreciation to my amazing husband, Vin, for not filing a missing persons report when I was in self-imposed office confinement for days at a time. All of those alien documentaries we've watched and discussed have been instrumental for creating this story. You are the love of my life.

ACKNOWLEDGMENTS

Thank you seems insufficient appreciation for my Mom, Jo, my number one fan in everything I do (including the humiliating gymnastics exposition of '78). Thank you for your encouragement and hours of reading a genre outside of your romance comfort zone. Yes, people really love science fiction, and I love you.

To my brother, the most creative writer in the family, thank you for your guidance and for sharing with me the love of reading. I aspire to your ability to make people gasp aloud when they reach that aha! part of a story.

Thank you to my sister for always being interested in my project and for helping me with the dilemma du jour. You are much appreciated. As the technical writer of the family, I won't tell you how many missing commas my editor corrected.

I'd like to thank my editor, Sam Wright, three hundred and seventy-nine times, but instead will settle for 379. (My pride wouldn't allow me to include the number of capitalized The's you gently persuaded me were a pain to read.) Your brilliant work caught the most glaring and minute of errors. Thank you from The Bottom of My Heart...yeah, that is painful to read.

Many thanks to Ranka Stevic for the gorgeous cover design. You are a genius, and I am so proud to have one of your creations! You captured exactly what I'd pictured in my head minus the crayon scribbles, crooked lines, and stick people.

To Roseanna White. Thank you for the amazing interior design of Habitat. What a horrible, complicated mess you were given! Thank you for waving your magic wand and creating loveliness.

Thank you to my school colleagues—my second family. Without your constant support, love, kindness, and tolerance of my antics, work wouldn't be nearly as much fun. You are a lifeline.

ACKNOWLEDGMENTS

For my current students, thank you for helping to choose a book cover and for fussing at me to 'hurry up and finish it.' Your enthusiasm and encouragement mean the world to me. ☮

For all of my students past, present, and future—life's possibilities are endless; never stop dreaming.

TO THE READER

If you are reading this, and I hope you are, thank you so very much. I hope you've enjoyed *Habitat*. In fact, I hope you enjoyed it so much you convinced someone else to buy it. Actually, I hope you enjoyed *Habitat* so much that you convinced someone else to buy it and eagerly await book number two in the series, *New Earth*. Okay—scratch that—I hope you enjoyed *Habitat* so much that you convinced someone else to buy it, you eagerly await book number two in the series, *New Earth*, and you are smiling right now. May you always have a reason to smile.

In loving memory of my dad,

Fred Lewis,

whose hilarious yarns continue to be spun.

The HABITAT will never be the same

new enemy   new danger
NEW REASON TO SURVIVE

NEW EARTH

The End Series, Book 2
available 2020

GET AN EXCLUSIVE SNEAK PEEK

December 24

Sign up for my newsletter

@ Fredalewislombardo.com